The Baby!

"Your, er, mother won't be gone long."

Beside himself, Colby reached out, flexed his fingers, then lightly patted the baby's blond head. The softness surprised him, as did the silky tickle of fine feathery hair. He'd never touched a baby before.

Little Megan was sobbing so hard Colby feared she might choke on her own tears. Panic-stricken, he was just about to dial 9-1-1 when he heard a knock at his front door.

"I guess I wasn't hearing things after all." His neighbor Dani McCullough regarded him strangely. "If it makes you feel any better, you're not the first man whose checkered past finally caught up with him."

"This is *not* my child."

"That's what they all say." She scooped the baby up as if it was the most natural thing in the world.

"This child is my niece. Her mother will be right—" realization hit him like a fist "—back."

Suddenly he knew she wasn't coming back. And little Megan was his responsibility!

Dear Reader,

In the spirit of blossoming love, Special Edition delivers a glorious April lineup that will leave you breathless!

This month's THAT'S MY BABY! title launches Diana Whitney's adorable new series duet, STORK EXPRESS. Surprise deliveries bring bachelors instant fatherhood...and sudden romance! The first installment, *Baby on His Doorstep,* is a heartwarming story about a take-charge CEO who suddenly finds himself at a loss when fatherhood—and love—come knocking on his door. Watch for the second exciting story in this series next month.

Two of our veteran authors deliver enthralling stories this month. First, *Wild Mustang Woman* by Lindsay McKenna—book one of her rollicking COWBOYS OF THE SOUTHWEST series—is an emotional romance about a hard-luck heroine desperately trying to save her family ranch and reclaim her lost love. And *Lucky in Love* by Tracy Sinclair is a whimsical tale about a sparring duo who find their perfect match—in each other!

Who can resist a wedding...even if it's in-name-only? *The Marriage Bargain* by Jennifer Mikels is a marriage-of-convenience saga about a journalist who unexpectedly falls for his "temporary" bride. And *With This Wedding Ring* by Trisha Alexander will captivate your heart with a tale about a noble hero who marries the girl of his dreams to protect her unborn child.

Finally, *Stay...* by talented debut author Allison Leigh is a poignant, stirring reunion romance about an endearingly innocent heroine who passionately vows to break down the walls around her brooding mystery man's heart.

I hope you enjoy this book, and each and every story to come!

Sincerely,

Tara Gavin
Senior Editor and Editorial Coordinator

Please address questions and book requests to:
Silhouette Reader Service
U.S.: 3010 Walden Ave., P.O. Box 1325, Buffalo, NY 14269
Canadian: P.O. Box 609, Fort Erie, Ont. L2A 5X3

DIANA WHITNEY

BABY ON HIS DOORSTEP

SPECIAL EDITION®

Published by Silhouette Books
America's Publisher of Contemporary Romance

To my husband, Carl, who ended up with his own "Babies on the Doorstep" when he married me. Thank you for all the years of support, acceptance and love.

SILHOUETTE BOOKS

ISBN 0-373-24165-8

BABY ON HIS DOORSTEP

Copyright © 1998 by Diana Hinz

Printed in U.S.A.

DIANA WHITNEY

says she loves "fat babies and warm puppies, mountain streams and California sunshine, camping, hiking and gold prospecting. Not to mention strong romantic heroes!" She married her own real-life hero twenty years ago. With his encouragement, she left her longtime career as a municipal finance director and pursued the dream that had haunted her since childhood—writing. To Diana, writing is a joy, the ultimate satisfaction. Reading, too, is her passion, from spine-chilling thrillers to sweeping sagas, but nothing can compare to the magic and wonder of romance. She loves to hear from readers. Write to her c/o Silhouette Books, 300 East 42nd Street, 6th Floor, New York, NY 10017.

Dear Reader,

Ah, babies! Who can resist them? Not me, certainly. I have always adored babies, been enchanted by that sweet powdery fragrance, the silky softness of delicate skin and adorable, drooly smiles. Then again, I'm a mom. Moms are notorious for being enamored of those precious little creatures we call children.

But what about, say, a stoic, high-powered bachelor executive like Colby Sinclair, who can create a billion-dollar business without breaking a sweat, face down hardened bankers with a steely stare and affect the stock market with a single swish of his mighty pen? What's a man to do when his fastidious life-style is chaotically upended by one befuddling bundle of tiny teething terror? The same thing any self-respecting corporate problem-solver would do. Find a wife. Fast.

But babies have a way of wriggling and giggling into the most reticent of hearts and opening it from within. These small diapered delights are love personified, treasures of the human soul. I love cuddling them, I love cooing over them, and I love writing about them. *Baby on His Doorstep* is the story of one such treasure. I hope you will enjoy reading it as much as I enjoyed writing it for you.

All the best,

Chapter One

Colby Sinclair didn't exactly hate children. He did, how-ever, consider their unbridled exuberance unnerving, which was why he'd chosen living quarters that specifically ex-cluded the noisy little beasts. Of course, he hadn't counted on residing next to a goofy Pollyanna who worked at the local food bank and harbored an annoying propensity for dragging home every forlorn unfortunate to stumble across her path.

Once again shrill shrieks reverberated Colby's private sanctum. The floor vibrated. He gritted his teeth, squinted at the colorful figures scrolling across his computer monitor and tried to concentrate on marketing projections predicting only moderate growth unless he took his chain of sporting goods stores public.

Colby puffed his cheeks, tapped a gold-plated ballpoint on the edge of his study desk. A stock auction was the last thing he wanted. Answering to greedy stockholders and a meddlesome board of directors wasn't his idea of financial security.

Still, the figures weren't encouraging.

Another childish squeal broke his concentration, followed by a deafening crash that rattled the adjoining apartment wall. Startled, Colby pushed away from the desk. By the time he noticed the quivering modem cord jiggle at the connector, it was too late. Hours of work disappeared into the irretrievable black hole of cyberspace.

Horrified, he swept a disbelieving gaze from the blank monitor to the limp modem cord kinked like a dead snake beneath the chair leg. *She* was to blame for this, that bleeding-heart liberal who insisted on turning the entire apartment complex into a flophouse for down-and-out losers.

Colby leapt to his feet, seething, strode across the immaculate ivory carpeting through the gleaming glass-and-chrome decor of his living room and yanked open the front door with enough force to rattle the hinges.

There she was, hustling down the apartment hallway hugging a grocery bag and fiddling with a fat ring of keys.

Colby folded his arms, stepped out to block her way.

The woman blinked, skidded to a stop so quickly that a loaf of bread flew out from a bag and dropped to the floor. Her eyes widened as an earsplitting shriek dissolved into childish squeals behind her apartment door.

Licking her lips, she fixed Colby with a bright grin. "Hi. Lovely afternoon, isn't it? I guess I should say 'Wasn't it?' because it's dark now, so I suppose afternoon is officially over, although that doesn't mean it won't be a lovely evening." She winced as something thumped against a wall somewhere in her apartment. "But it's supposed to rain later, so I guess a lovely afternoon is the best we're going to get—"

"The weather is not my concern, Ms. McCullough—"

"Call me Dani. Everyone does."

"That—" Colby jerked a thumb toward the continuing din of thumps and laughter inside his neighbor's apartment "—is my concern."

Her grin stiffened only slightly as a curt nod vibrated the waterfall of kinky brown curls fastened atop her head with a stretchy hunk of peculiar purple terry cloth. It looked like a sweat sock. "Ah, yes, it does sound as if like my, umm, guests are a little restless. I'm sorry if you were disturbed." She cleared her throat, avoided his gaze and added, "Again."

Colby unfolded his arms, ignored a tiny spasm of regret at having caused her unhappy expression. He reminded himself that *he* was the one being wronged here. "This is an adults-only apartment complex."

Danielle bit her lip, slid him the same coaxing look that had flustered him into submission in the past. When he didn't respond, she heaved a long-suffering sigh, flinched as a baby's furious wail filtered from behind her apartment door. "I know you're not particularly fond of children, Mr. Sinclair, but it's only temporary. They'll be leaving tomorrow."

"I have nothing against children per se," Colby assured her, although he realized that semantic vagaries were useless when dealing with a blind rescue mentality.

This certainly wasn't the first time he'd tried to discuss the problem with his quirky neighbor. She always responded by widening her guileless amber gaze, nodding with profound empathy, and promising to rectify the situation with a sincerity that inevitably left Colby feeling outfoxed, if not downright manipulated. For the president of a multimillion-dollar conglomerate, the sensation of being snookered by a rank amateur was not appreciated.

Besides, Colby had the law on his side. *He* was the wronged party. There was no logical reason for him to feel guilty about insisting that his neighbor live up to legally binding terms of her lease. And he *wouldn't* feel guilty...

If she'd only stop staring at him with those big, soulful eyes.

Buying a moment to mentally reinforce himself, Colby bent to retrieve the dropped loaf, which had landed a few inches from the woman's left foot. She shifted back a step, drawing attention to a pair of peculiar ankle boots that resembled mukluks glued onto squatty, two-inch heels. His gaze automatically followed a shapely calf upward to where the sheen of bare skin disappeared beneath a faded denim hem on which some kind of gingham ruffle had been stitched.

He studied the peculiar garment for a moment, then blew out a breath, straightened and stiffly tucked the bread back into the grocery bag, noting that she'd completed the bizarre ensemble with a black V-neck T-shirt emblazoned by some kind of garish cartoon. Not particularly fashionable, although he had to admit that the woman's avant-garde sense of style was oddly appealing.

Colby shook off the distraction, tightened his jaw and was fully prepared to communicate displeasure in no uncertain terms when Danielle McCullough flashed a grateful smile that fused the angry words to the tip of his tongue.

"Thank you," she whispered, and he wondered why he hadn't noticed how sensually rustic her voice was.

"Excuse me?"

A row of bright, even teeth flashed through a widening grin. "The bread. Thanks for picking it up."

Husky, he decided, yet melodic, rather like a bass oboe in a virtuoso's talented hands. It was enough to throw a man completely off stride, obliterate the righteousness of his cause. Fortunately, a rabble of thumping little feet vibrated the walls as a reminder. His resolve stiffened.

Colby drew up his shoulders, spoke brusquely. "As I

was saying, I have nothing against children. I do, however, draw the line at having my privacy violated. Your dubious choice of friends is none of my business, Ms. McCullough—''

"Dani."

"Except when it intrudes upon the quality of my life. I cannot tolerate—'' he winced as the baby's howls grew more shrill "—this bedlam.''

"I'm so sorry. I'll talk to them.'' Her golden brown eyes poured empathy, her full lower lip protruded in a sultry pout that Colby presumed was supposed to express sympathy, but succeeded only in emphasizing a subtle beauty that exuded equal measures of innocence and sensuality.

There was no doubt that Dani McCullough was an enormously appealing woman, which was probably why Colby had never reported her habit of harboring "guests" in violation of the building's strict policy. He recognized that weakness in himself, and was immensely annoyed by it. The first rule of business was to reveal nothing the competition could exploit.

As for his personal life...well, in point of fact Colby Sinclair didn't have much of a personal life, but presumed that the behavioral mandates were similar to those accepted in business. So he drew upon what he knew, and arranged his features into the expressionless mask that had propelled him to the apex of his profession. "I expect the problem to be resolved."

Danielle flinched, tried for a smile that had clearly lost its effectiveness. The last thing on earth she needed was another confrontation with Mr. Tall, Dark and Grumpy. In the year since they'd been neighbors, she had yet to see the man smile and had, in fact, seen mug shots with friendlier faces.

She sighed, met his gaze squarely. "Tomorrow morning, I promise."

Colby Sinclair's eyes were colder than a skid-row flophouse. At first Danielle feared he might insist tomorrow wasn't soon enough, but after regarding her for a hard moment, he nodded curtly, spun on his polished Italian heel and disappeared into his apartment.

Danielle's breath slid out all at once. The relationship with her grumpy neighbor had been uneasy at best. The man was impossible, an arrogant elitist without a bone of compassion in his entire body. The only reason Danielle hadn't told him off months ago was fear that he'd file a formal complaint with building management. So far he hadn't been inclined to do that, although she suspected his restraint was based more on a desire to avoid personal involvement rather than any altruistic motive.

Fisting her keys, Danielle wiped her moist forehead with the back of her hand then scuffled toward her noisy apartment wondering how charitable her pompous neighbor would be if she couldn't keep her promise. She'd already spent half the afternoon trying to find suitable quarters for the Risvold family, and had run into one bureaucratic brick wall after another.

Disappointed but never willing to accept defeat, Danielle pasted on a confident smile, keyed open the door lock. As she stepped inside her apartment, a throw pillow hit her square in the face.

"Ayee! Julian, no!" Marta Risvold scurried forward to scoop the feisty four-year-old under one arm, then extended her free hand in apology. "I am so sorry, Dani. My little ones, they are restless. It's been so long since they've had a warm place to play."

"I understand," Danielle murmured, numbed by the chaos. Her apartment looked like it had been bombed. Magazines and newspapers were strewn across the room as if they'd been used as projectiles; a plant stand had been overturned, spilling potting soil across the carpet; and her beleaguered cat, Whiskers, was hunched atop the étagère, watching the pandemonium with typical feline disdain.

Danielle flinched at the silent reproach in her pet's irked little eyes. It wasn't the first time the long-suffering animal had been relegated to the safety of a high shelf. Clearly, poor Whiskers didn't care for his owner's habit of dragging home human strays any more than her stuffy, kid-hating neighbor.

"I'm sorry," she whispered to the irritated cat, who promptly turned his back on her. She sighed, pressed a fingertip against the budding headache forming over her left eyebrow. Despite the problems, Danielle never had been able to turn her back on those who were temporarily down on their luck. The minor inconvenience of occasional overnight company paled in comparison to the satisfaction of helping people in crisis land on their feet.

Throughout her own austere childhood, Danielle and her five siblings had been raised with an abundance of love and an abiding respect for those less fortunate. The McCulloughs had always been a close, happy family despite having suffered the hardship of a disabled father and a mother who worked minimum-wage jobs to put food on the table. Times had been tough back then, but the kindness of strangers had often made the difference between survival and the disintegration of her family.

Danielle knew how much a helping hand meant to people in need. Some people were just needier than others.

Stepping over a toppled plant, she caught sight of a curly blond head disappearing into her bedroom. "Um, I think maybe you should check on Lily," she told Mrs. Risvold.

The harassed woman spun a look over her shoulder, muttered to herself. She released her wriggling son, who dashed into the kitchen while his mother tracked down his six-year-old sister. Baby Val sat on the living room floor, wailing miserably.

Danielle picked her way through the clutter, plopped the grocery bag on the kitchen counter and pulled Julian away from her utensil drawer. "Don't play with those things, honey. We're going to have to eat with them in a few minutes."

Julian brightened. "Want spaghetti."

"Hmm… Oh, well, how about macaroni and cheese instead?"

"Want spaghetti!"

"Okay, fine. Fat yellow spaghetti."

"Yeah!"

As Julian grinned in victory, his mother dragged her furious daughter out of the bedroom. "Behave yourself," Marta told the struggling girl. "If not for Miss McCullough, we would sleep in the park tonight. Look how you repay her kindness, eh? Shame on you."

Lily flopped into a kitchen chair, propped a grubby elbow on the faded laminate tabletop and fixed Dani with a "drop-dead" stare. Children, Danielle had discovered, didn't consider homelessness to be as disastrous as did their frightened, preoccupied parents. Oddly enough, kids usually found the experience to be a grand adventure, an exciting kind of camp-out.

At least for the first week or so. After that, the fun factor decreased dramatically. Danielle was determined to see the Risvold family safely tucked into a new home long before that happened.

"We're having spaghetti," Julian announced, scrambling into a chair across from his sister.

Lily skewered him with a look. "I hate spaghetti."

Julian grinned. "Uh-huh."

The girl's eyes narrowed into mean green slits. Before the argument could escalate, Dani reached into the grocery bag to retrieve her secret weapon.

"Truce," she said, wiggling the rented videotape in front

of the children's startled eyes. "Tell you what. If you two eat your dinner quietly then tiptoe to the sofa like polite little mice, you'll be treated to—" she squinted at the box blurb "—'a heartwarming animated classic for the entire family.'"

Danielle whipped the tape behind her back as Lily made a grab for it. A covert glance confirmed that the children's mother had moved out of hearing range to wipe baby Val's runny nose, so Danielle leaned over the table and lowered her voice.

"On the other hand, if there's any more fighting, screaming, running through the house like stampeding elephants, the very grumpy man who lives next door might just dice you both into bite-size morsels and feed you to the cat." She flashed a saccharine smile. "Do we understand each other?"

The children shared a wary look, then nodded.

Danielle straightened. "Good. Now, the sooner the living room gets shoveled out, the sooner you'll watch videos, so how about a little help?"

Both kids leapt from their chairs in sprint mode.

"Quietly," she added with a knowing nod toward the wall adjoining Sinclair's apartment. "We wouldn't want to disturb the neighbor."

Skidding to a stop, the children cast an apprehensive glance at the grumpy man's wall, then stared up at Whiskers, who hunkered on his high perch eyeing them with appropriate malevolence. Julian gulped. Lily sidled cautiously around the étagère, then lurched into a silent, clutter-gathering frenzy.

Their mother, clearly stunned by her children's abrupt attitude adjustment, angled a questioning glance. "How did you do that?"

"I just asked if they'd rather tidy the living room or feed

the cat," Danielle muttered, then returned to preparing a meal of fat, yellow spaghetti.

"It's the third time this month, Ms. Wilkins." Mildly irritated, Colby clamped the portable phone between his chin and shoulder, freeing his hands to perfect the knot in his silk necktie. "I'm not unsympathetic to your plight, but members of my management staff are expected to adequately organize their personal agendas. I've scheduled a department head meeting at one o'clock this afternoon. Your attendance is required."

Colby thumbed the power switch, laid the phone on the polished marble vanity. He fiddled with the necktie knot for another moment, smoothed a slight imperfection in the shape of his scissored executive haircut, then cast a quick glance at the extravagant wristwatch that his staff had presented to him the first time retail sales hit the five-million mark.

It was exactly 7:17 a.m. As always, Colby Sinclair was precisely on schedule.

Leaving the telephone on the vanity, Colby strode from the master bath, retrieved the suit coat he'd hung out the night before and slipped it on as he crossed the living room. His open briefcase was on the dining room table. He scanned the neatly organized interior, plucked a palm-size Dictaphone from one of the leather storage pockets and clicked the record button. "Memo to all department heads, copy to Mira Wilkins's personnel file."

Colby pressed the pause button, considering his options. He could, of course, reiterate written policy on abuse of personal time. He could even revise the policy to include appropriate salary deductions for excessive absenteeism, but a niggling doubt held him back. Mira Wilkins was a fine finance officer, one of the best he'd seen. She was a hard worker who frequently arrived early and stayed late.

At least, that had been her habit until the family au pair had suddenly returned to Switzerland, creating an instant child-care emergency in the Wilkins household.

Colby honestly believed that he'd been exceptionally lenient in responding to his finance officer's personal problems. His patience was, however, wearing thin. From his perspective, a phone call to any of the dozen domestic agencies in the Los Angeles area could have resolved the situation immediately. Certainly Colby's own parents had done so on numerous occasions without expressing the slightest angst. The Wilkins, however, had approached the task as if replacing a nanny was on par with appointing the secretary of state. Admirable, perhaps, but unacceptable.

Colby did, after all, have a business to run.

His thumb hovered over the record button. He pursed his lips, gave in to doubt. Erasing the previous entry, Colby tucked the Dictaphone back into the pocket, snapped the briefcase shut and carried it through the living room, rechecking his watch as he reached the front door. Precisely 7:22 a.m. The Wilkins matter had put him two minutes behind.

Scowling, Colby yanked the door open, stepped into the hall and came face-to-face with two towheaded youngsters who appeared to be arguing over possession of the neighbor's morning paper. The children snapped to attention, goggle-eyed. Before Colby could do more than blink, they let out a blood-curdling shriek, dropped the newspaper and dashed into the McCullough apartment just as Danielle was on her way out.

The youngsters churned past, spinning her around. "What on earth—?" Danielle McCullough tripped into the hallway, shoved a spiraling tangle of wild hair out of her face. Her confusion melted into a quirky smile when she saw Colby. "Oh," she murmured, as if the children's bizarre behavior had been magically explained. "It's you."

Baffled, Colby simply stood there like a smartly tailored lump while Danielle reached back to close her apartment door, then regarded him with a sparkle of amusement that he considered rather odd. Unless there was shaving cream smudged beneath his nose, quite unlikely considering his meticulous grooming routine, Colby figured that if anyone had a right to be amused by someone else's appearance, it was him.

The ever-fashionable Ms. McCullough, who was wearing a green-and-purple plaid miniskirt topped by a hot pink sweater, looked as if she'd been costumed by a color-blind vaudevillian. The garish ensemble was completed by lemon yellow tights, red high-top sneakers and a peculiar woven wicker shoulder pouch that he assumed to be some kind of a purse.

Impeccable manners forbade mentioning the garish attire, so Colby said simply, "I trust your guests slept well."

"Ah, yes. Thank you."

"You're out early this morning, presumably to assist in the relocation effort?"

"I promised that they'd be gone this morning, didn't I?" Her gaze flickered, an involuntary gesture Colby presumed to be one of concealment.

"So you did."

"Well." She managed a strained smile, then hoisted the lumpy woven bag higher on her shoulder. "Have a nice day," she murmured, heading toward the glass door at the end of the hallway.

"Ms. McCullough?"

She stiffened, glanced warily over her shoulder. "Yes?"

"Your newspaper."

Danielle followed his glance to the crumpled paper, still laying where the children had dropped it. She was so anxious to get away from Colby Sinclair's prying eyes that she considered leaving it and making a mad sprint for the parking lot. Instead, she hustled back down the hall, scooped up the paper and tossed it unceremoniously into her apartment.

She clicked the door shut, wincing as a cranky baby fuss filtered into the hall. Judging by the way Sinclair's eyes narrowed, Danielle had little doubt that he heard it, too. She edged toward the building exit, flashed a cheery smile. "Well, have a nice day."

"You said that."

"Did I?" She licked her lips, issued a limp shrug. "Then I guess I must really mean it."

Colby regarded her with an intensity that made her skin prickle. There was something about the man that made her crazy, and it wasn't just that smug, condescending expression he always wore. Danielle was used to being underestimated.

In fact, she thrived on it. She'd learned long ago that the best way for a woman—especially a very young and reasonably pretty woman—to get what she wanted in business was to make others think that *they* wanted what *she* wanted. A guileless expression and unique style of dress made her less threatening to those in power, gave them a sense of righteousness when they donated an extra pallet of canned goods, or added another zero to their tax-deductible check.

Danielle saw nothing wrong with manipulating the "haves" to benefit the "have nots." From her perspective, it was a win-win situation, with half of society feeling smugly charitable and the other half feeling as if they just might survive another day.

Her imperious neighbor was definitely one of the "haves." From the gleaming leather toe of his hand-stitched shoes to the polished onyx studs glittering on starched cuffs, and the silk designer tie that probably cost more than Danielle earned in a week, Colby Sinclair reeked of blue blood and old money.

Still, he was a bit of an enigma, an arrogant elitist with a blue-collar prickle that made him difficult to categorize with finality. There was a contradiction between his demeanor and his eyes, which had a tendency to display unnerving empathy despite his dispassionate brusqueness.

Yes, the unfathomable Mr. Sinclair was clearly a contradiction, yet Danielle suspected he was a man not easily swayed beyond the confines of his own conscience. Nor would he be duped by cheerily evasive small talk, so when he opened the glass exit door for her, she thanked him with a silent smile, then stepped into the brisk, bright Los Angeles sunrise.

A moment later, as Colby Sinclair's shadow fell over her, a chill slithered across her nape. The sensation was not unpleasant. There was a peculiar sense of anticipation to his nearness, a vague excitement that both intrigued and annoyed her.

He followed her toward the parking lot, hoisting that fancy leather briefcase as if it were a badge of honor. "You look tired," he said suddenly.

Startled, she looked up. It was a mistake. Sunlight sparkled in his gray eyes, changing them from formidable to incredibly erotic. She'd always thought his hair to be a nondescript brown similar to her own, but now realized that it was much lighter, a tawny, caramel shade streaked with paler hues of platinum and gold. Fine lines around his eyes were visible, too, evidence of laughter that somehow seemed incongruous with the man she'd perceived him to be. He was handsome, she realized. Truly drop-dead, movie-star gorgeous. Odd that she'd never noticed that before.

Apparently taking her silence for umbrage, he added, "I didn't mean to suggest that you don't look quite, ah, attractive."

"I took no offense, Mr. Sinclair. I was simply surprised that you noticed."

"Ordinarily I wouldn't have, but there was an innate curiosity as to whether or not I was the only one kept awake half the night by a crying infant."

Danielle's shoulders tightened as if spring-loaded. She licked her lips, looked away. "I'm sorry. Little Valerie is teething. She's quite uncomfortable."

"So I gathered."

Irritated by the reproach in his voice, she felt the telltale rush of blood through her veins that preceded imprudent behavior. The heated sensation was usually her cue to smile and remove herself from the situation before she said something she'd regret.

This time, however, she ignored the warning, snapped her head around and stared directly into Colby Sinclair's incredibly sexy eyes. "You've made your position quite clear, Mr. Sinclair, and I truly am sorry you were inconvenienced, but when it comes to a choice between the well-being of a homeless family and a few hours' beauty sleep, I think you know where I stand. Mrs. Risvold is a fine, hardworking woman who is quite simply at her wits' end. First she lost her husband, then she lost her job and now she's lost her home. She needs help, her children need help, and I don't need your approval to give it to them."

Sinclair regarded her thoughtfully, issued a subtle nod. "Quite commendable. A bit naive, perhaps, but a worthy effort nonetheless." Before Danielle could do more than sputter in surprise, he glanced at his watch, effectively dismissing her. "As for your unfortunate guests, I'll expect them to be housed elsewhere by the time I return this evening. Good day, Ms. McCullough." With a curt not, he strode to his sleekly extravagant automobile and drove away.

Alerted by a draft on her tongue, Danielle snapped her

mouth shut and flounced into the ten-year-old station wagon that had racked up more miles than *Air Force One*. She sat there, fuming.

In the course of her social welfare career, she'd met hundreds of people, perhaps thousands, with personalities running the gamut from open amiability to hostile reticence and everything in between. But personality had never mattered. Danielle prided herself on a God-given talent for getting along with anyone, and hadn't met a person who couldn't be accurately assessed and convincingly cajoled. Never. Not one.

Until now.

"Thanks, Nancy. I can't tell you how much I appreciate your help." Danielle plugged one ear as a forklift chugged past the cluttered warehouse counter that doubled as her desk. When the din eased, she shifted the telephone and hunched forward to jot a note on her calendar. "The Risvolds will only be with you for a few days until a public housing unit opens next week."

"Whatever," Nancy replied cheerfully. "My kids are in school all day, so it'll be nice to have company."

"You're a peach." Danielle tapped a pencil on the metal countertop. "Umm, you do realize that Marta has three children, including an eight-month-old."

"No problem."

"I know it might be a little crowded—"

"Oh, stop!" A pleasant chuckle filtered over the line. "Good grief, Dani, if it wasn't for you my kids and I wouldn't even have a roof over our head. Anytime you need anything, you just call, hear? You can always count on me."

Danielle dropped the pencil, rubbed the back of her neck. A smile eased the nervous twitch of her stomach. "I know that, Nancy. I just wish they could stay with me, but—"

She sighed, shifted the telephone to her right ear. "Never mind. I'll drive them over to your place around noon, if that's all right."

"Noon, huh?" Nancy chuckled again. "My, my, you *are* anxious."

Danielle issued an irked snort. "Believe me, the rush to mass exodus isn't my idea. It's just that I live in an adults-only building, and some tenants are complaining. Well, one tenant."

"Ah. For a moment there I was wondering if these were ordinary kids or catastrophes in sneakers." A long silence stretched over the line. "They *are* ordinary kids, right? I mean, I won't have to chain them down or anything?"

Danielle cleared her throat, fidgeted with the cord. "Do you by any chance have a cat?"

"Well, yeah."

"Then they'll be perfect angels."

"Uh?"

"I'll explain when I see you. Bye." Relieved to have resolved at least one of her problems, Dani quickly cradled the receiver, scooped up a pile of blank donation receipts and headed out to see a man about a pallet of day-old dinner rolls.

Colby returned home late that evening, as was his habit. Although most of his staff left the office between six and seven, Colby usually stayed until his concentration was broken by hunger.

Now he hung up his suit coat, replaced his cuff links in the cedar-lined accessory box that had been a gift from a client. He checked his personal mail, saw nothing of immediate importance and laid the envelopes aside. After rolling up his sleeves, he microwaved a quick supper, ate it at his desk while perusing the business wrap-up on an internet news group.

An hour later, he was in the midst of dictating a series of marketing memos when the grating howl of a disgruntled child again seeped into his sanctum.

Furious, he flipped off the Dictaphone. This, he decided, was absolutely the final straw. There was no way he'd spend another sleepless night listening to a screaming child, even if it meant piling the entire Risvold family into his car and personally delivering them to the nearest motel.

Colby marched to his front door, yanked it open and came face to stunned face with a gorgeous blonde draped in mink, dripping diamonds, cradling a cranky baby in her arms.

"Colby, darling." A thick awning of mascaraed lashes shuttered a sly smile. "Do you still like surprises?"

Chapter Two

The woman swept through the door in a choking cloud of cologne. "Kiss, kiss," she murmured, aiming a couple of chaste pecks in Colby's general direction. She immediately sat the baby on the floor, groomed her mussed mink lapel, then regarded Colby's sleek living quarters as if eyeing the inside of a hay barn. "So, this is your little nest, is it? How very rustic. Mother would be appalled."

A familiar throb spread from the base of Colby's skull, settled like a barbed-wire knot between his shoulder blades. "What are you doing here, Olivia?"

She glanced up with feigned dismay. "Since when do I need a reason to visit my favorite brother?"

Not bothering to point out that he was also her only brother, Colby closed the front door, rubbed his forehead and regarded the woman he'd last seen six years earlier when she'd pitched a fit at their uncle's funeral because she'd been excluded from the old geezer's will. "Cut the crap, Olivia. You wouldn't visit the pope on his deathbed unless there was something in it for you."

Scarlet lips pursed into a purposeful pout. "Don't be unpleasant, Colby dear. I simply thought you'd want to meet your niece."

"Niece?" His startled gaze slipped to the little blond gamin dripping drool on his immaculate ivory carpet. "That's *your* child?"

"Lovely, isn't she?" The offhand remark was delivered with a flip of her manicured hand, and the amused glance of one admiring a cute puppy. "Megan, sweetie, say hello to your uncle Colby."

Megan blinked, stuffed a fist in her sloppy wet mouth and emitted a cranky fuss. That, along with a disgusting slime oozing from tiny nostrils, diminished the cuteness factor considerably, at least as far as Colby was concerned.

Olivia turned away, clearly bored. "I suppose she's hungry again. The little vulture eats all the time."

Colby nodded stupidly, still trying to assimilate the shocking concept that his vain, avaricious sister—the same one who'd tied her three-year-old brother to a highway median with a Take Me, I'm Free sign tacked to his little shirt—could actually be a bonafide mother. "The child is adopted, right? I mean, you didn't actually give birth."

"I most certainly did. It was the most hideous experience of my life." Looking stung, Olivia allowed the mink coat to fall open, exposing a slinky red sheath that clung to every curve of a body that was only slightly more voluptuous than Colby remembered. "My figure is positively ruined. Even the best cosmetic surgeon in Brentwood couldn't tuck everything back the way it was." She held open the coat, pirouetted to study her own rounded hipline. "I still look like a peasant."

Since no question was posed, no response was issued. Colby knew perfectly well that the only opinion Olivia valued was her own. Meanwhile, little Megan's cranky fuss evolved into a wail of displeasure that almost but not quite drowned out a peculiar thumping outside the front door.

Frowning, Colby turned toward the noise when his sister grabbed his arm, spun him around.

"Silly me," Olivia cooed with a nervous giggle. "I seem to have left dear Megan's formula in the car. She just needs a little nip before bedtime. Not unlike her mum," she added with a sly wink, then swished around her startled brother and back toward the door. "No, no," she said, planting both palms against Colby's chest when he took a step to follow. "I'll just be a moment. Be a dear and keep an eye on the baby, will you? She crawls, you know."

A horrified glance revealed that the child was indeed motivating across the floor at alarming speed, heading straight toward Colby's study. He leapt forward, hurried over to shut the study door a moment before the baby reached the threshold.

Thwarted, the baby sat up, screwed her face into a wet purple mask and emitted a furious shriek that sent a chill of pure terror down Colby's spine.

"Oh, good Lord. Do something, Olivia. She'll rouse the entire building. Olivia—?" Colby stared at the empty foyer for several seconds before realizing that his sister had already left. He swallowed panic, turned his attention to the screaming baby at his feet. "Uh, there, there," he murmured, twisting his hands together. "Your, er, mother won't be gone long."

Megan sniffed, rubbed her eyes, choked on a sob.

Beside himself, Colby reached out, flexed his fingers, then lightly patted the baby's blond head. The softness surprised him, as did the silky tickle of fine feathery hair. He'd never touched a baby before. There'd never been reason to.

He was relieved that the child seemed comforted by the contact, because she raised her watery blue eyes and stopped crying. Emboldened, Colby stroked the baby's hair again. Megan shuddered, blinked, offered a thin smile that did peculiar things to his stomach. He felt his cheeks twitch and realized that he was smiling back.

He instantly straightened, feeling foolish for expecting a mere infant to respond to something as subtle as facial expression. Oddly enough, though, little Megan did appear to be responding. Her smile widened, and she issued what seemed to be a rather satisfied squeak.

"Well." Colby regarded the child more closely, decided that there was indeed a family resemblance. She was actually rather sweet looking, with eyes a bit bluer than Olivia's, and a pert little nose that was somewhat rounder—and wetter—than her mother's.

The infant was appealing enough, in a gooey kind of way. "Megan is a lovely name," he said, hoping the sound of a voice would keep her calm. "It's Irish, you know. Well, technically it's Greek, although the popularity of the Gaelic derivative eventually obscured a Mediterranean origin."

Megan studied him for a moment, then pitched forward and crawled under the dining table. Colby dropped to his knees in time to see a diapered bottom wiggle through a forest of polished chrome chair legs. He stood quickly, rounded the table just as the baby emerged from the other side, churning toward the kitchen.

Colby followed, keeping the curious child in sight but reluctant to pick her up. First, he seriously doubted that the baby would be pleased to have her exploration halted. More importantly, he feared that his own clumsy inexperience might inadvertently hurt a child so tiny and fragile.

So he simply kept little Megan in sight, removing items in her path and impatiently awaiting Olivia's return.

Five minutes later, he was still waiting. The baby was becoming fussy again.

Ten minutes ticked by.

Megan was now sobbing so hard, Colby feared she might choke on her own tears. Panic-stricken, he was just about to dial 9-1-1 when he heard a timid knock at his front door. He dropped the phone, hurdled the coffee table and nearly yanked off the doorknob. "Where the hell have you—?" The angry question died midair as Colby stared into Danielle McCullough's startled face. He sagged against the jamb. "What do you want?"

"Hello to you, too," she replied with a wry smile, then peered past his shoulder as Megan's distraught cries became more urgent. "I guess I wasn't hearing things after all."

He gave her a withering look. "See here, Ms. McCullough—"

"Dani."

"I'm rather busy at the moment, so if you'll excuse me."

"Sure, no problem, but if the fire marshal strolls by and sees all the stuff you have piled in the hall—"

"Stuff?" Colby straightened, stepped out and nearly fainted. A folded portable crib was propped beside his front door, along with a high chair, a stroller, a flattened net object that looked painfully like a playpen, a grocery bag filled with baby food, and a suitcase. "Oh, God."

Danielle regarded him strangely. "If it makes you feel any better, you're not the first man whose checkered past finally caught up with him."

"Hmm?" Colby blinked over, recognized reproach in her eyes as little Megan crawled toward the front door. "This is *not* my child."

"That's what they all say." She scooped the baby up as if it was the most natural thing in the world, retrieved a tissue from the lumpy woven shoulder bag and proceeded to wipe the slimy little face. "There, there, sweetie, your daddy didn't mean to make you cry."

Colby tossed up his hands in utter frustration. "This is absurd."

"Shh." Danielle angled a warning stare. "Even a baby can be traumatized by parental rejection."

"I am *not* that child's parent!"

"Oh, please. She looks just like you, right down to that silly chin crease."

Colby absently touched his chin, was chagrined to realize that he was more perturbed that she'd labeled his proudest feature as silly than by the insulting inference that he'd fathered an illegitimate child.

Thoroughly annoyed with himself, Colby yanked his hand away, balled his fist at his side. "Of course there's a family resemblance," he hissed through gritted teeth. "The child is my niece. Her mother will be right—" realization hit him like a fist "—back," he finished lamely, then sagged against the wall, eyeing the furniture piled in the hall. Clearly Olivia had no intention of returning anytime soon. "I'm going to kill her," he muttered. "My sister is a dead woman."

Danielle regarded the panicked man, noting the frantic twitch at the corner of his mouth, the bleak fear in his eyes. Judging people was her job, recognizing and properly interpreting the subtlest reaction, sifting the manipulative from the sincere. She had no doubt that Colby Sinclair was being truthful. This adorable, pink-cheeked child was indeed his niece, and for some odd reason, he was as terrified by the baby as he was frank about murderous intent toward his sister.

Still Danielle was perplexed by his reaction, which seemed completely out of proportion to what was clearly a practical joke, and rather an amusing one at that. After all, she was no stranger to the pranks kinfolk played on each other. Interfamily teasing and sibling squabbles were the most natural thing in the world, yet this poor man was behaving as if he'd never been subjected to such a thing. Quite peculiar, she thought. And a little sad.

She shifted the baby on her hip, regarded her distraught neighbor with a thoughtful eye. "I can see that you're a bit upset with your sister, although murder might be a bit extreme."

He shot a killing look at the cluttered hall. "Trust me, it's not."

"Oh, come on. It's not all that terrible. Why, one of my brothers once ripped the juiciest pages out of my diary and thumbtacked them to the high school bulletin board. Now *that* was definitely a case for capital punishment. In comparison, a sneak baby-sitting attack seems pretty tame." Danielle eyed the furniture, swallowed hard. "It's probably just a joke."

"I'm not laughing."

"I can see that." She shrugged, still unconcerned. "Well, I'm sure there's a perfectly good explanation." A glance around the clutter revealed a white envelope on the high-chair tray. "Aha, a clue."

Colby snatched up the envelope, on which his name had been penned in scrolling script.

Danielle peered around his shoulder. "Your sister's handwriting?" He nodded but made no attempt to open the envelope. She sighed. "Since you clearly would prefer to read your mail in private, I'll just take your niece... Ah, what's her name?"

"Megan," he mumbled, still staring at the envelope.

"Megan," she repeated, smiling when the child responded with a happy grin. "Well, Megan, what say we saunter inside and freshen up a bit?"

Megan giggled. When her distracted uncle offered no objection, Danielle scooped up a package of disposable diapers and carried the baby into Colby Sinclair's elusive lair.

She emerged into a gleaming wonderland of light reflecting from sparkling glass, polished chrome and oiled leather.

The apartment layout was a mirror image of hers, but that's where the resemblance ended. Danielle's home was plush with plump flowered cushions, warm wood tones, with every sunlit spot alive with lush foliage spilling from glazed ceramic pots. Her place was…well, homey. Sinclair's was an Art Deco museum, sleek and shiny, with glass surfaces that would attract tiny finger smudges the way a white sofa lures a muddy dog.

As for the spotless ivory carpet, she shuddered to think what a drooling little rug rat would do to that.

Sweeping a final glance around the room, Danielle decided that moisture-resistant leather was best suited for a diapering project, and headed toward the massive sofa. "Nothing like a pair of nice fresh undies to perk a girl up, right, precious?"

As she laid the baby down, a subtle scent of lemon wafted up from the supple leather. "I've never seen a man yet who could be bothered oiling a sofa," she told little Megan, who blinked up with curious blue eyes. "Your uncle must have a maid. Which makes me dislike him all the more, of course. I mean, I can certainly understand a man driving the fanciest car he can get his hairy, testosterone-soaked hands on. It's a guy thing. They can't really help themselves."

Danielle folded the damp diaper into its waterproof covering, laid it aside. "But it really galls me when they won't even clean up after themselves. I mean, how come expensive cars are a guy thing and housework is a gal thing? I hate housework. I've never met a woman yet who wouldn't choose piloting a Porsche over scraping mildew out of the shower stall." She tucked the fresh diaper into place, smoothed the baby's frilly dress. "Face it, sweetie, it's a sexist world out there. We gals have a rough road to hoe."

Megan giggled, shoved a tiny fist in her mouth.

Danielle's heart melted. "Has anyone every told you that you have the prettiest eyes in the entire world?"

The baby squeaked happily before her attention was captured by movement across the room. Following Megan's gaze, Danielle saw Colby standing in the doorway looking like he'd been shot. A slip of linen stationery was clutched in his hand.

Danielle scooped Megan up, carried her to the cramped foyer. "Well?"

Colby just stood there, ashen. After a moment, he cleared his throat. "It seems that nine months of motherhood has taken a toll. My sister has decided that she requires a break."

"A break?"

"Yes." Colby crimped the paper in his fist. "Apparently she's gone on holiday, and plans to spend the next few weeks touring Venice with an ex-gondolier named Paolo."

"You're kidding." Surprised laughter died in her throat. "You're not kidding." Danielle shifted the baby, took the note and read the awful truth for herself while Colby strode past her. She glanced up. "Where are you going?"

"To call the authorities."

"What?" She hurried over to grab the receiver out of his hand. "You can't do that."

He snatched the receiver back. "I most certainly can. This poor child has been abandoned."

"Shh." Danielle shot him a hard look, then took Megan to the other side of the living room, sat her on the floor and left her occupied with a ring of keys from her woven shoulder bag. "Now," she said in a low voice, "I'll agree that your sister was a bit presumptuous, but I guarantee that if you bring child welfare into this, Megan will regret it for the rest of her life."

His gaze flickered a moment, then he glanced over to

where the baby was happily playing with Danielle's keys. "I have no choice," he said finally.

"There's always a choice." She pried the telephone from his grasp, cradled it firmly. "How about the rest of your family?"

"Family?" He frowned as if unfamiliar with the word.

"Yes, family. You know, parents, other brothers and sisters, aunts, uncles, cousins, et cetera, et cetera. Surely there's someone you could call on for help."

Colby rolled his head, massaged the back of his neck. "The Sinclair bloodline is thankfully limited to Olivia and I."

"Your parents are deceased, then?"

"Not in the literal sense. They live in Brentwood."

Something in his shuttered gaze sent a chill down Danielle's spine. "That's only a few miles from here."

"Geographically." He folded his arms, clearly unnerved by the discussion. "They would not wish to be involved in this."

"That's ridiculous. Megan is their granddaughter."

"I doubt they're even aware of the child's existence." He avoided her incredulous stare, focusing instead on straightening a canvas of abstract art that was the only wall decoration in the room. "Our family is somewhat estranged."

Danielle narrowed her eyes. "Define *somewhat*."

He turned his attention to a loose thread on the inside seam of his folded sleeve. "I've had no communication with my parents in years. To the best of my knowledge, neither has Olivia."

If Colby Sinclair had just confessed to being a psychopathic serial dognapper, Danielle couldn't have been more shocked. Even though her own family was spread throughout several states, she'd always remained close to her siblings, telephoned her parents once a week. She loved her mother and father with all her heart, and couldn't even fathom what her life would be like if they hadn't been a huge, loving part of it.

Colby regarded her with wise eyes and a sad smile. "That shocks you, doesn't it?"

"Yes." She rubbed the chill from her upper arms, moistened her lips. "Most of the broken families I see are victims of poverty, violence or addiction. I guess I always figured that if we could just fix those three things, society would magically heal itself. But you...your family..." The words dissipated like so much steam.

Although Colby's gaze was not unkind, a steely glint added edge to his words. "But you can't fit my family into one of those imaginary pigeonholes, can you?"

She shook her head, offered a limp shrug.

"Categorizing people by public image or economic status has always been a foolish endeavor. No outsider can ever truly know what goes on behind closed doors." A poignant sadness touched his eyes, darkening the clear gray irises to cloudy charcoal. The sadness faded, replaced by an equal measure of surprise and wariness, as if he'd just realized how much he'd revealed about himself and regretted it. "You needn't regard me with such pity," he said with peculiar harshness. "My sister and I wanted for nothing during our formative years. Our parents were not drunks or drug addicts. They did not beat or abuse us. We lived a typical, upper-class suburban life-style."

Danielle considered that, chose her words carefully. "I never meant to imply otherwise. Clearly, however, something happened to change that, something wrenching enough to make both you and your sister presume that your parents wouldn't be interested in the well-being of their own grandchild."

Colby shifted, clearly uncomfortable. He hesitated, appeared to be considering how much to tell her, if anything at all. Finally he set his jaw, arranged his features into an unreadable expression and spoke with the calm dispassion of one reading aloud from a newspaper's weather column. "Olivia was an obstinate child," he said. "In those days my sister fancied herself champion of the downtrodden— not from social conscience, but because she derived such pleasure from parental outrage. The final break came when she was seventeen and eloped with a tattooed ruffian whose only mode of communication was limited to four-letter words and obscene gestures. Our parents were mortified, just as Olivia had known they would be. They never forgave her. She never expected them to."

"Not forgive their own daughter?" Danielle flicked that away as unthinkable. "I don't believe it." Colby's indifferent shrug indicated that he didn't much care what she believed. "At least call them," she implored. "Give them the opportunity to be a part of Megan's life."

Fire flashed in his eyes, white-hot and terrifying. "I'd rather chew my own arm off than subject another helpless child to their Machiavellian clutches. Clearly, my sister felt the same."

Stunned by the vehement response, Danielle immediately backed off. She realized there was more than met the eye in Colby's volatile relationship with the elder Sinclairs, but only a fool would ignore the warning in his furious eyes. Danielle was not a fool.

She was, however, deeply committed to save little Megan from being thrust into the arms of strangers. "Well, then, perhaps we could contact Megan's father." When Colby's response was a pained grimace, her heart sank. "You do know who her father is...don't you?"

Colby confirmed the worst. "Olivia was married and divorced three times before her thirtieth birthday. For all I know, there could have been three more husbands since then. We haven't kept in touch. I didn't even know I had a niece until a few minutes ago." He massaged his eyelids, heaved a sigh that was, she thought, tinged with regret. Straightening, he glanced at little Megan, then looked away quickly. "So you can see that my options in this matter are severely limited."

When he reached for the telephone again, Danielle caught his wrist. "Please, don't do this. You don't seem to understand the consequences."

"And you don't seem to understand that I have no choice—"

"There's always a choice."

Colby shook his head. "It's only temporary, until her mother returns."

"Nothing about the child welfare system is temporary. Child abandonment is a serious charge."

That seemed to sink in. "Are you saying that if I call the authorities, my sister may permanently lose custody of her child?"

"That's exactly what I'm saying, Mr. Sinclair, and let me tell you what will happen then." She paused, waiting until she had his undivided attention. "As long as Megan is little and cute she'll merely be shuttled from foster home to foster home, where if she's extraordinarily lucky, a few people will care enough to bless her with an occasional hug. As she grows older, though, chances are better than even that she'll become either angry and rebellious, in which case she'll be transferred to juvenile detention dormitory, or she'll become withdrawn and depressed, whereupon she'll probably be committed to an institutional facility."

"That sounds a bit exaggerated," Colby replied, although he'd paled considerably. "It's my understanding that the state's foster care system is one of the best in the country."

She shrugged. "I wouldn't know about other systems, but the one we have here, well-intentioned though it may be, is woefully underfunded and inadequately staffed. I see its results every day—young people who've given up on themselves, given up on life. They're human shells, Mr. Sinclair, empty husks. But even if Megan is one of the lucky ones who bucks the odds and grows up with the appearance of normalcy, she'll never completely shed the pain of having been neglected, unloved and unwanted.''

Colby didn't respond right away. Instead, he gazed at his cooing niece with a reflective thoughtfulness that contradicted the supercilious snob she'd initially judged him to be. When he finally spoke, a wistful softness touched her to the bone.

"Every child deserves to be loved," he said.

An hour later, little Megan had been fed, bathed, dressed in footed, cartoon-character pajamas. Colby had watched from a safe distance, awed that his lovely neighbor's expertise went far beyond a knowledge of diapering and measuring formula. Danielle McCullough had established an emotional bond with the baby that left Colby dumbfounded, and deeply grateful.

Not that he doubted his own ability to care for the child. A man didn't rise to his level of success without a certain flexibility and quickness to learn new skills. Children had basic needs for food, clothing, cleanliness that seemed simple enough. Olivia had also prepared a detailed set of instructions, complete with a list of food requirements, sleep regimen and other routine necessities, along with a notarized affidavit of temporary guardianship should, God forbid, the baby require medical attention during her mother's absence.

All in all, Colby was confident that the child could be well tended without much disruption to his own schedule for the day or so it would take for him to make other arrangements.

Meanwhile, irritation at his sister had dissipated into amazement at how his neighbor had turned an impossible situation into a tolerable one.

Colby stalked to the open door of his bedroom, peering inside as his helpful neighbor fastened the final snap on Megan's pajamas. "There you go, sweetums," Danielle cooed at the tiny blond babe, who was dwarfed in the middle of Colby's king-size bed. "All fresh and clean and ready for nightie-night."

Megan giggled. "Umm-m-m, yayayaya."

"What's that?" Danielle puckered her brows, bent over the bed until shiny brown spirals fell forward, concealing her profile. "You say you want a tummy tickle? Well, I don't know." She made a tsking sound with her tongue. "Tummy tickles are pretty intense. Think you're up to it?"

Megan replied by grabbing a tiny fistful of Danielle's hair.

"Yikes, you want to play rough, huh?" Laughing, she buried her face in the baby's gelatinous belly and made a peculiar, vibrating sound that elicited childish squeals of delight.

Colby watched in fascination, barely able to believe that the chortling nine-month-old was the same child who'd been shrieking in fury barely an hour ago. Clearly, Danielle McCullough had a magical way with children. He didn't understand her secret, but was nonetheless grateful for it.

"Okay, champ. You win." Straightening, Danielle pried her hair out of Megan's fingers, scooped the pajama-clad baby into her arms. "Time for beddie-bye."

"Be-ba," Megan said in baby gibberish that may or may not have been an attempt to parrot the word.

"Yup." She bounced the child on her hip, swung toward the doorway with a shrewd gleam that Colby spotted too late. "Let's give Uncle a be-ba kiss, okay?"

Before Colby could step back, the baby grabbed a hunk

of flesh from each of his cheeks, hauled his head down and pressed a wet, open mouth to his chin.

"Good girl," Danielle praised, grinning broadly as Colby pulled out of the baby's taloned grip and staggered backward, rubbing his stinging face. "Uncle just loves baby kisses—" she slid him an evil grin "—don't you, Uncle Colby?"

Megan giggled, clapped her fat hands.

Colby gave Danielle a look that could freeze meat, although she didn't seem particularly perturbed. Instead, she carried the baby to the portable crib which had been set up in the corner of the master bedroom. She tucked Megan in beside a stuffed patchwork turtle that according to Olivia's instructions was the child's special sleep toy.

Danielle glanced over her shoulder. "Are you sure you want the crib in your room? Babies can be noisy sleepers."

"That's rather the point, isn't it? If the child has a problem in the middle of the night, I should be close enough to hear her."

She cocked her head, regarding him with a rather odd expression. For a moment, he thought he saw a softening of her eyes that was surprisingly similar to admiration. Before he could dwell on that, she blinked, turned away and began murmuring softly to the baby.

"Sleepy girl," she whispered softly, repeating the gentle words almost like a mantra as she caressed the baby's soft hair until the tiny eyelids fluttered shut.

The scene was riveting, the most poignant display of maternal tenderness Colby had ever witnessed. There was an ethereal love to Danielle's soft whispers, a nurturing warmth to which the baby instantly responded.

Colby was also mesmerized, stunned that any woman could display such profound affection for a child that wasn't her own.

But as he watched with awestruck wonder, the loving scene began to fade, overshadowed by images of the past....

The two-year-old wandered through a room of chatting people, dodged a sea of unfamiliar legs. Other children were playing nearby, but the youngster was too shy to join them. Instead, he watched in fascination as a whining toddler was lifted in a smiling woman's lap. She held her baby, kissed him, cuddled him.

The youngster watched a moment, then scurried off in search of his own mother, who was seated on the parlor settee, engaged in conversation with a bald man in a stiff suit. Emboldened, the youngster climbed into her lap, but she stood so quickly that he rolled onto the floor. She gave the cowering boy a cold stare, then pivoted around the settee and disappeared into the milling crowd.

The youngster crawled under the coffee table, comforted himself by sucking his thumb. He knew he wasn't supposed to. He knew his mother would scold him, coat his thumb with an ugly liquid to make him throw up. The boy knew all of that, but he didn't care. His thumb couldn't turn its back on him; his thumb couldn't walk away. It was the only friend he had.

The lonely little two-year-old learned a lesson that day. He learned that the only person he could ever truly count on was himself.

The boy had never forgotten that lesson; and Colby Sinclair had never forgotten the youngster who'd learned it.

Chapter Three

When Danielle turned from the sleeping baby's crib, Colby was staring into space with a peculiar trancelike expression. She tiptoed across the room, whispering. "Mr. Sinclair...Colby?"

He blinked, glanced down as if he'd never seen her before. "Yes?"

"You looked a million miles away. Are you all right?"

His tongue darted out, his gaze skipped sideways. "Of course," he mumbled, dabbing his brow with the back of his hand. He took a shaky breath, eyed the little net-sided crib tucked in the corner of his bedroom. "Is she asleep?"

Danielle glanced across the room to make certain, was reassured by the rhythmic rise and fall of the stenciled blanket tucked around the dozing child. "Yes. Poor little thing was exhausted. It usually takes babies a few days to adjust to sleeping in strange places. Megan seems exceptionally adaptable."

Only for a moment did a flicker of softness light his eyes before dissolving into a mask of icy indifference. "Good. That will make things easier for her."

The sudden chill in his voice did not escape Danielle's notice, nor did the stiffness of his stride as he left the room. She turned off the bedroom light, then found him in the living room shuffling through his briefcase. "What things?"

"Your assistance has been appreciated, Ms. Mc-Cullough—"

"Dani."

"We've taken up enough of your time." As he spoke, he continued to rifle through the briefcase contents, then withdrew a thick document fastened at the margin. Notations on the blue cover sheet indicated that it was a budget document, but even if Danielle hadn't seen the title, she'd have recognized the girth, the telltale column of tedious figures revealed as the document sagged open in his hands. He folded back the cover, flipped through several pages and rudely turned his back on her. "Good night, Ms. Mc-Cullough."

Rankled by the curt dismissal, Danielle followed Colby into the study. "Why did you say that Megan's adaptability would make things easier for her?"

Colby laid the folded document on his desk, flipped on a computer monitor, studied the screen as he offered a carefully worded reply. "The ability to accommodate to changing circumstance is always a virtue."

A sick heaviness settled into the pit of her stomach. "You're going to send Megan away, aren't you?"

"I won't call child welfare, if that's your concern."

"Megan is my concern, Mr. Sinclair."

"She'll be well cared for."

"By whom?"

"I'm certain there are a variety of excellent boarding facilities available."

"Boarding facilities?" Danielle steadied herself on a file cabinet. "Megan is a child, not a dog."

"I'm aware of that."

"You can't just toss a baby into a cage and pick her up at the end of the week."

He straightened, frowning. "I went to boarding school, Ms. McCullough, and I can assure you that I wasn't kept in a cage."

If Danielle hadn't been so piqued, she might have caught a salient clue. Instead, she shook her head so hard that a kinky tendril of hair whipped into her mouth. She impatiently wiped it away. "A school is one thing, but Megan is a baby. You can't board a baby."

"You can't?" Genuine surprise was quickly replaced by real distress. "Then what is one supposed to do? I have a business to run."

Danielle shrugged. "Perhaps you could pay your maid extra to take care of her during the day."

Colby frowned, shook his head. "I don't employ the services of a maid."

That surprised her. "Who keeps your place so spotless?"

"I'm capable of picking up after myself," he replied testily. "I'll not have strangers pawing my belongings and invading my privacy."

"You actually oil your own sofa?" When his stung expression indicated that he did, Danielle swallowed a snort of surprised laughter. "All right, the maid idea is out, but there are still a number of good day-care facilities in the area."

"Day care."

"Yes. They offer a wide variety of supervised play programs, and most are open until early evening hours."

He considered that briefly, then discarded it with a disdainful flip of his hand. "Out of the question."

"Why?"

"In case you've forgotten, Ms. McCullough, children are not allowed in this complex."

"Oh, good grief, must you be so darned inflexible?" Heaving a frustrated sigh, Danielle knuckled a tangled mass of curls away from her face, then jammed her fists on her hips and faced him. "Look, there are only four apartments off this hallway. I'm not going to complain, you're certainly not going to complain, the neighbors to my right are good-hearted folks who'd be more than understanding if you simply explain your predicament and the elderly woman on your left is so deaf, she wouldn't know if the high school marching band held practice sessions in your living room."

"That's not the point."

"What, pray tell, *is* the point?"

"The point is that a contract is a contract, and the building's lease agreement contains no fine print indicating that the terms can be broken for the sake of convenience." Colby clasped her elbow, ignored her indignant sputter and escorted her into the living room. "Your opinion is, however, appreciated." He scooped up her woven purse on the way to the foyer. "I'll take it into consideration."

Vaguely aware that she was suddenly standing in the building's hallway, Danielle spun to face him. "But what about—?"

"Good night, Ms. McCullough. Thank you again for your help."

He handed over the purse, shut the door in her face.

Danielle stood there, gaping, then spun on her heel and stalked into her own apartment. She sagged against her front door, glaring at Whiskers, who'd abandoned his étagère perch after the Risvold family's departure and was now curled comfortably on the back of the sofa.

"That man is insufferable," she told the cat. "For a while there, I actually believed he possessed a modicum of human kindness." She flung the woven bag onto a nearby chair, crossed her arms and paced, fuming. "Obviously I was wrong. Colby Sinclair is the most pompous, the most arrogant, intractable, completely callous and insensitive individual I've ever met in my entire life."

Whiskers yawned.

"He is heartless, utterly heartless, and there will be icicles on the gates of hell before I ever set foot in that condescending cad's apartment again." She stomped past the sofa, pausing to shake a finger in front of the cat's wide yellow eyes. "Never, do you hear? Not ever."

Then she marched into her bedroom and slammed the door.

Hell froze at two o'clock the next morning.

Roused by a persistent pounding, Danielle snagged her robe from the foot of the bed, stumbled to the front door and saw Colby Sinclair's frantic face through the peephole. She opened the door a crack, realized he was wearing little more than a bathrobe and a terrified expression. "What's wrong?"

"It's Megan. She won't stop crying."

"Did you try giving her a bottle?"

"Yes, yes." He impatiently raked his fingers through his hair, cast a worried glance over his shoulder, to where his apartment door stood open. The baby's choked sobs spilled into the hall. "She chewed the nipple for a moment, then spit it out and started screaming again." He faced Danielle, wrung his hands. "Her face is turning purple. I think she's dying."

Danielle pushed past him, tying her robe sash as she hurried across the hall.

Colby caught up with her as she rushed through his living room. "I tried holding her. I bounced her, and walked her. I even offered to read her a story."

"I'm sure she was impressed," Danielle murmured, entering the distraught man's bedroom. She paused in the doorway, touched her throat. Little Megan had pulled herself into a sitting position, was clinging to the crib rail, red as a beet and wailing pitifully. "Oh, sweetums." Danielle hurried over, scooped the miserable child into her arms. "It's okay, precious girl, everything's going to be just fine."

Megan's chin quivered, her chest racked with the force of her sobs. She twisted crankily, rubbed her wet little fists against her mouth, into her mouth, chewed her fingers with familiar desperation. "Hmm, let's see what's going on in there. Are our gums a little sore?"

She carried Megan over to a lamp, urged the baby's hands down so she could investigate. "Aha."

Colby peered over her shoulder. "Has she swallowed something, poisoned herself? I knew it, oh, God, I knew it. There's an emergency hospital on Grand Avenue. I'll get the car."

"Forget the car," she said as the frenzied man snatched his car keys off the dresser. "We'll settle for an ice cube."

He jerked to a stop, eyes cloudy with confusion. A moment later, they popped open in pure fear. "Ice? She has a fever, doesn't she? Oh, Lord, I thought she felt warm. A fever is serious, isn't it? I'll fill the bathtub." He pivoted, rushed toward the master bath.

Danielle managed to snag the sleeve of his robe with her free hand. "Good grief, Colby, will you settle down? We don't need an emergency room and we don't need to dunk the poor child in ice water. All we need is a single ice cube to rub on her gums. Megan is teething.''

"Teething?" His bewildered gaze shifted from Danielle to Megan and back again. "But she already has teeth."

"A few," Danielle acknowledged with a smile. "Soon she'll have more. Won't you, sweet girl?" The final question was posed to the sniveling baby, whose tiny face was screwed into a shuddering mass of blotchy red frustration.

Danielle brushed a kiss across the child's rashy, wet cheek, crooned words of quiet reassurance that much to Colby's surprise had a calming effect nothing short of miraculous. Megan sniffed, shivered, hooked a slimy finger around her swollen gums, even managed a thin, teary smile.

Colby was astounded. "How on earth did you do that?" he demanded, following Danielle into the kitchen.

Bouncing Megan against her hip, Danielle retrieved a piece of crescent-shaped ice from the automatic ice maker, glanced over her shoulder. "Do what?"

"That child has been howling for nearly an hour. Five seconds with you and she's happy as a clam in mud. I demand to know why."

"First of all, clams aren't particularly fond of mud, despite long-standing rumors to the contrary. They much prefer sand."

"Ms. McCullough—"

"Dani."

Colby gritted his teeth. "Very well... Dani. Fascinated though I may be by such unique knowledge of ocean crustacea—"

"Clams are mollusks," she murmured, using the ice to urge the baby's lips apart. "Crabs are crustacean. There, precious, doesn't that feel better?"

The inane discussion of sea life abruptly ended when the annoying but indisputably efficient woman lightly stroked little Megan's swollen gums with the ice. Colby watched in abject fascination. "Are you sure that won't hurt her?"

"You have to be gentle, keep the ice moving with light strokes. Like this, see?"

Shifting Megan in her arms, Danielle stepped closer, until the sweet scent of baby powder mingled with strawberries heightened his senses. Although distracted by the oddly appealing fragrance, Colby studied the gum-icing technique with engineering precision. It seemed simple enough, and the child appeared pleased by the procedure.

Then his gaze slipped from the process to his neighbor's attire, a thick terry cloth bathrobe. The garment itself wasn't particularly sensual. It was, in fact, unusually bland, considering the woman's dramatic flare for garish street clothes. But it was nonetheless intimate.

The entire situation was uncomfortably intimate. Occupying a kitchen in the wee hours of the morning was a distinctly personal activity, one Colby had never chosen to share. Guests invited to his sanctuary for certain social activities were made aware of the rules. No overnight visitors allowed.

He didn't consider that particularly unreasonable, nor did he view it as a symptom of antisocial behavior. Even if he hadn't battled insomnia since childhood, Colby was simply the type of person who required privacy, space to prowl his own abode whenever he chose, wearing whatever he chose to wear. Or not wear, since he'd always considered pajamas as loathsome and restrictive.

Colby's world was replete with restrictions, most imposed by his own unyielding expectations. Night allowed him to throw off the yoke of intractable ethics, indulge the illusion of unfettered freedom for which he secretly yearned. He'd never shared that. He didn't want to share it now.

"Some people use brandy."

Colby blinked. "Excuse me?"

"I'm not sure I like the idea of putting liquor into a baby's mouth, but my mother swore by it." Danielle gazed up with eyes that were, he now realized, more amber than brown, fringed by lashes that despite being rather short and stubby, gleamed with the same subtle coppery gold sheen that highlighted her hair in sunlight. "Personally, I recommend you pick up a bottle of teething anesthetic at the drugstore. Ms. Risvold used it on baby Val. It seemed to help."

The scent of strawberries intensified with Danielle's movements. Colby stepped back, not because the fragrance was unpleasant, but because it was distracting. "I'll purchase some in the morning."

"Good." Flipping the drippy ice cube into the sink, Danielle hoisted Megan to her shoulder, retrieved a pacifier from the refrigerated portion of Colby's large, side-by-side unit. "I found this when I was unpacking Megan's suitcase," she said as the baby recognized the pacifier, let out a delighted squeal and snatched it out of Danielle's hand. "Mama always chilled them, so I tossed Megan's in the fridge out of habit. Getting sleepy, precious? Ready for beddie-bye?"

"Be-ba," Megan replied happily, then popped the cold pacifier into her mouth.

Feeling uncomfortably helpless and out of his element, Colby followed as Danielle returned the baby to the crib, repeated the same tuck-in routine he'd witnessed earlier that evening. When Megan's breathing slowed in slumber, they turned off the bedroom light, exited quietly.

Danielle took a step toward the front door, held up her palms as Colby approached. "I'm leaving on my own, partner. No force is necessary this time."

Embarrassed by the reminder of her earlier, rather unceremonious exit, Colby struggled with the unfamiliar verbiage of apology. "I'll admit a tendency toward brusqueness, but it was never my intention to be ill-mannered. You've been most helpful." She cocked her head, regarding him as if expecting something more substantial. He managed a stiff smile, added, "Thank you again."

"You're welcome again." She reached for the doorknob.

"Ms. McCullough...ah, Dani?"

Pausing at the door, she angled a glance over her shoulder.

Colby fidgeted with his robe sash, suddenly terrified without reason. "This teething situation, it's not, ah, serious, is it? I mean, what if the child's immune system has been weakened, putting her at higher risk of viral infection—"

Danielle laid a hand on his wrist, stunning him into silence. Her fingers were soft, warm, electrically charged. She flashed a devastating smile. "Your niece is fine, just fine."

A surge of relief relaxed his shoulders. "Thank God," he murmured before he caught himself. Colby Sinclair rarely indulged himself with emotional utterings. They served no practical purpose, offered personal insights that others could use for their own advantage.

The slip did not go unnoticed by Danielle McCullough, who eyed him as if studying a strange new species. "Why, Mr. Sinclair," she murmured, eyes sparkling. "I do believe there truly is a streak of tenderness lurking beneath that arrogant veneer."

"Please keep it to yourself. I have a reputation to maintain."

"Your secret is safe with me. I'm the absolute soul of discretion." She opened the door, gave him a flirty wink. "By the way, the food bank relies on the generosity of corporate donors. We should talk about that. I'll call your office for an appointment."

Before Colby could muster a response, she issued a cheery good-night and disappeared into her apartment.

He stood there, having been thwarted by a daffy snip of the woman who'd usurped his privilege of not only controlling conversation, but had actually gotten the last word. Perhaps that shouldn't have irked him, but it did. Colby despised losing control, even on an admittedly inconsequential level. It had been a day of such losses, of utter anarchy, a chaos not of his own choosing.

In business, he could deal with turmoil. A perverse part of his nature almost admired pandemonium, that explosive, formless freedom of expression that neither served a purpose nor required one. He studied it; he admired it; then he tamed it.

Now Colby's safe, structured existence had been thrown into a turmoil he couldn't tame. A man who'd created a multimillion-dollar business without breaking a sweat, who could face down hardened bankers with a steely stare and implement corporate policy with a single swish of his mighty pen now found himself completely overwhelmed by one tiny bundle of teething terror.

Feeling totally inadequate for the first time in his adult life, Colby Sinclair spent the rest of the night staring into the crib, watching the baby breathe and plotting revenge on his sister.

"They're here early this morning," Danielle murmured as the slouching throng eased through the front gate of the food bank.

Beside her Madeline Rodriguez, a middle-aged community activist, volunteer extraordinaire and Danielle's best friend, glanced up from the clipboard on which she kept an informal head count of those served by the food distribution program. "We ran out of sugar and cornmeal yesterday. We've only got a two-day supply of flour, and barely enough bread to supply half of the people who are already here.''

''Three pallets of day-old baked goods will be here by noon, along with fifty pounds of sugar that should be repackaged and ready for distribution by tomorrow morning.''

''Donation or charge?''

''The baked goods were donated.''

Madeline sighed. ''Which means we'll be getting a bill for the sugar.''

''Not until next week.'' Shading her eyes against the early-morning glare, Danielle focused on a familiar battered station wagon pulling up beyond the chain-link fence. Two adults emerged, and four shabbily dressed children, who were promptly lined up and scrutinized by their parents. Thin sweaters were straightened. Shoelaces were tied. Untidy hair was smoothed, and little faces were inspected for cleanliness.

It was a routine Danielle had seen before, and it never failed to touch her. Frank Lonnigan and his family had been food bank regulars for the past three months, ever since the gasket factory on Figueroa closed down and threw three hundred people out of work.

The Lonnigans were a proud family; so were the Cruzes, the Herndens, the Archibalds, the Monaldos and all the other desperate families struggling to survive. These weren't lazy people looking for a handout. Many had jobs, usually minimum wage or day work that barely brought in enough to keep a roof over their heads. Sometimes it came down to a choice between having a place to live or having enough to eat.

Danielle knew how it felt to be hungry and homeless.

Suddenly the milling crowd surged forward as the dock doors opened, exposing packed boxes of groceries ready for distribution. Several burly volunteers positioned themselves to validate food-bank eligibility cards and pass out cartons that weren't nearly as full as they'd once been.

The process was quiet, organized, policed by the people themselves who followed strict rules of etiquette despite the fear in their eyes. Fear that there wouldn't be enough.

It was their fear that drove Danielle, that kept her pleading with merchants for just one more contribution, begging the city for just one more increase in funding that would allow more people to be fed, clothed, given hope.

The line moved quickly, efficiently. The Lonnigans inched forward, stood stoic, eyes forward, faces grim. The children clasped their hands, chewed their lips. They anxiously watched each box handed off, then studied the remaining stack of donations as if calculating how much was left versus the number of people ahead of them.

Behind the fence, more people arrived. A few tried to push through the gate out of turn. One of the volunteers hurried over to calm, to soothe, to escort them toward the end of a line that snaked beyond the fence through an asphalt parking lot littered by the debris of those who'd spent the night to assure their place in line.

There were too many people today. Some would leave empty-handed. Again.

The realization broke Dani's heart.

"Do you know that girl?" Madeline asked.

Danielle followed her gaze, saw a grubby teenager with stringy blond hair lurking outside the chain-link gate. "No."

"She was here a few days ago, but Jonas sent her away because she didn't have an eligibility card."

"Why wasn't I informed? I could have made arrangements—"

"She took off before we could page you." Madeline shaded her eyes, pursed her lips. "I think she's a runaway."

"Yes," Danielle murmured, studying the girl's gaunt features and torn clothing. "I'm going to talk to her."

"She won't go to the shelter," Madeline warned. "She's already hardened. Pulled a knife on one of the packers."

"That only means that she's been on the street long enough to be frightened and cynical. No child is beyond help."

Ignoring Madeline's weary shrug, Danielle shifted her jacket collar against the bitter chill, headed down the concrete steps. She reached the distribution area just as the Lonnigan family returned to the parking lot carrying their precious cargo of groceries. The gaunt teenager slid a wary glance around, then followed.

Danielle increased her stride, hurried toward the gate. Before she reached it, the girl snatched a loaf of bread from the Lonnigans' grocery box, sprinted across the parking lot and vaulted a fence. One of the Lonnigan boys gave chase, only to be called back by his father, who spoke softly to the youngster then hustled his family into the dented station wagon and drove away.

Danielle couldn't hear what Frank Lonnigan told his family, but knew what her own charitable father would have said. He would have reminded his children that anyone who stole food needed it more than they did. Clearly, the young runaway had needed food desperately, and Danielle was disappointed to have missed the opportunity to help her.

"She'll be back," Madeline said when Danielle had returned to the loading dock.

"I know, but not before she spends at least one more night on the street."

Madeline heaved an indifferent shrug, tucked the clipboard under her arm. "You can't save them all, Dani. Be thankful you were able to save some of them."

"What do you mean 'were'?"

"Word is out that the food bank is folding. That's why people are so desperate to stock up."

Since street rumors were the bane of the barrio, Danielle wasn't exactly shocked by the news. She was, however, disheartened by it. "We're not folding," she said firmly. "Things have been a little tight lately, but our quarterly grant from the city is due next week."

"Have you checked your messages this morning?"

"Not yet. Why?"

"The city finance director called to give you a heads-up. Food bank funding has been added to this week's council agenda." Madeline blinked away tears, gazed across the sea of hopeful faces below. "It's over, Dani. They're closing us down."

"I'm Colby Sinclair, Ms. Glickman. We spoke on the telephone."

"Of course, Mr. Sinclair. This must be little Megan." All smiles, the petite redhead extended her arms. "Come here, sweetheart, and I'll introduce you to all your new playmates."

Pulling away, Megan squirmed on her uncle's arm, clutched at his shirt and buried her face against his neck.

The redhead chuckled, stepped out onto a freshly painted, gingerbread-style porch stenciled with bunnies and bonnet-clad geese. "A bashful beauty, hmm? Well, we'll soon fix that. Shyness is not an option at Happy Home Day Care."

Colby shifted his grip, encircling the child in a protective embrace. "I'd like to inspect the facilities now."

"Ah, yes," she murmured, a knowing twinkle in her eye. "I understand how difficult the first day can be, but I assure you, my staff and I will do everything possible to make the transition as painless as possible for you and your lovely little niece." She stepped aside, held the screen door open. "Please, come in."

After a hesitant moment, Colby entered a long foyer lined by colorful wooden pegs on which a variety of tiny jackets, sweaters and child-size outerwear had been hung. Beneath the pegs were painted cubicles containing boots, mittens, toys and an occasional lunch box. A din of childish squeals, not all of them happy, emanated from a huge open room to the left of the foyer and caused Megan to dig her frantic little fingers even deeper into the flesh of her uncle's shoulder.

"This is our coat room," Ms. Glickman was saying, automatically raising her voice as the playroom shrieks grew louder. "Each child is assigned a peg and a cubicle where personal possessions can be kept. As you can see, some of the children bring their own lunch, but most prefer to take advantage of our nutritionally complete hot meal program, which is available for a modest fee. Naturally, special dietary needs can be accommodated...er, but I can see you're more interested in the playroom."

Colby was already marching down the hall, into an expansive arena exploding in pandemonium. Hyperactive youngsters, ages three or four, chased each other through an obstacle course of bewildered toddlers, some of whom were wailing pitifully. Infants of varying age were buckled into wind-up baby swings lined along one wall; some slept; some gazed into space; one was trying to swallow its own hand.

Above the fray, a television set affixed to the wall displayed a video of a six-foot feathered bird engaged in rapt conversation with a freckled woman dressed like a rag doll and wearing a red yarn-mop wig.

Ms. Glickman stepped inside, beaming. "Our playroom is equipped with only the highest-quality, educator-tested toys, games and videos. We encourage unstructured activities here, and also in our outside playground, which has been specially designed to blend healthy physical exercise with the creative fantasies of curious little minds.''

The final word had barely left her lips before a rambunctious preschooler accidentally elbowed a toddler, knocking the startled baby to the floor. One of only two adult supervisors in the room leapt forward to scoop up and comfort the sobbing child.

Stunned speechless, Colby could do little more than tighten his grip on Megan, who sneaked a quick peak at the chaos, let out a sharp wail, then grabbed hold of his necktie and darned near strangled him before he could pry her frantic fingers loose.

''As you can see,'' Ms. Glickman added proudly, ''our staff of dedicated professionals is committed to the emotional and physical well-being of each and every Happy Home child.'' She pivoted, hooked her hand around Colby's elbow, spun him back into the hallway, led him toward a deserted room of brightly colored plastic tables and matching miniature chairs. ''Our quiet room, where we have story time, craft time and other structured activities. When the older children return from school, we also use this area to assist with their lessons.''

Colby was appalled. ''Good Lord, there must be thirty children out there as it is. Are you telling me that there will be even more?''

''From three to six is our busiest time, but we take extra precautions to make certain our babies aren't forgotten in the rush.'' She opened yet another door, stood back with a satisfied smile. ''We schedule baby nap time for late afternoon. That way, the little ones are protected from the, er, exuberance of older children, and they're rested and refreshed when their parents arrive.''

Colby didn't hear the last part of Ms. Glickman's explanation. He was frozen in shock, staring into a room in which row after row after row of slatted cribs were lined like open-topped cages.

"This is our sleepy-time room," she informed him proudly. "The decor has been scrupulously chosen to soothe and comfort the youngest members of our Happy Home family."

Colby was not impressed. "It's a human kennel."

"Excuse me?"

"Cages with bars." He spun, strode down the hall, furious with himself, furious with Olivia, furious at the frantic woman who scurried behind him.

"Our cribs are quite safe," Ms. Glickman assured him. "The design has been certified by the consumer council on child safety and approved by—"

"A safe cage is still a cage." Colby shouldered open the screen door. "Thank you for your time. I'll be making other arrangements."

But as he carried his suddenly happy and bright-eyed niece to the car, Colby would have relinquished every stock option in his portfolio for the merest clue as to what those arrangements could possibly be.

Chapter Four

It was shortly after noon when Danielle returned to the apartment complex clutching a bag of colored marking pens and a thin ream of poster board. She hurried down the short hallway, pausing at Colby Sinclair's apartment. The door was open a few inches, which struck her as odd. Inside, a phone was ringing, a pager was beeping. She heard voices. Male voices.

She set the bag and poster board in the hall, eased Colby's door open and peeked inside. The gleaming chrome-and-glass living room looked like a war zone, with crumpled magazine pages littering the ivory carpet, wooden spoons, spatulas and plastic mixing bowls strewn about the floor.

Danielle stepped warily inside, hovered in the foyer. In the study, the ringing of a telephone was replaced by a series of odd clicks, beeps and electronic wails. The fax machine, she realized.

A grainy male voice filtered from the kitchen. "The budget committee is scheduled to meet at three, and you have an appointment with Golf-Pro Manufacturing at four-thirty."

"Cancel the four-thirty" came the gruff, but familiar reply. "I'll try to make the budget meeting. If I can't, we'll just have to arrange a conference call."

Danielle instantly relaxed, realizing that Colby was using the kitchen speaker phone. Judging by the snippet of conversation she'd heard, he was most likely conversing with his office, which was a major relief considering that she'd initially thought his apartment had been burglarized.

Nothing nefarious appeared to be happening, although it occurred to her that Colby probably wouldn't be thrilled to find her lurking in his foyer. Before she could beat a furtive retreat, all hell broke loose.

Behind her, someone pounded on the front door. She spun around, clutched her chest.

"Delivery!"

She flattened against the foyer wall, cast a frantic glance toward the kitchen just as Megan came scooting out, her little hands and knees churning. She grabbed a wooden spoon, sat up, happily whacked her shoe.

Colby called out from the kitchen. "Leave the package. There's a twenty on the coffee table."

The front door swung all the way open, pinning Danielle in place as a whistling delivery man sauntered through the cluttered living room, laid a red-and-white express envelope on the table, pocketed the bill and sauntered out, tipping his hat to Danielle as if a wild-eyed woman squashed behind a door was no big deal.

Thankfully, Colby was still in the kitchen. "The contracts just arrived," he was saying. "Put the new cash-flow projections on-line. I'll check them out from here."

A dial tone buzzed for a moment, then there was a click

as the speaker phone was silenced. Colby burst through the kitchen door, scooped Megan under his arm as if she was a towheaded football and dashed into the study. A split second later, he reappeared, stared straight at Danielle, who was easing out of her hidey-hole.

She squirmed, flashed a smile. "Your, ah, door was open."

"So you considered that an invitation?"

"Well, umm—"

"Good." He hurried over, plopped the baby in Danielle's arms. "Her lunch is on the counter."

"Wait—"

Colby disappeared into his study.

"—a minute." Danielle sighed, shifted the grinning baby. "Well, sweet girl, it looks like I've been commandeered."

Megan, clearly thrilled, giggled, pinched a fistful of Danielle's face in each hand and slopped a soggy kiss square on her mouth.

Danielle laughed, gave the baby a warm hug. "When you ask that nicely, how can I refuse? Let's go see what Uncle has cooked up for you."

On the way to the kitchen, Danielle glanced into the study and saw Colby hunched over the computer. She watched for a few seconds, knowing he wouldn't look up. He didn't. Still, she was fascinated by his ability to completely focus his concentration on the task at hand. Behind him, the fax whirred and clicked. He ignored the din, silenced his beeping pager, picked up the desk telephone, dialed a number, all without taking his eyes off the computer screen.

Colby Sinclair was in his element, Danielle realized. He was confident, decisive, exuding the raw power and magnetism of a man who took authority for granted, commanded respect as his due. He was impressive. He was fascinating. He was the most exciting man she'd ever met.

He was also impossibly arrogant. But nobody was perfect.

Alerted by Megan's restless wiggle, Danielle continued into the kitchen, placed the baby in the high chair, glanced around for a bib. Finding none, she tucked a paper towel around the baby's fat little neck, and eyed a compartmentalized plastic toddler plate into which the contents of several open baby food jars had already been spooned. "Applesauce, puree of green stuff and strained mystery meat. Personally, I'd rather have a burrito, but all things considered, looks like Uncle Colby did all right by you."

Megan smiled.

Danielle had just placed the empty plate in the sink when Colby appeared in the doorway. "Good timing," she told him. "Lunch is officially over."

He frowned slightly, calling attention to the fact that his tawny brows and lashes were considerably lighter than his hair. Odd, Danielle thought, that she hadn't noticed that peculiarity, nor had she noticed the rugged creases bracketing his mouth. If he hadn't been wearing a slick dress shirt and tailored wool slacks, Colby Sinclair could easily be mistaken for an outdoorsman, one of those rugged individualists whose photos grace the cover of extreme sport magazines.

Eyes narrowed, he nodded at Megan. "How did you do that?"

"Do what?"

"Keep her so clean. After breakfast, every inch was lathered in oatmeal. I had to change her clothes and give her another bath."

"You didn't put the cereal bowl on the high chair tray, did you?" When he straightened defensively, Danielle shrugged. "Ah. Well, I suppose there's a creative aspect to letting kids squish their fingers through their food." She snatched a clean paper towel to wipe the sticky baby mouth, removed Megan from the high chair and handed her to Colby. "I hate to feed and run—"

"Then don't." Ignoring the fact that Megan's goopy little fingers were twisting in his designer necktie, Colby shifted his stance, moistened his lips. "I mean, the least I could do is offer you lunch."

She regarded him for a moment, saw the furtive flick of his lashes, the way his gray eyes avoided her gaze. "You need a baby-sitter, don't you?"

"Just for a couple of hours," he confessed, looking massively relieved. "I'll pay you, of course."

"Sorry." She brushed by him, headed toward the front door.

"You don't understand. I have an appointment this afternoon."

"So do I."

"Yes, yes, but mine is important."

She jerked to a stop, tossed an incredulous look over her shoulder. "Mine is a matter of life and death, Mr. Sinclair. As far as I'm concerned, it doesn't get more important than that."

"Mr. Sinclair?" The woman slapped an agency card in Colby's hand, stalked through the front door sniffing air like a shark on a blood trail. "I don't work weekends or holidays. I'm a licensed au pair, not a short-order cook, so I shall expect my meals to be catered." She thrust a sheet of paper at him. "My dietary requirements."

Colby juggled the paper and the business card, laid both on the dining room table. "You understand that the position is temporary—"

"My hours are from eight to five, precisely. Should I be

required to stay longer, I'll expect double my hourly wage, triple if I'm required to supervise the child's evening meal.''

''Supervise?''

The woman cast him a withering look. ''I thought I made myself clear, Mr. Sinclair. I am not a cook.''

Colby puffed his cheeks, blew out a breath. ''Thank you for coming,'' he said. ''I'll be in touch.''

''Sure, I really, you know, love kids and stuff. That's why I'm doing the nanny thing, like, to pull in a few extra bucks. College is the pits, you know? Like, everything is so expensive.'' The young woman flipped her bobbed hair, snapped her gum. ''Yeah, I can stay late sometimes, but like, I mean, the buses don't run forever, you know? I could, like, take a cab maybe, but you'd hafta, like, pay for it.''

Colby sighed. ''Thank you. Goodbye.''

''The child is spoiled. Look how she clings to your leg, sniveling like an animal. Discipline is the key, Mr. Sinclair. You will not even recognize your niece when I've completed my training regimen.''

Colby opened the front door. ''Goodbye.''

''Jeez, that's a real big television you got there. I'm really glad you got such a big television. I can't work without one, on account of Melissa and Melvin are going to have a baby anyday now, only they don't know that Melissa's evil twin, Melody, is going to sneak into the delivery room and— Hey!''

Colby shut the front door, considered beating his head against it. He would have, except that Megan was pulling herself up on his pants leg and he thought bashing his brains out in frustration might set a bad example for the child.

The baby hugged his knee, grinning proudly. "Yaya," she said happily.

"You're right," he murmured, lifting the child into his arms. "The last one was a real 'yaya.'" He spun her around until she giggled, then carried her to a stack of plastic mixing bowls of which she was particularly fond. Megan chortled, flung the nested bowls across the room, then lurched into chase-crawl mode, squealing cheerfully.

Colby collapsed on the sofa, grimly recounted the past two days in his mind. Out of a dozen au pair applicants, only one had seemed reasonably normal. A warm, friendly middle-aged woman who'd been well-groomed, articulate, and actually seemed more interested in the baby than the perks of the job itself. Even Megan, who'd eyed every other applicant with blatant disapproval, had liked her. So had Colby, until he'd excused himself to answer the phone then returned to find her sucking a silver flask and reeking of vodka.

It seemed hopeless, utterly hopeless. Colby's empathy for Ms. Wilkins, his harried finance director, had increased to the point that he was contemplating the establishment of an office child-care facility. Considering how much company time was lost each year in pursuit of parental concerns, Colby suspected such a project might actually be fiscally prudent.

Thinking he should appoint a committee to study the concept, Colby glanced at his watch, was disappointed to realize that the office had been closed for over an hour. It was, in fact, Megan's dinnertime. He sighed. It seemed like only moments ago he'd finished cleaning up the lunch mess. Colby was discouraged, and he was tired to the bone. Who'd have ever thought that following the myriad machinations of one tiny human would prove more exhausting than the sixteen-hour work schedule of a high-powered corporate executive?

No wonder Olivia needed a break.

Not that Colby's sense of forgiveness had been sharpened, at least not where his sister was concerned. Olivia would pay dearly for what she'd done. Colby would see to that personally, although the direction of resentment had shifted from anger at the chaos his sister had caused in his own life to absolute outrage at the harm she could have caused her beautiful child. Megan deserved better.

And if Colby had anything to say about it, his selfish sister and his precious niece would each get exactly what they deserved.

At the moment, however, Colby wished nothing more than a few minutes peace before revving up for another pitifully lacking Mr. Mom performance. A quick glance at Megan confirmed she was playing happily, so Colby retrieved the remote, powered up the big television set that had so enamored the last nanny applicant and flipped to a local news station.

Normally he followed current events with avid enthusiasm. This evening, however, he was distracted, barely able to concentrate on the news anchor's droning recitation of Middle East tensions, world trade deficits and the latest political shenanigans in the nation's capital. Colby's mind wandered even as his gaze was glued to the screen.

Then something caught his attention. It was a protest of sorts, a group of sign-wielding malcontents picketing city hall. Not unusual in itself, except that there had apparently been some kind of roughhousing in the ranks. The television station had video to prove it.

He sat up, leaned forward, blinked in disbelief.

There was no mistaking the woman wearing a lime Santa Claus sweater, violet stretch pants and a floppy, flaming red beret. Danielle McCullough, who stood out in the surging crowd like a rainbow-colored jelly bean in a rice bowl, was struggling to keep a picket sign out of the hands of a burly dockworker-type who apparently took umbrage at her message.

What the message was, Colby hadn't a clue. The picket sign was ripped out of her grasp before he could read it. A moment later, Danielle, too, was knocked to the ground. Horrified, Colby leapt to his feet just as the news anchor returned with a recap, explaining that the protest had been held earlier by a group lobbying the council to continue funding for the local food bank.

"Good Lord." Colby snatched Megan up and strode straight to Danielle's apartment. Their paths hadn't crossed since his clumsy baby-sitting request had sent her marching off in a fit of righteous anger. He'd regretted the incident, but had been too harried the past few days to set aside enough time to rectify the situation.

Now he was reacting on impulse, along with a deeper, more curious emotion that he dared not examine too closely. When he'd seen the tape of Danielle being attacked, something inside him had exploded with rage. And with fear.

Protective anger was a new experience for him. He didn't much care for the sensation, but he couldn't seem to control it, either. All he knew was that he absolutely had to see Danielle. Now. This very minute.

Colby shifted Megan in his arms, knocked on Danielle's door and waited. After several seconds he knocked again. Harder, this time. More insistent. He knew she was home. He'd heard her moving behind the wall that divided their apartments, and had no intention of leaving until he'd assured himself that she hadn't been injured in the melee.

On the third knock, the door cracked open. A gaunt young woman peered out. "Yes?"

"Er, I'd like to speak with Ms. McCullough, please."

"She's not here."

Colby regarded the young woman a moment, realizing that she wasn't a woman at all. She was a girl, perhaps fifteen at the most, with huge, frightened eyes and stringy blond hair that looked as if it hadn't been shampooed in weeks. "May I ask what you are doing in Ms. Mc-Cullough's apartment?"

"The shelter was full. Dani said I could stay here for a couple of days." The girl's eyes flickered, flinched at a thump from somewhere inside the apartment. "Umm, she's at a city council meeting. I'll tell her you came by."

Colby stuffed his foot in the door before she could close it. "That might be difficult, since you haven't bothered to ask who I am."

"Oh. Yeah." The girl stiffened, allowed the door to open far enough to reveal a pathetically thin frame draped in gaudy, mismatched clothing that was vaguely familiar, and much too large for the teenager who now wore them. "So, who are you?"

Colby stared past the girl, toward a sliver of light emanating from a room that he judged from the layout of his own apartment to be the master bedroom. "I thought I heard a noise. Are you alone?"

"Uh-huh." The girl tossed a disinterested glance over her shoulder, then faced Colby with a bland shrug. "It's probably the cat. He gets into everything."

The words had barely left her mouth when the sliver of light suddenly widened. A hissing ball of black fur shot out, charged into the living room and leapt onto the top shelf of a polished wood étagère cluttered with framed snapshots and dime-store bric-a-brac.

"You see?" The girl smiled sweetly. "Cats are such a pain."

Colby couldn't dispute that. Personally, he considered felines to be annoying, destructive creatures without a single redeeming feature. He'd rather stick his hand in a blender than touch one of the ferocious, skin-shredding little beasts. "When do you expect Ms. McCullough to return?"

"Late."

"How late?"

"Real late." The girl shifted, cast a brief glance over her shoulder. "Look, mister, I got supper on the stove."

Since the girl clearly wasn't inclined to provide any further information, Colby took the hint and left. But he wasn't happy. He wasn't happy about spotting his neighbor on the six o'clock news, nor was he pleased by her habit of hauling home strays who looked and smelled as if they'd been dragged through the trash. Most of all, he wasn't happy with himself, because he couldn't keep out of affairs that were none of his business; and because he couldn't keep thoughts of Danielle McCullough from invading his mind.

Danielle returned home, bruised, psychologically battered and weary to the bone. Her lobbying campaign had been successful beyond her wildest dreams, but in winning the war she'd become a casualty of it. The food bank would survive. Her career wouldn't.

A light sliver beckoned from beneath Colby Sinclair's front door. Danielle hesitated, suppressed an urge to ring his bell. It was nearly midnight, and she doubted he'd appreciate the intrusion. Besides, she needed comfort, understanding, perhaps even a smidgeon of sympathy. These were not emotions with which Colby Sinclair had more than a passing acquaintance.

Except when it came to his niece. Danielle doubted Colby would admit even to himself how attached he'd become to little Megan. Danielle saw it, though. She saw it in his tenacity, his determination to meet each and every one of the baby's needs regardless of how those needs impacted or conflicted with his own. She recognized his hidden tenderness, admired it deeply.

In truth, there was much about Colby Sinclair she admired, although she'd rot on ice before she'd admit it out loud. Despite his good traits—everyone had a few—Colby Sinclair was still oppressive and condescending, a man so certain of his own superiority that he was blinded to the misfortune of others.

Danielle could forgive many faults; a lack of compassion was not one of them.

She passed by Colby's apartment, unlocked her own, stepped into the dark foyer. A shadowed lump on the sofa drew her attention. "Sheila?" She fumbled for the light switch. "You don't have to sleep on the sofa. I told you to use the guest room— Oh my God!"

Danielle stiffened, stared at the stack of drawers from her bedroom dresser that had been emptied and piled on the sofa. Lingerie, socks, clothing and personal items, including her empty jewelry box, were strewn around the room. Except for a few snapshots and a visibly shaken cat, the étagère was empty. The crystal vase that her brother bought from Europe was gone, along with the hand-painted egg her mother had made for her birthday, and the china tea cups she'd collected since childhood.

So was the television and VCR, a small stereo, her portable CD player.

Clutching her stomach, she knelt by a broken plant container, caressed the wilted leaves of her favorite *Pothos,* and was stupidly sweeping spilled potting soil into her palm when a gruff voice boomed from the doorway.

"It's about time you got home. Good Lord! What on earth did that girl—?" Colby bit off the question, stepped inside to help Danielle to her feet. She rose shakily, brushing dirt from her palms. He steadied her with a firm arm, tossed a contemptuous glance around the room. "The little thief robbed you."

Danielle licked her lips, couldn't reply.

"Have you notified the authorities?" The question was posed with surprising softness. When she shook her head, he squeezed her shoulders, a compassionate gesture that startled her and conflicted with the harsh anger in his eyes. "I'll call them."

"No, please." She turned as he stepped around her, stopped him with a light touch on his sleeve. "I don't want the police involved. Poor Sheila has enough problems."

Colby regarded her as if she'd completely lost her mind. "Poor *Sheila*—" he spit the name out like a bad taste "—just repaid your kindness by stealing you blind."

"I doubt she wanted to." Sighing, Danielle picked up the cracked plant pot, laid it on a table. "Sheila is a fourteen-year-old runaway who hooked up with a crowd of hard-core criminals. After they took her in, they gave her a choice of earning her keep as either a thief or a prostitute. Guess which she chose." She straightened, brushed her palms on her thighs, avoided his gaze. "I didn't think they'd find her here."

Colby wandered toward the kitchen, where every cabinet was opened, every drawer pulled out. "Perhaps she gave them directions."

Danielle flinched, violently shook her head. "No, Sheila wouldn't have done that. She wanted to get away from them, wanted a better life for herself. They must have followed her or—" she waggled her hand, sighed, let it drop to her side "—or something."

"Indeed."

"What are you doing?" Danielle asked as he strode toward the telephone.

"Since you're quite certain this Sheila person had no

nefarious motive in accepting your hospitality, you surely won't object to verifying the last number dialed.''

Irritated by his all-knowing smugness, Danielle stepped aside, folded her arms and glared at him. ''Go ahead, knock yourself out.''

Colby issued a curt nod, dialed the call-return code. After a moment, he asked what number had been reached, listened to the response, then hung up. ''Have you placed any calls to a public telephone booth on Sepulveda Boulevard?''

She swayed as if gut punched, turned away.

Colby spoke quietly. ''I didn't think so.''

The evidence of Sheila's duplicity was mounting; still Danielle couldn't accept it. She'd looked into the girl's eyes and seen a frightened child, a child who yearned to be safe, to be loved. There had been no deceptive flicker, no avoidance, nothing to hint a lack of veracity. Danielle had measured Sheila's words, her body language, then had drawn upon years of experience assessing morals and motives of those with whom she worked.

Any social worker's effectiveness depended on the accuracy of those personal appraisals. Although deeply wounded by Sheila's betrayal, Danielle was shattered by the realization that her own judgment of the teenager had been so blatantly flawed.

A warm palm settled on her shoulder, a firm touch, surprisingly gentle. ''Let me call the police, Dani. Perhaps they can recover some of your things.''

''No.'' She bit her lip, dragged off the floppy felt hat and dropped it into one of the empty drawers on the sofa. ''Most of the stuff has probably changed hands three times by now. It doesn't matter. Things aren't important.'' She cast a wistful glance at the étagère. ''Except for Mama's birthday egg, and my brother's crystal vase, and…'' She knelt to touch the shattered remnants of a plaster handprint, proudly presented by a homeless child whose family Danielle had helped last year.

Tears spurted before she could stop them.

Whiskers leapt down from his perch, rubbed his head on her leg as if offering comfort, then issued a warning hiss as Colby approached.

"Scat," he muttered, easing the angry cat aside with his shoe. He helped Danielle to her feet, embraced her awkwardly, patted her back as she wept. "You're all right," he murmured in a voice roughened by hesitance. "That's all that matters."

From the depth of despair, Danielle noticed strange heat tingling beneath his touch, spiraling from between her shoulders to her nape, then encircling her chest like an electric noose. His scent overwhelmed her, an alluring fragrance of expensive soap mingled with musky, imported cologne.

She rested her cheek against Colby's chest, felt the rapid pulse of his heartbeat beneath the crisp cotton broadcloth shirt. His muscles flexed, tightened. The comforting movement of his palm on her back slowed, gentled, like the erotic caress of a lover.

Tension melted into buttery softness, the dizzying luxury of being cocooned in soothing warmth, of gliding beneath the silken waters of a hot, steaming bath.

Automatically she burrowed closer to the comforting heat, her hands curled beside her face while her fingertips lightly scraped the cotton fabric. A sob vibrated her shoulders, quivered her heart.

Colby drew her closer, murmured words of comfort that she felt rather than heard. His breath was soft against her hair, lifting light tendrils, warming the scalp beneath. A gentle pressure touched her temple as he stroked, caressed. Comforted.

The moment was eerily intimate, so erotic it took her breath away.

An angry growl emanated from somewhere around her ankles, then evolved into a furious hiss. Colby stiffened, stepped away, glared down as the cat, its back arched in outrage, slunk beneath the coffee table, regarding the interloper with slitty-eyed disdain.

Danielle ducked her head, wiped her wet face. "Sorry," she murmured, still shaken by the peculiar sensations his nearness had evoked. "I'm not usually such a drip."

Clasping his hands behind his back, Colby cleared his throat, rocked back on his heels. "Your trust was betrayed and your privacy violated. A certain emotional response is to be expected."

She shrugged, fingered a silky scarf that was draped over the sofa, said nothing.

Colby's jaw hardened as he scanned the cluttered room. "I suspected there was someone else in the apartment," he muttered, more to himself than to Danielle. "I should have followed my instincts and called the police when I had the chance."

"What are you talking about?"

"Hmm? Oh, I came to see you earlier this evening. When your, ah, guest informed me that you weren't at home, I thought I heard movements in the back bedroom." He glanced away, looked chagrined. "The young woman insisted it was the cat. Unfortunately, I believed her."

"Don't beat yourself up," Danielle replied grimly. "Sheila has a talent for believability. She fooled me, too. So, what did you want?"

"Want?"

"When you came over earlier."

"Oh." He furrowed his brow, shifted uncomfortably. "It was nothing."

"It certainly must have been something, or you wouldn't have been here. Is Megan all right?"

"Megan's quite well, thank you."

"Good." Folding her arms, Danielle regarded him curiously. "Were you going to ask me out on a date?"

His head snapped around. "A date? Good heavens, no."

"Well, you don't need to look so horrified. Men have been known to ask me out occasionally."

"Yes, of course," he murmured, although a perplexed glint in his eye indicated that he wasn't the least bit comfortable with the concept. "The truth is that I witnessed your disgraceful debut on the six o'clock news."

"Disgraceful, huh?" She chuckled, busied herself by tossing strewn personal items back into the emptied drawers. "To each his own, I guess. Actually, that wasn't exactly my television debut. I've been on the news quite a bit." She angled a flirty glance, winked at him. "When it comes to fighting city hall, a few minutes of action news airtime can be a girl's best friend."

"Do you mean that you've actually done that before?"

"Sure. A publicly embarrassed politician can be amazingly open-minded."

Colby was clearly appalled. "You actually created a riot for political purposes?"

"Let's just call it a minor disturbance."

"Let's call it utterly ludicrous. You're lucky you weren't seriously injured when that muscle-bound idiot attacked you—"

"You mean George? Oh, heavens, George wouldn't hurt me."

Colby stared at her. "You staged the entire incident, didn't you? The man who was trying to beat you senseless with your own picket sign, that was all an act?"

"I should mention that aside from being one of the food bank's most dedicated volunteers, George also does performance art for the cultural arts theater.'' She quickly tucked a pair of gloves, two scarves and a box of grape-colored tights into a drawer, skimmed a glance at the scowling man. ''You don't approve, do you?''

''Approve?'' His brows crunched together at the bridge of his nose. ''Now why wouldn't I approve of my tax dollars being doled out for fraudulent purposes?''

''There was no fraud involved. The city was going to close down the food bank, allow hundreds of families to starve in the street. I simply wanted the opportunity to plead their case in a public forum.''

''By manipulation and blackmail.''

''By whatever it takes.'' Danielle flung a handful of colorful socks into the drawer, jammed her hands on her hips, spun to face him. ''If it makes you feel any better, the good guys won tonight, and the bad guys lost. The food bank stays open.''

Colby regarded her thoughtfully. ''Congratulations.''

''Thanks.'' She raked her hair, brushed past him on her way to the kitchen.

He stood in the doorway, watched her shove boxes back into the cupboard, toss utensils back into open drawers. There was a vulnerability in her anger, a hurt in her eyes that touched him, although he didn't know why it should. Purity of motive notwithstanding, Danielle McCullough had been foolish to allow strangers into her home. Now she was paying the price for that foolishness. Causing one's own misery was not, in Colby's mind, worthy of eliciting empathy.

Still, he felt bad for her. He just didn't know exactly why. ''You can't stay here tonight.''

Without responding, Danielle knelt to study a splatter of blue ceramic on the kitchen floor. Her lip quivered before she caught it between her teeth and began picking up fragments, placing them lovingly in the palm of her hand.

"I said you can't stay here tonight, Dani. The thieves could return."

"They took what they wanted. There's nothing left."

Argument died on his tongue. He swallowed, widened his stance, nodded at the pottery fragments she was holding with peculiar poignancy. "Did that, ah, item have special significance?"

"In a way." She sighed, stood, dumped the pieces in the trash. "There was a couple hundred dollars in it."

That was not what he'd expected. "You kept cash in the house? Good Lord, why?" The answer popped into Colby's mind at the moment it was reflected in her sad eyes. "You gave it away, didn't you? You used it for motels and for food and for spending money for people like the Risvolds, and Sheila, and God knows how many other rescued strays." He tossed up his hands, fingered his hair and wondered why in hell he felt such a sharp sense of frustration. The woman wasn't his problem. If she wanted to throw cash out the window, it wasn't Colby's place to stop her.

Her safety, however, was another matter.

"At least have the locks changed," he said. "Thugs like that will wait for insurance to replace the losses, then they'll come back and rob their victims all over again."

Danielle managed a thin smile, twirled a lock of hair around her finger. "They wouldn't find much. I'm not insured."

Colby stifled a moan, rubbed his eyelids.

"But it doesn't matter anyway." She issued a dry laugh. "Maybe this is all poetic justice. I told you that the city agreed to keep the food bank open, but I didn't mention that they had one teensy condition. They want to take it over, run it with city staff. It's perfect, really. Almost like the plot of a melodramatic television movie. One week I'm executive director of a facility for the homeless and hungry, the next week I'm just another one of its clients."

Colby just stood there in stunned silence while Danielle continued to muse the irony of her changing circumstance. "So you can see why it doesn't matter that I'm not insured, or if I don't run out and get the locks changed."

He found his voice, or at least a raspy thread of it. "No, actually, I can't."

She sagged against the counter, met his eyes with an expression of exquisite sadness. "It doesn't matter because I'm leaving, Colby. I don't have a job. I don't have any money. I simply can't afford to live here anymore."

Chapter Five

Colby swiped a damp cloth over Megan's sticky mouth, hustled her into the living room and plopped her down beside a pile of her favorite toys. "Playtime," he announced, glancing at his watch. "You have twelve minutes."

Megan giggled, lurched forward and crawled under the coffee table.

"No, no." Colby dropped to his knees, snagged her legs and received an annoyed grunt for his trouble. After a moment's struggle, he retrieved the wriggling baby, who clutched a drool-soaked ream of crumpled papers to which tattered cover remnants dangled like wet blue confetti. "Oh, good grief."

Prying out of her greedy little hands what was left of the budget document, Colby sat back on his stained ivory carpet, heaved a sigh of utter frustration. He wiggled the soggy sheets in front of Megan's face. "This is not a toy," he said firmly. "This belongs to Uncle Colby. These—" he jerked a thumb at the colorful heap of fat plastic blocks and pull toys "—belong to Megan. Understand?"

Megan emitted an ear-piercing shriek, clapped her hands.

"Good. Now play fast. You have eleven minutes." Colby returned his niece to the toy pile, heaved a disheartened sigh as the baby crawled right past it, heading toward the dining area.

Colby watched glumly, knowing he should retrieve the tireless child, but was too weary to haul his aching bones into an upright position. So there he sat, cross-legged on the floor, clutching his ruined budget and completely oblivious to the lint and carpet dust burrowing a permanent home in his expensive, custom-tailored slacks.

He didn't know how much more of this he could take. Babies, he'd discovered, were utterly unpredictable little beings, giggling one moment and heartbroken the next for reasons far beyond the grasp of his eminently logical mind. A crawling infant was as volatile as derivatives, more unruly than junk bonds, less controllable than farm futures in a drought year.

And they will eat anything. Colby had learned that the hard way when Megan had managed to open the sink cupboard and helped herself to a mouthful of kitchen cleanser. Baby-proof drawer and cabinet latches had been installed within an hour after their return from the emergency hospital.

Childproofing the kitchen, however, was not the end of his woes since anything and everything within three feet of floor level was at risk. Including business documents carelessly left on the coffee table.

A knock on the door startled him. He hurried to answer it. "You're early."

"Yes, I know. Nine minutes, thirty-six seconds. Sue me." Danielle entered, tossed a neon orange backpack and a folded sheet of classified ads on the foyer table. "The good news is that public media exposure has made me so popular with one segment of society that I'm stopped on the street to give autographs. The bad news is that the rest of the world has my mug shot plastered in Personnel with an implied death threat to anyone who even thinks about hiring me. For some odd reason, I've garnered the reputation as a picket-toting troublemaker."

"I'm sorry to hear that," Colby lied.

She tossed a "Yeah, right" look over her shoulder, sauntered into the dining room, where Megan was weaving through the obstacle course of chair legs. "Peekaboo, sweet girl, I see you."

At the sound of Danielle's voice, Megan squealed and moved out from under the table, sat up with her little arms in the air, grunting madly. Danielle scooped the baby up, covered her face with happy kisses.

Colby savored the moment, awestruck as always by the loving interaction between Danielle and Megan. The child adored Danielle; clearly the feeling was mutual, which never failed to perplex Colby at the same time that it fascinated him.

As it turned out, Danielle's employment misfortunes had been a godsend for Colby, who hadn't risen to the top of his profession by neglecting to recognize opportunity when it stared him square in the face.

After an exhilarating negotiating session during which he'd been delighted to discover that his quirky neighbor was actually a surprisingly astute businesswoman, they'd struck a mutually beneficial deal. Danielle would provide afternoon care for Megan, which allowed Colby to spend the busiest part of his business day in the office while permitting his financially strapped neighbor the morning hours to job search.

For the past two weeks, the arrangement had proceeded smoothly, with splendid results.

"Has she had lunch?" Danielle asked.

"Hmm? Oh. Of course." Glancing at his watch, he hustled across the room, tossed the ruined budget into his briefcase. "I'll be in meetings most of the afternoon. My secretary can reach me if there's an emergency, or you can page me directly."

"I know the drill." Danielle blew a juicy raspberry against Megan's cheek to elicit a renewed round of happy giggles, then glanced up curiously. "Are you going to be late again?"

"Perhaps. I'll call you." He snapped the briefcase shut, hurried toward the door, grabbing his suit coat from a rack in the foyer.

"Ah, Colby?"

He stopped at the door, shot an irritable glance over his shoulder. "Yes?"

"Did Megan by any chance have strained carrots for lunch?"

"As a matter of fact she did. Why?"

"Because you're wearing some of them on your ear. Oh, and unless you're trying to make an innovative fashion statement, you might want to dispense with the apron."

Colby followed her gaze, groaned, then yanked off the blotchy towel that had been tucked in his waistband, mopped his ear with it and tossed it aside. "There. Am I presentable?"

"Turn around."

"I beg your pardon?"

"Hey, it's no skin off my nose if you trot off to the office with heaven-knows-what stuck to the seat of your pants."

He shot her a killing look, held his arms out and rotated

like a turkey on a spit. When she gave him a thumbs-up, he yanked open the door and stalked out.

Danielle burst into laughter, hugged Megan tightly. "You know, sweetums, if your uncle wasn't so uptight, he wouldn't be nearly so much fun to tease."

"Umm, mum, mum," Megan said.

"Absolutely. Ready for a nap?"

Megan shook her head so hard, she nearly launched out of Danielle's grasp. "Well, okay. You can play for a little while longer, but only if you promise not to tell Uncle Colby that we scrapped the schedule again." She carried the baby over to her toys, then sat down to play with her.

Danielle enjoyed her afternoons with Megan, so much so that she could almost forget that she was unemployed, unemployable and nearly bankrupt.

Despite hardship, life went on. At least, that's what she'd always told others who'd found themselves in apparently hopeless situations. Danielle missed that, missed working with people whose pride and courage enlightened her own spirit. She missed it so much that she spent a few hours every morning at the food bank as an unpaid volunteer, hours she probably should be using for more financially productive endeavors.

But things would work out. They always did. Her father used to say that change was the only certainty in life, and he'd been right. Danielle had learned to anticipate change, welcome it with open arms. Perhaps that's why upheavals weren't as traumatic for her as they were for Colby, who became rattled at the slightest variation in his precious schedule.

On the other hand, Danielle had to admit that going from high-powered executive to bachelor daddy in the space of a heartbeat was a complication bizarre enough to traumatize the mellowest soul. She also had to concede that he'd handled the inconvenience admirably, approaching temporary child-care duties as he would any other problem—with meticulous research and logical resolve.

Unfortunately, Colby had learned rather quickly that babies aren't terribly logical creatures, and the parenting books stacked up in the cluttered expanse of his once-pristine apartment depended more on generalities than the specific intent of one very determined, distinctly individualistic little rug rat.

She had to respect the man's tenacity, though, and Danielle secretly acknowledged that the awkward tenderness he displayed with his niece had turned him from executive robot to one of the most appealing men she'd ever met. He was still irksome, of course, and overbearing, not to mention much too imperious for his own good. Yet beneath the arrogant veneer lurked a tender soul, one that Danielle was determined to expose to the world.

That wouldn't be an easy task. Colby Sinclair had spent a lifetime reinforcing that protective shell around his emotions. He'd be a tough nut to crack, but that only made him a bigger challenge.

Danielle never could resist a challenge.

"What a wet girl," Danielle murmured, hoisting the drippy child out of the tub. "You like your bath, don't you? Yes, you do. You like playing splash-the-ducky and let's-drown-Dani."

Megan chortled, squeezed Dani's face, planted a familiar sloppy kiss on her chin.

"Ouch, those little pinchers hurt." Dani flinched, twisted away from the baby's painful grasp while struggling to wrap her wriggling charge in a fluffy bath towel. "You'll have to learn to be a bit gentler with that kissy-kissy thing. Otherwise you'll drive all the boys away, and end up a lonesome, shriveled old spinster like me. We wouldn't want that, would we?"

Megan blew a wreath of soggy spit-bubbles.

"I didn't think so. Oops, what's that I hear in the living room?" Dani hoisted the wrapped baby, carried her into the hall. "Well, well, look who's finally home."

Megan spotted Colby laying his briefcase on the dining table, threw her arms out, bucking madly. "Ungee, ungee, ungee!" she squealed, then instantly dissolved into a fit of baby giggles.

Colby looked up, flashed a smile that just about stopped Danielle's heart. "What on earth have you done to that poor child's head?"

"Spiked hair is all the rage," Danielle explained, using the tail of the towel to blot a few stray drips from the excited baby's face. "Besides, it suits her prickly personality."

Megan reared back, squirmed against Dani's shoulder, thrust her arms out with increased urgency. "Ungee," she insisted, her lip quivering.

"Let's get our jammies on first." Danielle smiled as tears spurted into the thwarted baby's big blue eyes. "Uh-oh, someone's getting sleepy."

"Would you like me to prepare Megan for bed?" Colby suddenly asked.

Since the chore in question had been hotly contested during employment negotiations, Danielle was surprised by the offer. She was also pleased, because she had a cross-town appointment in an hour to check out a listing for a garage apartment rental. "If you really wouldn't mind—"

The telephone's grating buzz had her sighing in disappointment. Colby answered on the second ring. "Hello? Yes, it is."

Since Danielle had clearly lost the opportunity for an early respite, she retreated to the bedroom where she dressed the cranky baby, who was less than enthralled with either the process or the entertainment provided—a slightly skewered recitation of *Goldilocks and the Three Bears*. "So Papa Bear said, 'Look, kid, breaking and entering is a first-class felony. Let me take you to a nice, warm shelter where you'll get free legal advice and all the porridge you can eat.'"

Danielle fastened the final snap, brushed Megan's wet hair into smooth feathers around her tiny ears, then scooped her up and smacked a kiss on the baby's flushed cheek. "All dressed and ready for sweet dreams. That wasn't so bad, was it?"

Megan rubbed her eyes, grunted peevishly.

"Hmm, I see we've got a tough audience tonight. Let's go see Uncle Colby, okay? That ought to cheer you up."

Danielle found Colby where she'd left him, still clutching the portable telephone. The conversation, however, was clearly over. Colby was staring into space, the phone dangling from his hand like an afterthought.

"We're ready for bed," Danielle announced cheerily. When he didn't respond, she noted the distance in his eyes, the peculiar slackening around his mouth. Her heart sank. "Do you have to go back to the office?"

He blinked, stared down at the phone in his hand as if he'd never seen it before, then laid it aside without another glance.

Danielle stepped forward, absently massaging Megan's back as the sleepy child snuggled against her shoulder. "What is it, Colby? Is something wrong?"

He frowned, clasped his hands behind his back, spoke without turning. "It's Olivia," he said quietly. "She's... dead."

The memorial service was somber, attended by only a few of Olivia's acquaintances and her latest ex-husband, who'd arrived with a frowsy, drunken woman on his arm, stayed long enough to learn that his ex-wife hadn't left a will, then shuffled out without a backward glance.

Colby knew none of the other mourners, which wasn't surprising since Olivia had lived in Manhattan for nearly a decade. At least, he thought she had. Colby hadn't actually kept up with his sister's whereabouts, nor had he believed that she'd kept up with his until the day she'd sauntered into his living room to abandon her only child.

Of the few darkly attired people milling about, only one seemed remotely familiar, a gaunt but stylish woman he recognized as one of his sister's high school friends. She hurried over, clasped his hand in her gloved palms. "I'm so sorry," she murmured. "It's tragic, absolutely tragic. You and your parents must be devastated."

Colby said nothing, although he felt Danielle's questioning gaze scalding the side of his face. He suspected that she was waiting for him to exhibit an expected response—the choked, grief-stricken platitude of a bereaved brother. But Colby's feelings were private. He kept his emotions to himself, preferred others to do the same.

The woman, whom he believed was named Lynn or Linda or perhaps even Lydia, continued to squeeze his captured hand while gazing moist-eyed at the carpet of roses adorning the closed casket. "I heard it happened outside of Rome. Some kind of automobile mishap, wasn't it?" She clucked her tongue, furrowed her penciled brows. "Terribly tragic."

Colby's chest tightened, pressed the air out of his lungs. He managed to shake off the woman's taloned grip, murmured a curt "Thank you for coming," then pushed his way out of the chapel, loosening his tie and sucking great gulps of air.

The dizziness eased. He sagged against the stone wall, closed his eyes. Barely a half-dozen mourners were inside, offering respect for his sister's memory. Frankly, he was surprised to see so many. Not only had Olivia spent most of her adult life flitting between the East Coast and Europe, she'd never been one to nurture personal relationships. On more than one occasion, she'd espoused a belief that "friendship" was nothing less than a sentimental fraud, a socially correct excuse for shameless mutual exploitation.

And so she'd surrounded herself with usable people, giving of herself only when necessary, discarding those who could no longer meet her needs. A pathetic woman. A pitiful life. It was hard to believe that once Colby had admired both.

Behind him, the chapel's chunky wooden door squeaked open as Danielle emerged carrying Megan, who dozed against her shoulder.

Colby glanced away, focusing on the lush garden at the gateway of the cemetery. "It's past Megan's nap time. I shouldn't have allowed you to bring her."

"Olivia was her mother," Danielle whispered. "Megan has a right to say goodbye."

"Megan is a baby. She doesn't even understand what's going on."

"In that case, there's no harm done, is there—? Colby, what's wrong? You look ill." Danielle followed his furious gaze, saw an older couple striding purposefully down the cobble walkway.

They didn't spare Colby a glance until they'd reached the chapel door. A distinguished man nodded a greeting, received none in return. The woman held her coiffed head high, coolly appraised Colby without comment. She turned, regarded the sleeping child in Danielle's arms with routine curiosity. "Is that Olivia's child?" When Danielle replied with an affirmative nod, the woman studied the baby with peculiar intensity. "She's smaller than I'd imagined. Her hair is quite blond, isn't it?"

"If you'll excuse us," Colby said brusquely, then took

Danielle's arm, ushered her up the cobble sidewalk, pressed his keys into her palm. "Take Megan home."

"Now?"

"Now."

"But what about you?"

"I have some financial arrangements to complete with the funeral director, then I'll call a cab." The urgency in his eyes broached no argument.

"All right, if it's that important to you."

"It is."

Danielle regarded him, then glanced at the older couple, who stared back with chilling intensity. "Those people don't seem particularly fond of you."

"They despise me," he replied blandly.

Danielle didn't know whether she was more shocked by the harshness of the message or the indifference with which it was delivered. "But why?"

Colby glanced at the couple, then looked away with a trace of sadness in his eyes. "They're my parents."

Sunset found Colby at his sister's grave site, pondering the freshly dug earth with clinical circumspection. There should be no emotion, no raw sensation of loss. They were strangers, really, although they'd grown up in the same house, shared the same pain.

Nonetheless, there was a stirring inside him, a flicker of feeling, and memories he'd thought forever lost.

At nine, the boy saw his teenage sister being harassed by ruffians. Something snapped inside of him. He threw his skinny frame at the group, flailing his fists ineffectually. The teenagers laughed at him. Then they beat him to a pulp.

Afterward his sister wiped his bloodied face. She called him a dumb little twerp, said he was stupid for putting himself in danger. She said she could take care of herself, but there were tears in her eyes, and she held her brother's hand while they walked home.

She'd never held his hand again. The boy pretended not to care. But he did care. He always cared.

It was the caring that made him weak.

"No, she doesn't like beets." Danielle plucked the small jar from Colby's hand, placed it back on the shelf. "Green beans are good, or peas— Ah, not that. Upsets her tummy."

Colby clasped his hands behind his back, scowled at the rows of colorful baby food jars lining the grocery aisle. "It all looks the same to me. Disgusting mush. One wonders how she can stomach any of it."

"Actually, she might be ready to move on to some of the junior foods." Danielle held up a jar labeled Toddler Lunch. "See, spaghetti in sauce, or beefy macaroni. Looks more palatable, doesn't it?"

Colby eyed it without interest. "I suppose." He felt rather than saw Danielle's questioning stare. Turning away, he absently fussed with Megan's Winnie the Pooh T-shirt, smoothing the hem which had rolled beneath the restraining belt of the grocery cart's baby seat. "Don't chew your fingers," he murmured, urging her hand out of her mouth. "It's a bad habit."

Megan pulled away, grabbed for a bright little jar that was thankfully out of reach. Thwarted, she grunted, muttered baby gibberish, pounded the cart's plastic handle. Colby absently reached into the diaper bag for a cookie, which Megan snatched up and chewed happily.

She was such a sweet child, Colby thought. Affectionate and trusting. So young to have been cruelly betrayed. Someday she'd be old enough to understand what had happened to her, to grasp the cold reality of having been abandoned by the one person on earth who should have showered her with unconditional love.

Colby knew what it was like to grow up unloved and unwanted. The last thing on earth he wanted was for his sweet, vulnerable little niece to share that fate. He simply didn't know how to stop it.

Danielle, who'd just dumped a load of baby food jars into the belly of the cart, glanced up, regarded him quietly. Her gaze warmed him like a touch, didn't waver as he met it. Instead, she continued to study him with an unreadable expression that was neither admiring nor disapproving, neither flirtatious nor shy; rather, it was a peculiar combination that left him bewildered, unsteady, uncomfortably hesitant. She was, he realized, not sending any message at all. She was receiving one.

Right in the middle of the grocery aisle, Danielle McCullough was analyzing *him*, dissecting the nuance of body language, evaluating his emotional aura much as he appraised the motive and intent of others in his day-to-day business life.

Colby had never been scrutinized with such intensity, nor had he ever been so physically affected by a mere look. There was a depth to Danielle's gaze that penetrated his soul, as if she alone possessed the power to peel away his protective shield and study the inner workings of the hidden man, the man held hostage from the world. He didn't like that. The problem was that he didn't exactly dislike it, either.

"Diapers," she murmured without breaking the visual stalemate. "You're almost out."

It took a moment for Colby's numbed mind to digest that information. "Ah, yes. Of course." He swallowed hard, absently pried Megan's sticky fingers from his necktie, then swung the grocery cart around, letting Danielle lead him to the proper aisle.

She hoisted on tiptoe, snagged a fat package from the top shelf, then squinted at row upon row of other colorful plastic-wrapped bundles. "Do you want to stay with the same kind, or try something new?"

Colby frowned at the displays, noting diapers with Velcro tabs, diapers with sticky tabs, diapers with pink stenciled baby dolls and blue stenciled bears. Some had elastic legs; some had pleated waistbands; some were touted as biodegradable, others were declared positively leakproof. So many choices boggled the mind, particularly in a product which, under the best of circumstances, was destined to be peed upon.

"Whatever," he said finally.

Danielle tossed two packages in the cart. "Anything else?"

"Hmm?"

"Do you need anything else?"

"I'm not sure. I don't think so."

She smiled, a slow, sensual, steamy smile that shifted the rhythm of his heart. "Anyone who believes that high-powered executive types are naturally decisive has never taken one grocery shopping." Her smile softened, saddened. "I take it that you haven't had any luck locating Megan's father."

The muscles in Colby's neck snapped taut. "No."

"Couldn't your lawyer find a copy of her birth certificate?"

"He found it." Colby flexed his fingers around the cart handle. "Care to speculate as to which line was left blank?"

Danielle's expression crumbled. "You're kidding." She spun around as Colby pushed the cart past, ran to catch up. "Maybe it was an oversight. The hospital records—"

"Reflect the same information as the birth certificate. Registered under her maiden name in a New York City hospital, Olivia gave birth to a daughter, whom she christened Megan Louise Elizabeth Sinclair. The father was declared to be unknown.'' Colby wheeled into the checkout line, began tossing baby food jars onto a humming conveyor. ''My lawyer contacted dozens of people with whom Olivia had contact in the months prior to Megan's birth. The one thing upon which they all agreed was that my sister traveled extensively and had the morals of an alley cat.''

''Oh, Colby, I'm so sorry.'' Danielle touched his arm, her eyes bright with moisture. ''But it's only been a few days since Olivia passed on. Someone may come forward.''

He straightened, shook his head. No one would come forward. Colby had learned that after Olivia's third divorce, she'd launched into a series of one-night stands and brief affairs with men from nearly every major city in the United States and Europe.

Colby studied his beautiful little niece, who was intently fiddling with the woven tail of the cart's toddler safety belt, then looked away as a lump caught in his throat, threatened to choke him. He coughed it away, squared his shoulders. ''Legally and logistically, my niece is an orphan. Someday she'll have to come to terms with that, and she'll have her mother to thank for it.''

Danielle withdrew her hand. ''I know you're angry with your sister. You have every right to be, but I don't believe that Olivia was quite as flighty and heartless as you seem to think she was.''

Colby stared at Danielle as if she'd sprouted antlers. ''On what basis could you possibly make such an inane statement? You never even met the woman.''

''True, but I've met Megan. She's a happy child, Colby, one who knows how to love and be loved. I believe that sense of security and comfort came from her mother.''

Colby shrugged that off, reached for his wallet as the cashier totaled his purchase. ''All it means is that Olivia was astute enough to secure proper child care while she flitted the globe. Look how quickly Megan bonded with you."

Now it was Danielle's turn to glance away. "Yes, well, we've already discussed how adaptable she is. I'm sure she'll be just as quick to form a bond with her next sitter."

"Her next sitter?"

"Umm." Danielle fidgeted with the safety belt buckle, lifted Megan out of the cart. "We discussed at the outset that our arrangement would be temporary."

"Yes, yes, but circumstances have changed."

"My circumstances haven't changed." Danielle smoothed Megan's hair, brushed a kiss on her cheek. "I've been offered a social service position in South El Monte."

"El Monte? Good Lord, that's miles from here."

"I know. I found an apartment in the area. It's not much, but at least I can afford it."

"If it's a matter of funding, perhaps I can—"

"No. Thank you, but no."

"I see." Colby felt like he'd been gut-punched. "When will you be leaving?"

She met his gaze, wavered. "Tomorrow."

For the second time in a week, Colby's world came crashing down.

Danielle trudged up the complex's outside walkway, shifted Megan in her arms. "Oh, come on, it's not like I'm abandoning you. I've arranged to work part-time for the first few days so I can continue to spend afternoons with Megan. That gives you a week to find someone else."

"You know perfectly well that a week isn't nearly long enough." Balancing the grocery bags, Colby strode up to the glassed entrance doors leading to their wing of the apartment building and was awkwardly trying to reach the knob without dropping his parcels when a man in a business suit stepped out, held the door open.

Colby stood back, allowing Danielle to enter first, then nodded brusque thanks to the well-dressed door holder before entering the hallway himself. "I don't understand why you feel compelled to rush into a job you admit is not what you were looking for in the first place."

"I have to work, Colby."

"Yes, but—"

"Mr. Sinclair?"

Colby and Danielle simultaneously glanced back to see that the fellow from the front entrance had followed them inside.

"Colby Eugene Sinclair?" Upon receiving an affirmative nod, the man tucked a folded document in one of the grocery bags. "You've been served, sir. Have a nice day."

"Here you go, sweet thing."

Megan snatched the bottle Danielle offered, sucked greedily, gazing up with great goggle eyes. Danielle smoothed a lick of blond fuzz at the apex of the baby's silky forehead, murmured soft, sleepy-time words that flowed so naturally, an onlooker would never believe that she hadn't borne the child herself.

She smoothed the flannel blanket with loving tucks, tiptoed quietly across the room, hesitating at the light switch. Her gaze swept the master suite, the sleek chromed headboard of the massive bed piled high with fluffy pillows and coordinated earth-tone comforter. The dresser, too, was ultramodern, with a sparkling glass mirror jutting like crystal from a gleaming square of frosted ice.

When Danielle had first seen the room, it had smelled of spicy musk and masculinity, and had been so tidy as to seem sterile. Now the smooth dresser was cluttered with tubes of rash cream, squeeze bottles of lotion and powder, teething anesthetic, a drape of pleated elastic studded with a fussy satin bow. Fat diaper packages were piled in the corner, within easy reach of the small, net-sided crib. Tiny folded garments were heaped on a nightstand.

The room was a dichotomy now, a paradoxical mingling of seductive bachelor retreat with the unique chaos of a nursery. For some peculiar reason, Danielle found the peculiar combination extraordinarily appealing.

She would miss it.

Flipping off the light, Danielle left the door ajar, moved quietly through the hall. Colby's angry voice filtered from the study, where he was on the telephone with his lawyer. Apparently the conversation wasn't going well.

"I don't give a damn what my parents want. Olivia's intent was that I have sole guardianship of Megan. No, dammit, I'm not going to relinquish custody." Muffled footsteps, rustling papers. "Of course I'm willing to fight it. Look, I don't care what it costs. I'm not going to let them destroy Megan the same way—"

Colby's voice cracked, fell silent. Danielle moved forward, hovered at the kitchen door, which was only a few feet from the entrance to the study. She heard faint movement, the squeak of a chair.

Tension oozed from the silence, so thick she could almost see it. Something horrible was happening. Danielle didn't understand it, but she knew that the stakes were inexplicably high.

Earlier, after reading the summons, Colby had flown into a rage that had frightened her half to death. She'd gotten ahold of the legal document long enough to see that Colby's parents, Eugenia and Kingsley Sinclair, were suing for custody of Megan. Danielle hadn't been terribly surprised by that. To her it seemed quite natural that grandparents would want to raise their only grandchild, and since caring for Megan had put a tremendous strain not only on

Colby's personal life, but on his business, as well, Danielle had initially presumed that a transfer of custody would probably be best for all concerned.

But that was before she saw the cold fury in Colby's eyes.

Now she leaned forward, straining to hear.

"All right." He sounded tired. "Yes, I understand. I don't care, Jack. File the papers."

Colby clicked off the portable phone, tossed it onto his desk. He was furious; he was frantic, seething with memories of his own childhood, of having been raised by servants and ignored by parents who viewed emotionalism as weakness, worshiped wealth as a god.

And there was more, much more.

Now they wanted Megan, wanted to subject his bright, loving niece to the same emotionally barren environment that had turned Colby into a man unable to express love, and his sister into a desperate woman who couldn't get enough of it.

He wasn't about to let them do that to Megan. He'd burn in hell first.

A muffled "ahem" caught his attention. He swiveled his chair around, saw Danielle in the doorway.

"Is everything all right?" she asked.

"No."

"I'm sorry." She stepped inside, fidgeted with the doorjamb. "Is there anything I can do?"

"Yes, as a matter of fact, there is." Colby regarded her for a moment, leaned back in his chair, steepling his fingers. "You can marry me."

Chapter Six

Shock slipped into a snicker, then a guffaw that died on Danielle's lips when she realized Colby wasn't smiling. "You're serious."

"Quite." He leaned forward, his hands still steepled in that annoying manner powerful men use to enhance their illusion of control. "According to my lawyer, courts do not favor single-parent homes."

"You mean that your parents might be awarded custody of Megan?"

"Exactly." He bowed his head, rubbed his eyelids, then peered over his fingertips with renewed determination. "I have no intention of allowing that to happen."

"Oh, Colby." Danielle extended a hand, let it drop with a resigned sigh. "This divisiveness between you and your parents is very sad. I don't pretend to understand it, but I do know that a custody battle can only have a negative affect on Megan. There must be some kind of compromise—"

"There isn't," Colby growled. He rose from his chair, his gray eyes colder than winter fog. "My sister and I weren't close, but she knew that if the worst happened she could trust me to keep her child from falling into enemy hands."

"Enemy hands? Oh, good grief, Colby, we're talking about your parents here. What could they have possibly done to evoke such hatred?"

The ice melted from Colby's eyes as suddenly as it had appeared. He seemed startled by her statement, almost hurt by it. "I never said that I hated them."

Taken aback, Danielle folded her arms, tried to reconcile the contradiction. Where his parents were concerned, Colby was clearly conflicted. Conflict, however, could be resolved. Danielle firmly believed that, just as she was utterly convinced that healing the shattered Sinclair family was crucial for Megan's physical and emotional growth.

Meanwhile, Colby had rearranged his features into the unreadable mask she recognized as his business face.

"The arrangement will be mutually beneficial," he intoned. "You need work and a place to live. I need a wife. It will all be legally documented, the terms and conditions of which will be agreed upon in advance, and will automatically terminate when the custody issue has been permanently resolved. My lawyer will prepare the contract, of course, but I expect you'll wish to consult your own legal counsel to finalize the details."

It was ludicrous, Danielle thought, positively absurd. Only Colby's impeccable solemnity kept her from laughing out loud. But as her mind formulated a dignified refusal, an outlandish question rolled off her tongue. "So, where would we put my sofa?"

Colby didn't blink. "Our new residence will have adequate facilities to house your possessions and ensure your privacy."

"New residence?"

"Certainly we can't stay here. Even if the complex allowed an exception to the adults-only rule, the apartment is much too small for three people."

"Much," Danielle agreed weakly, beginning to realize that this marriage idea wasn't quite as impulsive as she'd first presumed.

Across the room, Colby flicked his wrist as if to banish any lingering doubt. "Besides, my parents have a large home with fenced acreage that they will no doubt offer as evidence of environmentally superior atmosphere in which to raise a child…" His words trailed off, he stared into thin air for a moment, as if remembering that home, that yard. Then he blinked, began to fuss with papers on his desk, seeming nonplussed by whatever thoughts had entered his mind. "I've contacted a real estate agent and been assured that there are several fine suburban properties available that would suit our purpose. All have large yards and are located in a school district considered to be one of the best in the state."

"You're concerned about schools?"

Colby glanced up, frowned. "Of course. Academic excellence is crucial to a child's development. Don't you agree?"

"Well, certainly I agree, but Megan isn't even out of diapers."

"Children grow quickly," he reminded her. "And I have no intention of uprooting the child in her formative years simply because I lacked the foresight to assure proper educational opportunities."

Danielle shook her head, laughed softly. "I can't believe this. Three weeks ago you were horrified by the mere thought of baby drool on your rug, now you're considering college options. This isn't just about settling an ancient grudge against your parents, is it? I mean, you're actually planning to be around for the long haul.''

"Raising a child is a lifetime commitment," he said simply.

"And it's a commitment you're willing to make?"

"Yes, it is." He expanded his lungs, studied Danielle with unnerving intensity. "Will you help me?"

"By marrying you?" When he nodded, Danielle turned away, not wanting her thoughts to be swayed by the distraction of his intense gaze. It was foolish even to consider a marriage of convenience. This wasn't the sixteenth century. People simply didn't do that sort of thing anymore. Except to get green cards, perhaps. Or to fulfill the terms of an inheritance.

Or for political reasons.

She sighed. Okay, so there were perfectly modern reasons to fake a marriage, but the entire idea grated on her nerves. It seemed so sterile, a slap at her own dream of someday falling in love and having a family of her own.

Of course, that could still happen. What Colby was proposing was a business venture that would run its course in a few months. It would have nothing whatsoever to do with her personal life. At the moment, she didn't have a personal life, although that wasn't exactly by choice, and Danielle was nothing if not optimistic.

Besides, Colby *had* indicated that her privacy would be respected. The man had his faults, but dishonesty wasn't one of them. Danielle trusted him without question. Unfortunately she trusted most people without question, but that was beside the point. She knew Colby well enough to understand that he kept his promises, and his word was his bond.

There was an upside to Colby's bizarre proposal. Danielle had become irrevocably bonded with little Megan. She adored the child, and had to admit that the idea of spending more time with her beloved little sweetums was definitely appealing.

Even more tempting was the unprecedented opportunity of observing the Sinclair family on an intimate level. As an insider, she'd be privy to personal details, to clues to what had precipitated such a catastrophic rift between the elder Sinclairs and their children. Once Danielle had isolated the cause, she could furtively work on a cure. In her own mind, this was crucial. No matter what the court did regarding the custody issue, Danielle was convinced that Megan could never be truly happy unless her family was healed.

It wouldn't be easy, but bringing families together was what Danielle had been trained for; it's what gave her the greatest joy. As far as living under the same roof with a man who probably set his watch timer to brush his teeth, well, there was always that challenge thing that she found so-o-o irresistible.

Danielle glanced over her shoulder, dazzled him with a smile. "Congratulations, Mr. Sinclair. You're engaged."

Twenty-four hours later Danielle and Colby bundled Megan into traveling clothes to catch a red-eye to Las Vegas, were married in a dull-as-dirt ceremony performed by a weary justice of the peace who yawned between vows, then they flew back to meet a chatty real estate agent with a gluttonous grin and a briefcase full of listings.

That had been a week ago. For the past seven days, Colby's strictly scheduled life-style had spiraled into utter chaos. Even his office, formerly an island of indisputable control in a world gone mad, was suffering its own upheaval, primarily because of Colby himself. Things simply weren't the same anymore. Colby wasn't the same.

He just wasn't certain as to why.

"Mr. Sinclair?" Mira Wilkins peeked around the office door just as Colby's private line rang.

He waved her in, grabbed for the phone. It was his stockbroker. Disappointed, he handled the matter deftly, hung up, glaring at the telephone. Today was moving day. Danielle was supposed to call—

"Ah, is this a bad time?"

"Hmm?" He swiveled, saw his finance officer hovering uncomfortably beyond the polished mahogany barrier that had been scrupulously positioned to maintain executive distance. "Have a seat." Colby frowned, tried to focus, then finally recalled why he'd summoned her. "What's the status of the office day-care project?"

Beyond the expansive desk, Ms. Wilkins sat gingerly, so stiff that her weight barely dented the plush cushion of the guest chair. "The committee has met twice this week, and is in the process of preparing—"

Colby's executive assistant appeared in the open doorway. "Your attorney is on line three, in reference to the terms of a contract termination document he's preparing at your request."

A fancy way of saying divorce, Colby thought, and wasn't even struck by the irony of preparing for the imminent demise of a week-old marriage. "I'll return the call." He flicked his wrist, refocused on his rigid finance officer. "Now, Ms. Wilkins, regarding the day-care situation—"

The marketing manager poked his head in. "Got a minute?" When Colby cowed him with a look, the chastised man backed away, mumbling, "I'll, umm, make an appointment."

Colby pinched the bridge of his nose, tried to concentrate on the day-care committee's preliminary report. "A suitable location has been found?"

"Yes, sir." Ms. Wilkins snapped even straighter. "There

were no suites available on this floor, but there's a lovely facility on level three that would suit the purpose admirably."

"Cost projections?"

"They're in the report, sir." She leaned forward, clearly stressed. "I realize the cost is quite high, but I've taken the liberty of preparing some alternative strategies, including a fee schedule for employees taking advantage of the center."

Colby flipped the document closed, pushed it away. "Cut to the chase, Mira. Can it be self-sustaining?"

The woman, who'd never heard her first name spoken within these hallowed walls, vibrated with surprise, stuttered only slightly. "Why, yes."

"Then do it."

"Excuse me, sir?"

"Do it. Sign a lease, hire a staff, get it on-line." Colby stood, signaling an end to the meeting.

Ms. Wilkins shot to her feet. "I beg your pardon, Mr. Sinclair, but I'm not quite clear on this. You want me to hire the day-care staff without your input?"

Colby hiked a brow. "There's no need for me to become involved in the interview process. When it comes to assessing child care providers, you're far more capable than I."

"But you've always insisted on personal involvement in any hiring process—"

The intercom squawked. "Golf-Pro on line two," came the scratchy reminder from his ever-efficient assistant. "You have a budget meeting in ten minutes, and a three-thirty with the banking commission."

Colby glanced at his watch, shot out of his chair. "Good Lord." He shook his wrist, held it to his ear. "There's something wrong. It can't be after two."

Ms. Wilkins eyed him warily. "Yes, sir, it's 2:10."

"Impossible. I left precise instructions to be notified—" Colby bit off the words, leaned over his desk to punch the intercom button. "Have you been able to reach Ms. McCull— Er, my wife?"

"There's been no answer."

"What do you mean, no answer? I've given her my cell phone with explicit instructions that she must have it on her person at all times."

"I'm sorry, Mr. Sinclair. Perhaps there's a problem with the cell phone server—"

"Contact them at once."

"Yes, sir."

Colby released the intercom button, snatched up the phone and dialed his cellular number. With each unanswered ring Colby raked his hair, paced behind his desk, pivoted without thinking and nearly strangled himself with the phone cord.

He untangled himself, ignoring Mira Wilkins's wide-eyed stare. Ordinarily he'd have conducted himself with meticulous calm, a comfortably dispassionate shield that he always displayed during moments of crisis. His staff had never seen their president visibly upset. That was the way he wanted it.

Judging by his finance officer's gaping mouth, fear must be etched all over his face. For the first time since he was a child, Colby couldn't control that fear. Danielle wasn't answering the cell phone. He was terrified that something had gone horribly wrong.

Perhaps there had been an accident during the moving process. After all, there were all those heavy boxes to pack, all that furniture to be loaded for transport. Anything could have happened. Anything.

On the twelfth ring a bland recording informed Colby that the party he was calling was unavailable, then disconnected the line.

He hung up, fuming, fearful. Danielle was supposed to notify him the moment the moving van arrived at the new house, which was scheduled at precisely two o'clock. No earlier, no later. Two o'clock.

Allowing her to handle the project on her own had clearly been a mistake. What if she'd procured an unlicensed moving firm? What if she'd been victimized by some kind of scam? Colby had been so relieved to rid himself of the problem that he hadn't even made certain that the moving company's business license had been validated, or that appropriate reference checks had been conducted—

"Mr. Sinclair?"

He snapped around, scowled at the hapless Ms. Wilkins, who hovered by the doorway, wringing her hands. "Do we have further business?" he asked curtly.

"Ah, no, sir, I just wanted to offer my congratulations on your marriage."

"My what—? Oh, of course. Thank you."

"I must say, we were all taken by surprise. No one in the office had the slightest inkling that you were involved in a serious relationship."

"Yes, well." Colby cleared his throat, snatched up the phone again. "It was an impulsive decision."

"Impulsive… You?" The woman vibrated as if struck, then suddenly smiled, as if she'd just gotten the joke. "You're right, of course. It's none of my business."

Colby, having just completed dialing his cell phone number for the second time, glanced up as Ms. Wilkins left the office, shaking her head and chuckling softly.

The cell phone rang. Colby paced, muttering to himself. The phone rang again, and again, and again. "Come on, come on."

The intercom buzzed. "The budget committee meeting begins in two minutes, sir."

Colby shifted the receiver, cursed under his breath. He

should have handled the moving arrangements himself. Danielle was too gullible, too woefully naive to weed out those with nefarious intent. Perhaps she'd inadvertently hired a truck full of thieves who'd loaded up their goods and driven away, never to be seen again. That would be inconvenient, but hardly catastrophic. Colby's deepest fear was that the thieves would have taken more than material possessions. What if Danielle had tried to stop them? What if they'd become violent?

Dear God, what if they'd hurt her? Or Megan?

The automatic recording kicked in. *"The party you are trying to reach is not available."*

The intercom squawked. "Your banker is on line two."

"Please try again—"

"The budget committee is waiting, Mr. Sinclair."

"—later."

"May I tell them you're on your way?"

Beep. Click.

Colby slammed down the phone, snatched his coat off a nearby rack and strode past his startled assistant, who was still pleading through the intercom. She stood quickly. "Sir?"

"Continue your attempts to reach Ms. McCu—my wife."

"But the budget meeting—"

"Can wait." Colby pushed through the gleaming glass doors, marched past the elevator and hit the stairs running.

"Uh, whaddaya want us to do with this?"

Danielle, crouched beside a canvas jump chair to wash smeared cookie remnants from Megan's gooey face, glanced at the sweaty pair juggling Colby's prized leather sofa. "That goes in the parlor, along with all the chrome and glass stuff. And be care—" she flinched as the sofa arm clipped the doorjamb "—ful of the walls."

"Sorry," mumbled the leaner of the two men, a denim-clad stud-muffin with tattooed biceps and the long, flowing mane of a beefcake cover model. His bald-as-a-cue-ball partner, whose gelatinous beer belly oozed over his belt like an occupied marsupial pouch, shifted one end of the sofa, grunted, staggered forward.

A thud emanated from the parlor, followed by masculine mutterings. The two men emerged, flushed and huffing.

Danielle gave the hapless movers a bright smile. "You're doing great, guys."

The big man grunted again, heaved his gut and waddled out the open front door, presumably to retrieve another load. The swaggering stud-muffin, an ex-heroine addict whom Danielle had urged into recovery a couple of years earlier, hovered in the expansive, slate-tiled foyer long enough to wipe his sweaty forehead, flash a sexy grin. "So, how 'bout another beer?"

"Work first, Bounder. Drink later." Danielle stood, tossed the sticky facecloth on the kitchen pass-through counter, bent down to unfasten Megan's bib. "Besides, someone's got to drive the truck back to the food bank."

"That would be me." Madeline Rodriguez popped out of the hallway, toting a carton bristling with kitchen appliances. "I don't like beer anyway," she murmured, gazing at Bounder as if he were God in a ripped T-shirt.

Bounder winked at her, flexed his biceps to create a unique undulation of a tattooed jaguar on his upper arm, then sauntered out the door with a cocky butt swing exaggerated for the enjoyment of a clearly appreciative audience.

Madeline heaved a wistful sigh. "Makes me wish I was ten years younger."

"From the way Bounder was flaunting his assets, I doubt he considers age a problem." Danielle tossed the bib aside, hoisted Megan out of the canvas chair. "Nap time, sweetums. Look at those sleepy little eyes.'' She glanced around, frowning. ''Where's the diaper bag?''

''I put it in Megan's room,'' Madeline said, hoisting the appliance box onto the counter. ''Do you need it?''

''No. Just wanted to make sure it didn't get lost. Megan's binky is in there.''

''Ah, the beloved binky.'' Madeline nodded knowingly. ''A misplaced pacifier, the scourge of parenthood.''

''So I've discovered— There's that noise again.'' Settling Megan against her hip, Danielle pivoted toward the direction of the sound. ''It's kind of a funny buzz. Do you hear it?''

''I think it's coming from somewhere down the hall.'' Madeline cocked her head. ''That's weird. Last time I heard it, I could have sworn it was in the kitchen.''

''I thought so, too,'' Danielle muttered, heading for the hall. ''But it stopped before I could find it.'' She followed the peculiar intermittent buzz into the bedroom wing of the house, which was strewn with unpacked cartons of every size and description. Some were carefully sealed, neatly labeled. Those were, of course, Colby's. Her own cartons were left open, with jumbled contents poking out. That way, she'd reasoned, she'd be able to see what was inside without having to waste time labeling everything.

''It's coming from the nursery,'' Madeline said, stepping over a pile of folded bedding at the same time she ducked beneath the upper linen cupboard's open door. ''Yes, yes. I'm sure it's in Megan's room....'' Madeline paused midstep, tilted her curly head like a curious poodle. ''Uh-oh, it stopped again.''

Danielle entered the nursery, a cheery, open space with sunlit windows and cushy carpeting to provide a soft surface for delicate little knees. After settling Megan in the crib, she eyed an unobtrusive disk mounted on the ceiling.

"The smoke detector in my apartment used to beep when the battery got low. Maybe I should check—"

Bounder's voice bellowed from the foyer. "Hey, whaddaya want us to do with this?"

Danielle sighed, made a mental note to check the alarm battery later, then gave Megan a kiss. She left the nursery to find her beefy movers struggling to keep a tenuous grip on her comfy flowered sofa with the oversize cushions.

"That goes in the family room," she told them, sidling alongside to point out exactly where she wanted the furniture arranged. "Remember, the upholstered furniture and oak tables with nice rounded edges belong in the family room. The sharp metal stuff, and anything with a glass top goes in the parlor. That way, we can keep the parlor doors shut so the baby can't get in and break something, or hurt herself. Got it?"

Bounder gave her a glazed look, then covered his confusion with a sexy smile. "So, how 'bout that beer?"

Danielle sighed, jammed her hands on her hip and turned to the big-bellied fellow who was propped against the wall, gasping. "Maybe Jonas can tell the difference between wood and metal."

Jonas sucked a wheezing breath, wiped a meaty hand across his mouth. "Wood, here. Metal, there." He pushed away from the wall, sucked in his fleshy gut. "Got it." The pooped fellow staggered off, followed by his swaggering buddy.

Madeline watched until Bounder was out of sight, then fanned her face with her hand, sagged against the flowered sofa. "Only an old married woman like yourself could possibly be immune to that."

Danielle followed the woman's rapt gaze, smiled as Bounder's swiveling, denim-clad rear rotated out the front door. "I'm preoccupied, not immune. There's just so much to do to get this place organized."

"It *is* a glorious house," Madeline acknowledged, scanning the cozy family area that opened into a gleaming white-tiled kitchen. "You must be thrilled."

"Hmm? Oh." She avoided her friend's gaze, fiddled with the fleecy Dallas fern sprucing up the center shelf of her crowded étagère. "Yes, it's a lovely house."

Madeline regarded her shrewdly, aimed a pointed stare at the plain gold band gleaming on Danielle's left ring finger. "You know, everyone's talking about your marriage. It came as quite a shock."

"Did it?"

"Mmm-hmm. I mean, no one had even heard you mention this dreamboat of yours, then poof! Suddenly, you're Mrs. Dreamboat."

"These things happen," Danielle murmured, madly fluffing fern fronds.

"Some people are a bit cheesed off at not being invited to the wedding." Madeline sniffed, reached down to stroke Whiskers, who'd finally mustered enough courage to sidle down from his étagère perch. "Not me, you understand. But some people."

A guilty twinge prickled Danielle's nape. Madeline was her dearest friend in the whole world. She hated deceiving her, hated deceiving all of her friends, but the stakes were too high for Danielle to trust anyone. If word of the ruse got back to the elder Sinclairs' lawyers before Danielle had a chance to bring the family together, Colby could lose custody of Megan forever. That would be a tragedy Danielle wasn't willing to risk, even if it meant hurting her best friend's feelings.

She laid an empathetic hand on Madeline's plump shoulder. "No one was invited. We just kind of, well, eloped."

"How romantic," Madeline mumbled, fingering the cat's neck fur. "In that case, I can certainly see why I wasn't wanted."

"Oh, Maddie—"

"Hey!" Bounder stood in the foyer, grinning. He held up a glass-and-chrome lamp table. "Whaddaya want me to do with this?"

Danielle rubbed her eyes, swallowed temptation by reminding herself that he was actually doing her a favor. She looked up, forced a smile. "In the parlor, please."

He nodded, sauntered off while Madeline watched and sighed. "Face it," she murmured. "Sometimes it just doesn't matter if they can think."

"I know what you mean." The women communed with a look, then heaved simultaneous sighs. "Well, back to work."

"Right. Your linens await stacking, madam." Madeline headed off, wavered at the hall entrance. She snapped her fingers, spun around. "By the way, did you know that your clothes were put in the guest room?"

Danielle moistened her lips, ducked below the counter and made a production of tossing small appliances into a corner carousel cabinet. "Don't worry about it," she called out in her cheeriest, everything-is-wonderful voice. "Things are pretty chaotic right now."

"But it's a mistake," Madeline purred. "Right?"

Swallowing hard, Danielle peered over the counter, wide-eyed and hopefully convincing. "Of course it's a mistake."

The woman cocked her head, smirked, disappeared into the hall, chuckling.

Danielle sat back on her heels, glared at a battered, harvest gold blender, then stuffed it into the cupboard. "Don't get comfortable," she told the ugly appliance. "Your travels aren't over."

Puffing her cheeks, she blew out a breath, continued shuffling carton contents into cupboards. She was trying to find a place for the never-used battery-powered whipping wand her optimistic mother had sent three Christmases ago when a familiar voice boomed from the foyer.

"What in the hell is going on here?"

She shot to her feet, clutching the wand like a small club. "Er, hi."

Colby whirled, regarded her with a peculiar combination of frustration and relief. "There's a thrift shop truck in the driveway."

"Well, yes, there is—" Her gaze darted to the hall, where Madeline peered out with bright little eyes. Mustering her best come-hither smile, Danielle dropped the whipping wand on the counter, threw out her arms and swooped at the startled man like a sparrow on a worm. "Welcome home, sweetheart. I've missed you so much!" Tossing her arms around his rigid neck, she planted a firm kiss on his cheek, then nuzzled his ear. "Pretend you like it," she whispered. "We're being watched."

Stunned, Colby turned to stare at the woman who leaned against the doorjamb, studying them with folded arms and a suspicious expression. "Who are—?"

The question died as Danielle grabbed his face in her hands, and planted a firm kiss on his mouth. She hadn't expected sparks, but sparks was exactly what she got. Instantly she released him, took a shaky step back and saw that Colby, too, seemed somewhat unnerved. Danielle recovered first, tossing her head, raking her hair, then feigning surprise when her gaze met Madeline's, as if she'd actually forgotten the woman was there.

"Whoa," Madeline mumbled. "Mr. Dreamboat in the flesh. No wonder you couldn't wait."

Danielle shot her a look. "Colby, *darling*, this is Madeline Rodriguez, my trusted friend and the best volunteer the food bank has ever seen…"

The introduction trailed away as Jonas puffed through the front door carrying Danielle's favorite potted ficus. A man of few words, Jonas paused long enough to acknowledge Colby with a muttered "Hey" then turned to Danielle. "Where?"

"In the family room," she instructed, feeling Colby's narrowed gaze on the back of her neck. "By the sliding glass door, where it will get lots of light." She took a deep breath, glanced over her shoulder and managed not to flinch at her husband's dark scowl. "That's Jonas."

"I see." His gaze hardened as it settled beyond Danielle's shoulder, a clear indication that Madeline's favorite heartbreak in blue jeans had just made his presence known.

Bounder swaggered inside, flexed his tattoos and held up a neatly sealed carton with the word *Office* printed in block letters on all four sides. "Where d'ya want it?"

"Tough choice," she muttered. "Let's try the office."

"Cool." Bounder eyed Colby, bobbed his head in what could be loosely interpreted as a greeting. "How's it happening, man?"

Colby's eyes narrowed into stormy gray slits. "I beg your pardon?"

"Nah, you ain't in my way." With an oblivious grin, Bounder said, "Catch you later," then rotated his denim-clad buns in the general direction of Colby's new office.

A firm hand wrapped around her elbow. "If Ms. Rodriguez will excuse us for a moment, I'd like a word with you."

Danielle tried for a weak smile. "Be careful which word you use. Megan may not be asleep yet."

Not amused, Colby ushered her into the family room just as Jonas trudged out with a weary expression and ficus leaves stuck to his sweaty arms. Colby waited until the big man was out of hearing range, then whirled on her. "Why didn't you call me?"

"Call?" She frowned, glanced around. "The telephone man hasn't come yet."

"Which is why I gave you the cell phone."

"Ah, yes, the cell phone." She nodded, frantically trying to remember what the devil she'd done with it. "I'm sure it's around somewhere."

"Never mind." He massaged his forehead, took a calming breath that didn't work very well. "Let's try another subject, shall we? We can start with the thrift shop truck in the driveway."

"Oh, that. I kind of borrowed it."

"I see." Clearly he didn't. "And your scruffy friends, did you borrow them, as well?"

"Not exactly," Danielle replied, irked by the unflattering description of Bounder and Jonas, but unable to refute it. They actually were her friends, after all, and of all the adjectives one might use to describe their appearance, "scruffy" was probably the kindest. Still, his haughty tone rankled. "I hired them."

"You *what?*"

"I hired them. They needed the work." She shrugged. "Look, you put me in charge of getting our stuff from point A to point B, and that's exactly what I've done. What's the big deal?"

"The big deal is that these men are not licensed or insured."

"Oh, pish." She flicked her wrist as if shooing a pesky fly. "Friends help other friends move all the time. It's like a rite of passage—" She stiffened, her head spinning around. "There it is again. Good grief, every smoke detector in the house must have low batteries."

"Smoke detector," Colby repeated, eyeing her as if she'd lost her mind.

"Yes, the darn things have been going off every few minutes. They're driving me nuts."

"How can you tell?" he inquired politely, then pivoted smartly and followed the sound down the hall. A moment later he reappeared carrying Megan's diaper bag. It was beeping. "Is this the sound you've been hearing?"

"Uh-oh." She curled her fingers in front of her mouth, winced as he pulled out the cell phone, told whoever was on the line that the matter had been resolved, then flicked off the power switch and stared at her. She managed a thin smile. "Whew, that's a relief. Replacing all those alarm batteries would have cost a fortune."

Colby dropped the diaper bag, tucked the phone into his coat pocket. "I've been trying to reach you all afternoon."

"He was worried," Madeline blurted, grinning madly. "Isn't that sweet?"

Beside her, Jonas nodded. "Real sweet."

Colby cast them a long-suffering look, took one step toward Danielle and tripped over Whiskers, who'd just darted out from behind the flowered couch.

The cat yowled. The man swore. The audience behind them gasped.

Danielle leapt forward, scooped the hissing cat into her arms. "There, there, that big bad man didn't mean to scare you." She batted her eyes at Colby, who was steadying himself on the sofa with one hand and clutching his chest with the other. "You didn't, did you? Mean to kick a defenseless animal, that is."

Colby took a wheezing breath, glared at the cat nested comfortably in her arms. "What is that creature doing here?"

"He lives here, don't you, snookums-wookums?" She rubbed her nose against the cat's bristly whiskers. "Yes, you do, and you like your new house, don't you?"

Straightening, Colby tugged at his necktie, slipped a wary glance at their fascinated audience, then sidled close enough to Danielle that he could whisper to her without being heard. "Our agreement was that the, er, animal is to remain in your portion of the residence."

"And he is," she replied sweetly. "The family room is mine. The parlor is yours. The kitchen and laundry room are neutral territory, so naturally Whiskers is allowed there, as well."

"Naturally," he repeated dryly. The cat hissed.

Danielle covered the animal's ears with her hand. "He didn't mean that, snookums. He's really a very nice man. Look, I'll show you." She held the cat up. It growled. Colby stepped away. "Aw, go on," she urged, moving a step closer with the snarling feline. "Pet him."

"I'd rather floss a shark."

She shrugged, allowed Whiskers to hop onto the sofa, where he gave Colby an eat-dirt-and-die look before leaping atop his beloved étagère to sulk. "Our first fight," she mumbled with a warning glance at the curious group that was bunched at the edge of the kitchen counter, straining to hear. "What will our guests think?"

Before she realized Colby was moving, he'd snagged her waist, pressed her to his chest, cupped her face with his palm. "They will think," he whispered against her lips, "that I am an extremely fortunate man."

Then he kissed her with such power and passion that her knees turned to steam and her spine melted into an electrified puddle of pure sensation. She couldn't move, couldn't breathe, couldn't think of anything beyond the taste of him, the sizzling caress of his fingers on her cheek, her throat, the delicate curve at her nape.

He released her slowly, allowing his mouth to linger against her lips, then finally breaking away with a regretful shudder that was more sensual than a poet's whispered verse. Their eyes met, held. "I'll be home for dinner," he said quietly.

A moment later, he was gone, leaving Danielle standing where he'd left her, stunned, breathless. No one had ever kissed her with such fervor, such intensity; and no kiss had ever affected her so profoundly. At that moment, Danielle was suddenly aware that life as she knew it would never be the same. She would never be the same. Something had changed inside her.

Something wonderful.

Chapter Seven

Colby tied his robe sash, creaked the bedroom door open and was surprised by a diffusion of soft light emanating into the hallway. Moving toward the light, he emerged into the foyer that served as the hub of the home's floor plan, a connection point for the bedroom wing as well as the parlor, kitchen and family areas. Only his office, accessible via the parlor, could not be reached directly from the entrance.

Beyond the kitchen counter, a hooded crystal drop lamp in the breakfast nook was illuminated by a wreath of amber diffusion bulbs flickering like tiny flames. Danielle, wearing the same terry-cloth robe he'd seen during Megan's teething crisis, was hunkered over the kitchen table snipping pieces out of a newspaper.

She looked so natural, so comfortable, so completely at ease in her new surroundings. The mellow light bathed her face in softness, accentuating the sleek curve of her throat, the tantalizing glimmer of skin exposed by the robe's loose bodice. Her chestnut hair glowed with golden highlights, wild spirals sprang forth to tangle at her shoulders, tease the shadowed cheekbones of a face that he'd considered attractive, but never particularly beautiful. Until now.

He quietly rounded the counter, cleared his throat, startling her.

She shifted in her chair, the scissors poised midair. "I'm sorry. Did I wake you up?"

"No." Actually, she had. More precisely, she'd kept him from falling asleep in the first place. His lovely pretend-wife had invaded his mind, which had replayed the memory of that shattering kiss earlier in the day, a kiss that had been designed to surprise, shock, perhaps even exact a small retribution for the unexpected attack she'd launched by propelling herself into his arms when he'd first walked through the door.

In retrospect, he realized that she'd simply been abiding by terms of an agreement specifically designed to protect the sanctity of their marital sham. At the time, however, he'd been embarrassed, taken by surprise and had responded in kind. Unfortunately, revenge had ricocheted into something he'd never expected and wouldn't soon forget.

"I couldn't sleep," he said.

"I couldn't, either. Probably just the newness of everything." Danielle laid down the scissors beside a neat pile of rectangular clippings stacked beside her elbow. "Megan doesn't seem to mind, though. She took a lovely nap this afternoon, and went to bed tonight without a peep. I think she likes it here."

"Good. I want her to be happy." He hovered there a moment, compelled to continue the conversation. "Interesting articles?"

"Hmm?" She glanced up, followed his gaze to the stack

of newspaper clippings in her hand. "Coupons," she explained, flipping through them, holding one up. "Diapers. A dollar off. Not bad, huh? And this is good for free gum."

"I didn't realize you were fond of gum."

"Kids at the shelter like it."

"Seems like a great deal of effort to save a few cents."

"Every little bit helps." She put the coupons aside, angled a wary glance. "You don't mind, do you? I mean, it's yesterday's newspaper, so I thought you were through with it. If you haven't read it yet..." The words trailed off as he held up the paper, peered through a rectangular hole in the front page. She smiled, shrugged. "I guess you're out of luck."

He laid the paper aside, seated himself across from her. "I've read it. You're welcome to all the coupons you want, although you needn't creep about in the middle of the night to clip them."

"Usually I'm not much of a creeper. Most of the time I'm asleep before I hit the pillow. Today was just, well, kind of hectic. I guess I'm still a little wired."

Colby touched his finger to the rim of a chocolate-smeared bowl on his side of the table. "Ice cream?"

"A weakness."

"We all have them, I suppose."

"You don't."

The sadness in her voice startled him. "I'm hardly perfect."

"I didn't say you were perfect, I said you had no weaknesses. At least, none that I've noticed. Then again, perhaps having no weaknesses is a weakness in itself." A poignant smile took the edge off her comment. She leaned back in the chair, stifled a yawn.

"You should get some sleep."

"I suppose." She made no move to leave.

Colby hesitated, then stood and went into the kitchen.

He flexed his fingers at the light switch, thought better of it. For some odd reason he didn't want to break the fragile mood of soft light and golden shadows, so he used reflected illumination from the nook to peruse the contents of unfamiliar cupboards.

Danielle propped her chin on her hand, watched for a moment. "Are you looking for—?" She gasped as Colby lurched forward.

Something bounced across the floor, leaving a treacherous trail of slippery little balls scattered beneath his slippered feet. As he steadied himself on the counter, Danielle leapt up, flipped on the overhead fluorescent. Colby stared down, appalled. "What on earth is that?"

Danielle heaved a long-suffering sigh, yanked a small brush and dustpan out of the broom closet. "You stepped in the cat's bowl," she muttered, sweeping up the strewn kitty kibble. "At least you missed the water dish. That would have made a real mess."

"This mess isn't real enough for you?"

She glanced up, narrowed her eyes. "Whiskers has to eat, you know."

"But does he have to eat in *here?*"

"Silly me. All these years I've been under the delusion that kitchens were meant for food preparation and consumption."

"For people, not animals."

"Ah, I see." She straightened, emptied the dustpan into a wastebasket under the sink. "And where, pray tell, do you in your infinite wisdom believe that animals should dine?"

"Outside."

"Whiskers is a house cat. He's not allowed outside, and even if he was, I certainly wouldn't stick his food out there to be rained on and attacked by disgusting bugs." She returned the brush and dustpan to the broom closet, then regarded Colby with folded arms and an irked frown. "Whiskers and I are not unreasonable. If you're bothered by a couple of teensy-weensy pet bowls tucked in the farthest corner of the kitchen where any clumsy, inattentive clod could trip over them, I'm certain we can find a mutually agreeable compromise."

He, too, folded his arms, and performed the function with considerably more panache. "Exactly what kind of compromise did you have in mind?"

Danielle shrugged, scanned the kitchen. "How about the counter?"

"Good Lord, no!"

"The kitchen table?"

"You're being ridiculous. That's were *we* eat. I will not have a dirty animal traipsing the same surface where—" Colby bit off the words as a glance toward the nook revealed the animal in question seated atop the table placidly grooming himself. Even worse, the inner surface of the empty ice cream bowl was considerably cleaner than it had been moments ago. "Oh, good heavens," Colby sputtered. "That is disgusting."

Danielle followed his horrified gaze, tried to cover a smile behind her hand, but didn't quite make it. She retrieved the bowl, shook a scolding finger at the cat. "Bad kitty. Chocolate isn't good for you."

Whiskers blinked up, yawned. The animal stretched, then hopped off the table and ambled away.

Colby could barely speak. "That is completely unacceptable. It's unsanitary."

"I know. I'll talk to him."

"You find this amusing?"

"I find you amusing, Colby." She sighed, rubbed the back of her neck, suddenly looking so tired and vulnerable that Colby was struck by the urge to take her into his arms, use his body to shield her from a world she was too guileless to understand. She rolled her head, studied him quietly. "I'm sorry. This is your house, after all, and there's no reason you should suffer any more inconvenience than absolutely necessary."

He shifted, taken aback by her unexpected acquiescence. "I didn't mean to imply that your presence is inconvenient. It's just that I haven't had any experience with animals, and I find their habits a bit, ah, distasteful."

She nodded, rubbed her forearms beneath the floppy robe sleeves. "I'll put the food bowls in the laundry room with the litter box. That way—"

"*Litter box?*"

"You'll hardly notice it."

"Except when I do laundry, which I despise quite enough without the added unpleasantry of stepping over a pan of used toilet sand."

Danielle grimaced. "You do have a way with words."

"I'll not tolerate it."

"How about if I promise to clean up every time he, er, does his business and squirt the place with air freshener?"

Colby folded his arms so tightly that his ribs ached. "I'd still have to look at it."

"Not if I did the laundry."

"Absolutely not—" He blinked. "All of the laundry?"

She sighed. "Sure, why not?"

"Well…"

"Aw, c'mon." She nudged him playfully. "You better take me up on it while I'm in a giving mood. Who knows how annoyed we may be with each other in another week."

He pretended to ponder the offer, although he knew perfectly well that only a fool would refuse it. Colby detested laundry. And he was most certainly not a fool. "Very well."

"You needn't look so pained. After all, I'm the one who got the short end of the deal."

"It's your cat," he observed dryly. "If you wish to re-negotiate our agreement, I'd like to reopen discussions on outside feeding— Is that a whipping wand?" Colby scooped the item from a clutter of gadgets that had been unboxed and strewn across the counter. "Three speeds, battery powered. I've always wanted one of these."

"You're kidding."

"They're quite versatile," he mumbled, turning the unit in his palm to examine the molded handle. "I understand they make marvelous meringue."

"What on earth would a man like you know about meringue?"

"I know that if one whips it at the wrong speed, it will be dry as foam." He turned the appliance over, admired the sleek convenience, the stainless-steel blades tucked below a molded plastic collar. "Excellent," he murmured. "Perfectly designed to prevent marring of plastic mixing bowls."

Danielle eyed the whipping wand as if seeing it for the first time. "That's a good thing?"

"Of course. A tremendous time-saver, too. Think of all the dishes one could prepare without dragging out a bulky blender or bowl mixer."

"Ah, yes, the mind boggles." She snickered, shook her head. "Take it, it's yours."

"Really?"

"My mother would be thrilled."

"Your mother?"

"Mmm-hmm. She held high hopes that if she showered me with enough kitchen gadgets, I might break down and use one of them. Unfortunately, I didn't inherit her love of cooking."

"You don't cook?"

"Well, you needn't say it like that. I'm hell on wheels with a microwave." She angled a glance, apparently read the horror on his face and was amused by it. "Lucky for you that our agreement called only for sharing the kitchen and not what's prepared in it."

He regarded her for a moment. "Do you like corn soufflé?"

"I have no idea."

"It's delightful," he murmured, stroking the molded plastic handle. "I'll whip one up this weekend."

"You'd actually cook for me?"

"Why not?"

"I don't know. I guess I'm just having trouble picturing you in an apron."

"I do not wear an apron." He returned the wand to the counter, teased her with the hint of a smile. "I do, however, roll up my sleeves in a most casual manner."

"Bare forearms? Goodness, I can hardly wait." She feigned a shiver of excitement, cocked her head in a girlish manner that was oddly appealing. "So what else were you looking for?"

"Excuse me?"

"When you were going through the cupboards."

"Oh. My Scotch."

"The stuff in that crystal decanter? It's in the parlor." Returning to the table, Danielle refolded what was left of the newspaper, absently squared the little pile of clippings. "I figured the parlor was where you'd be most comfortable, kind of a private retreat where you'd be able to unwind in peace and quiet."

"Oh. That was thoughtful. Thank you." He clasped his hands behind his back, made no move to leave. "About this afternoon…"

The phrase dangled there like a curious scent. Danielle glanced up. "What about it?"

"You, ah, did a good job." He cleared his throat. "With the moving and everything."

She straightened slightly, squirmed in her seat. "There are still a lot of boxes to unload. Things are still pretty cluttered."

He'd noticed, of course, but hadn't been particularly bothered by the cartons heaped in the family area. A lack of annoyance was strange in itself, since tidiness had always been crucial to Colby's comfort. "I just wanted you to know that I appreciated your efforts."

"Thanks."

He filled his lungs, exhaled slowly. "I also wanted to apologize for my behavior."

At first, Danielle seemed bewildered by that, then her eyes widened, her gaze skittered away. She was remembering the kiss, he thought, and misread her embarrassed expression as annoyance. "Forget it," she murmured. "I know you were just pretending."

"Yes, of course." The moment their lips had touched, Colby's heart had raced so wildly that he'd feared he might pass out. "To keep up appearances in front of your friends. Still, it was unseemly, and I apologize."

She nodded, avoided his gaze. When she remained silent, Colby made a production of straightening the lapels of his robe. "Well, good night." He turned away quickly, strode to the parlor, turned on a lamp and closed the double doors.

The silence surrounded him like familiar arms. His room. His furniture, all gleaming, polished, sparkling clean. Big bay windows to let in morning light. Sophisticated sheers over custom privacy blinds, accented by a twist of earth-toned jacquard at the corners. The cut crystal decanter and matching glasses were positioned perfectly on the glass coffee table. Everything was perfectly arranged, exactly what he wanted in a personal retreat. Danielle had done well.

He moved past the leather sofa, to the entertainment center where the massive television stood dark and silent. A twinge of guilt gnawed him. Except for the news, he rarely

If offer card is missing write to: Silhouette Reader Service, 3010 Walden Ave., P.O. Box 1867, Buffalo, NY 14240-1867

BUSINESS REPLY MAIL
FIRST-CLASS MAIL   PERMIT NO. 717   BUFFALO, NY

POSTAGE WILL BE PAID BY ADDRESSEE

SILHOUETTE READER SERVICE
3010 WALDEN AVE
PO BOX 1867
BUFFALO NY 14240-9952

NO POSTAGE
NECESSARY
IF MAILED
IN THE
UNITED STATES

watched television. Since Danielle's set had been stolen, he considered moving his into the family room where she and Megan could enjoy it.

Lowering himself onto the stiff leather cushions, he poured two fingers of Scotch, swirled the amber liquid, watching the rainbow refraction of light bounce on diamond-cut glass. He leaned back, crossed his legs, eyed the modern abstract painting that had graced his apartment dining area. It looked nice.

The entire room was nice. It was private. Tidy. Quiet. Just what he needed.

He sipped the Scotch, tapped his fingers on his knee. Aloneness, it seemed, had lost much of its appeal. He flipped off the lamp, carried his glass to the kitchen nook and was disappointed to find that Danielle was gone. Foolish of him to feel deserted, he supposed. After all, it was well past midnight.

He turned on another lamp, wandered around the family room reeking of Danielle's influence. There were plants everywhere, some lush and healthy, others sickly and pathetic. Crisp leaves littered the carpet. Messy boxes with odd items protruding like chaotic little soldiers had been shoved in every corner, and behind a thick, flowered sofa that looked more like an upholstered garden than a piece of furniture.

Colby ran a hand across the sofa's back cushion, pinched the softness with his fingertips. A sweet fragrance wafted up, the familiar scent of strawberries and spice. He took another sip of Scotch, glanced back toward the gleaming parlor, then for some reason he couldn't quite fathom, he settled into the plush softness of the fragrant flowered sofa.

Whiskers hopped on the oak coffee table, delicately maneuvered around a clutter of plants and bric-a-brac, then sat directly in front of Colby with a reproachful stare.

"What is your problem?"

The cat uttered a thin meow.

"Yes, I suppose the move has been stressful for you, too." Colby sipped, felt the soothing warmth slide through his bones. The sofa was ugly, but exceedingly comfortable. He felt he was sinking into a sweetly scented cloud. Feeling mellower, he regarded the cat with more charitable intent. "It was an accident, you know. I certainly didn't mean to contaminate your supper dish with my foot."

Whiskers trilled softly. Colby yawned, nestled down into luxurious, soft cushions and drifted off to sleep.

Danielle found him there in the morning, sprawled in blissful slumber with the cat comfortably curled in his lap. One sleepy yellow eye opened.

"Don't get your hopes up," she whispered to the drowsy animal. "He's only pretending to like you."

Whiskers stretched, tossed a lazy paw over his eyes. Danielle could have sworn that silly cat was smiling.

"Your lawyer on two."

Colby took the call quickly. "Jack, has the ruling come down?"

"It's what we expected," came the droning reply. "The judge upheld your guardianship pending the final hearing next month."

The interim order was indeed anticipated since the Sinclairs' perfunctory request for temporary custody had not specified substantial cause as required by statute. Still, Colby was relieved that this small step had gone his way, although there were other questions that remained to be answered, questions that kept his shoulders rigid and his focus intense. "Were my parents awarded visitation privileges?"

"Oddly enough, they didn't request any."

Colby exhaled all at once, massaged his moist forehead.

"I hadn't expected they would. They're not fond of children."

"That seems a bit paradoxical," Jack replied. "Why would people who don't care for children turn around and sue for custody of one?"

"Their motivation is not my concern."

"It should be. If your parents are striving to fulfill some kind of clandestine agenda, we should certainly be aware of that before the hearing." Jack paused, waiting for Colby's response. When none was forthcoming, he sighed. "I like to think that our relationship goes beyond that of attorney and client," he said. "So I'm going to draw upon our friendship, and cut right to the chase. What's going on between you and your parents that I don't know about?"

"Nothing."

"Come on, Colby. From what you've told me, neither you nor your sister have had contact with your parents for nearly a decade. Now out of the blue, they've come forward to claim the illegitimate child of a daughter who according to you was disowned by them years ago. Why would they do that?"

A sharp pain stabbed between Colby's brows. He pinched the bridge of his nose, searched his desk drawer for an aspirin. "That's a good question, Jack. I suggest you pose it during their deposition."

A sigh whistled past the phone like exhaled cigarette smoke. "I don't like surprises, Colby, which is why I make a point of inspecting family closets for old bones before someone starts flinging skeletons from the witness stand."

"I've told you all you need to know," Colby snapped with more force than he'd intended. He swallowed two aspirin dry, took a moment to compose himself. Clearly his lawyer wasn't going to let the matter drop. Today, tomorrow, next week, sooner or later Jack would insist on answers, so Colby decided to throw out an explanation that was close enough to the truth to be accepted. "I can't imagine anything Eugenia and Kingsley would abhor more than learning their blue blood runs in the veins of a bastard grandchild. Since Megan quite clearly exists, their only recourse is to control the world's access to her."

"You believe they're only seeking custody in order to send her away?"

"Yes," he replied firmly. "I do."

"Can you prove it?"

"No."

"Speculation isn't evidence, Colby."

"Then ask how they raised their own children," Colby shot back. "Ask about the boarding schools, the holidays spent in Europe while their kids stayed home with servants, or even worse, spent Christmases alone in deserted dorm rooms. Ask how many school functions they attended, how many birthday parties they arranged, how many hugs they gave—" Colby snapped his jaw, pulled away from the phone, breathing hard. His anger had betrayed him. Again.

He took a deep calming breath, then another, and raised the receiver to his ear. "I want my parents prohibited from coming within a thousand feet of Megan."

"That's not realistic."

"I don't care how you do it, Jack, but I want a legal order that keeps Megan from ever laying eyes on those people."

"She's their grandchild, Colby. Regardless of the custody issue, the judge will certainly award some kind of visitation arrangements."

"No," he said simply. "I won't allow it."

Ivy clung to the aged brick wall, a living fence between the stately manor and the bustling Brentwood boulevard. Danielle pulled her car up the short driveway, just far enough to peer through the imposing wrought-iron gate. A small speaker was positioned on the driver's side, along with a red button with which one presumably announced one's presence.

Behind the barred gate the Sinclair estate sprawled like a medieval fortress—impressive, imposing, intimidating. "Wow," she murmured to Megan's reflection in the rear-view mirror. "Your grandparents really know how to live."

Megan, who was trying to dismantle a ring of fat plastic keys with her mouth, paid no attention to the view beyond the windshield. Instead, she grinned at Danielle, squeaked happily and whacked the keys on the tray of her car seat.

Danielle pivoted, draped an arm over the backrest. "Pretty fancy digs, huh? Someday, you'll be scampering around that plush lawn, plucking roses from the garden and drinking lemonade freshly squeezed, no doubt, by one of your personal servants."

Megan clicked her teeth, drooled on her chin.

"Hmm. Maybe we'll have to wait until your manners improve a bit." She retrieved a cloth from the diaper bag on the passenger seat, dabbed the baby's slippery little jaw. "More importantly, we'll have to wait until your uncle and your grandparents grow up enough to stop acting like children themselves."

Danielle tucked the damp cloth back in the bag, then scanned what she could see of the manicured estate. The two-story home was stucco, with red tile roofing and old Southern-style architecture. A formal lawn area was accented by brick planters from which a profusion of white blossoms spilled like sparkling spring snow. Huge trees shaded a marble fountain glazed with a patina of fine moss.

It was splendid, lush, yet somehow not particularly inviting. Stiff formality gave a museumlike quality to the grounds, a perfection of form and substance that seemed unlived in, if not unlivable.

"This is where Uncle Colby and your mommy grew

up," Danielle told Megan, who wasn't the least bit impressed. "It's part of your heritage, sweetie, part of who you are. Someday, knowing that will be important to you."

Megan yawned, started to fuss.

"I know, I know. It's getting close to nap time, and we still have to pick up Uncle Colby's suits at the cleaner's. Say bye-bye to Nanna and Poppa."

"Be-ba," Megan mumbled, waving her fat little hand.

Smiling, Danielle shifted into Reverse, backed out of the driveway and headed toward the freeway. Today had just been a scouting mission to satisfy her own curiosity and see what she was dealing with. During the past week since they'd moved into the new house, Danielle had discovered that the mere mention of Eugenia and Kingsley Sinclair turned Colby into a breathing block of stone. Undaunted, she'd simply switched to her backup plan for reconciling the feuding family.

The foundation of that plan had already been laid. It was nearly time for the elder Sinclairs to meet their beautiful grandchild. Danielle could hardly wait.

Colby snapped his briefcase shut, then strode past his assistant, who was still working on her computer. He stopped, frowned. "It's past five."

The revelation didn't seem to startle her as much as his comment. "I'm not finished transcribing your dictation."

"It can wait," he told her. "You should go home to your family."

She stared at him. "Yes, sir."

Colby shifted, feeling a twinge of guilt. After all, his policy had always been that employees stayed until the work was completed, and his harried assistant had always followed that edict to the letter. "You have children, don't you?"

"Three."

"Ah, well, I imagine they need their mother more than I do." An odd sensation prickled his cheeks. He realized that he was smiling. "Turn off the computer." He waited until she'd done so, then bid her a cheery good-night, whistled his way to the elevator.

On the drive home, he flipped the car radio from business news to soft music, then mentally sorted a list of favorite recipes he'd like to prepare for Danielle, whose appreciation of his culinary expertise made him feel rather godlike. As much as he enjoyed preparing exotic fare, it was her blatant delight with his creations that gave him the most pleasure.

In return, she'd taken over those errands and chores he found mundane and unpleasant. All in all, their living arrangements had proven mutually beneficial beyond his wildest imagination. For the first time in his life, Colby Sinclair was content. No, beyond content.

He was actually happy.

After a quick stop at the grocery store to pick up fresh ingredients for the evening meal, Colby drove directly to the sprawling, suburban home that he shared with Danielle and Megan. He pulled into the driveway, buzzed the garage door open, then took a moment to savor the sensation of normalcy. For that moment he was like everyone else, an everyday working man returning home for a quiet evening with his family.

It was fake, of course. Everything was fake. His home. His marriage. His family. Fake or not, it was the first time Colby had ever experienced a normal, happy life, and he relished every moment.

He parked the car, entered the kitchen from the garage door, put the grocery bag and his briefcase on the counter. Whiskers jumped up, meowed a greeting. "Off." The order was reinforced by pointing to the floor. Whiskers rubbed against him, leaving an affectionate trail of hair on his sleeve. Colby pulled his arm away, shook his finger in the animal's face. "No, bad cat. You're not allowed on the counter."

The cat's ears flattened. When Colby reached for the creature, he received a warning hiss from ten black-and-white pounds of hairy, in-your-face feline attitude. He was contemplating the wisdom of using a wooden spoon to herd the animal when Danielle's voice filtered from the hallway. "Look, sweetums, that's your mommy! Wasn't she pretty?"

A chill slithered down Colby's spine. He spun around the counter, raced down the hall and found what he'd feared—Danielle and Megan seated on the floor of his bedroom, hunched over an old photo album.

Danielle looked up, smiled brightly. "You're early." Her smile died as she followed his gaze to the album laying open on the floor. "I was hanging your suits from the cleaners and saw this on your closet shelf."

"So naturally you decided to pry into my personal affairs."

She straightened, bewildered. "I was looking for pictures of Olivia to put up in Megan's room. I didn't think you'd mind."

"I do mind."

"I can see that. I'm sorry." She contritely closed the album, stood as if to put it away.

"Leave it."

Danielle wavered a moment, still clutching the worn leather book in her arms, then she laid it on the bed, scooped up Megan and regarded Colby with peculiar sadness. "I didn't mean to upset you. I simply thought that someday Megan would want photographs of her mother."

"That really isn't your concern, is it?"

She flinched as if slapped, then hardened her gaze. "No, I guess not."

Colby waited until Danielle had taken Megan out of the room, then he closed the door and went to the bed, where the shabby leather photo album beckoned like a portal to the past. He should have disposed of it years ago, couldn't explain why he'd kept it. At the sight of it images strobed his mind with painful memories. He knew every photograph in that book, remembered each captured moment as if it happened yesterday. There were very few pictures of his childhood, most taken by servants who'd mistakenly believed his parents would enjoy mementos of birthdays and holidays missed during their many European tours.

But his parents hadn't cared. Danielle couldn't understand that, would never understand that. The loving relationship she'd cultivated with Megan proved her incapable of grasping the cruel reality that he and his sister had experienced. Danielle was too nurturing, too naive, too willing to give her heart, her love to a child who desperately needed both. Although that love still amazed Colby, it also provided a sad reminder of his own emotionally deprived childhood, and the secrets that still haunted him.

The crayoned drawing was a gift to his mother. The boy had spent hours on it, and his kindergarten teacher said it was the finest picture in the whole class. He arranged it on the kitchen table, then sat in a chair and waited for Mother to emerge from her bedroom. He waited a long time, until Cook chased him out so she could prepare the evening meal.

He took his picture into the parlor, laid it carefully on the coffee table, smoothing the corners, ironing tiny wrinkles with his hand. When it was perfect, he sat on the davenport as he'd been taught, with his hands clasped quietly in his lap.

He waited for Mother, refusing supper for fear he'd miss her monumental appearance. The au pair shrugged and gave him a strange look. But the boy didn't care. He knew his mother would love the drawing, love him for having created it.

So he waited, and he waited. He fell asleep waiting.

When he awoke, the picture was gone. His sister was standing there with a smug grin. She told him Mother had thrown the drawing in the trash. The boy cried. He cried all night long.

Then he never cried again.

Chapter Eight

"Next week isn't good for me. How about—" Colby noted today's appointment with representatives from the Family Unity Coalition, presumably a charitable organization seeking donations, then flipped his desk calendar forward to next week, scanned for empty lines. "The eleventh, around two."

Muttered agreement filtered over the line, although Colby's attention was distracted by a familiar voice outside his office door. He swiveled, leaned, saw nothing but the corner of his assistant's desk, heard a soft, raspy chuckle that sent chills down his spine.

The phone crackled. "So we're on for the eleventh?"

"Hmm? Oh, yes, three o'clock."

"I thought you said two."

"Sure, right. See you then." Cradling the receiver, Colby pocketed the calendar without noting his new appointment, stood to investigate that distinctive laugh. He peered around the doorjamb, steadied himself. It *was* her. Here. In his office, his professional sanctum, the only place on earth over which he still held a modicum of control.

Or had, until now.

"You look beautiful today," gushed his assistant. "Such a chic outfit. Red really complements that lovely blond hair."

Colby sagged against the door molding, rubbed his eyelids. This couldn't be happening. But of course, it was.

"Ya-ya oooo!" Megan squeaked, clapping her hands. "Ungee be-ba."

"Yes, Uncle is taking us bye-bye." Danielle, outrageously attired in a floppy brimmed hat, a garish crocheted vest that looked like it had been ripped from an old afghan, and a faded plaid dress that hung halfway to her ankles, glanced up to spot Colby lurking in the doorway. So did Megan, who squealed in excitement. Danielle's eyes lit, her voice softened. "Hi, there."

Colby cleared his throat, acutely aware that half his staff had been struck by a sudden urge to surround a nearby water cooler to observe the unfolding scene with undisguised curiosity. "I, er, wasn't expecting you."

"Aren't surprises fun?"

"Actually, I find them distracting." An angled glance revealed a guilty flush creeping up his assistant's cheeks. She fiddled with a desk calendar, peeked over the rim of her glasses.

An irritable question was poised on Colby's tongue when Danielle leapt to the woman's defense. "Now don't you dare scold Jo-Jo. This isn't her fault."

Colby's head snapped around. "Who's Jo-Jo?"

His assistant moistened her lips, managed a thin smile. "My friends call me that sometimes."

"Your friends?" Bewildered, he realized that his efficient assistant's first name was JoAnna, although during their eight-year association he'd never referred to her as anything except Ms. Reese. "I didn't realize you and, ah, my wife were acquainted."

It was Danielle who responded. "Jo-Jo and I met last week, when Megan and I dropped in to take you to lunch."

"You were here? Last week?"

"Mmm-hmm." She shifted the baby, smoothing her ruffled gingham dress. "You were in a meeting or something."

Colby swallowed, glared at his hapless assistant, who glowed like a neon tomato. "Why was I not informed?"

"Now, darling," Danielle cooed. Much to Colby's horror, she patted his cheek. "There's no need to get upset. It just makes your veins bulge, which is really quite unattractive. Oh! That reminds me. Is Mira here? I just stopped by to see how construction of the day-care center is coming, and it's going to be absolutely marvelous. She's done a splendid job. And so have you," she added quickly. "After all, it was your idea, you sweet old softie."

Colby gazed around helplessly, saw smiles hidden behind raised hands and heard the unmistakable crack of his carefully cultivated professional image shattering into a thousand irretrievable shards.

"James!" Danielle said suddenly, whirling toward the snickering staff at the break room door. "How's your wife feeling?"

James Malony, Colby's crackerjack marketing manager, grinned stupidly, smoothed his nearly bare scalp. "Much better, Dani. That psoriasis cream you recommended really helped."

"Good. Give her my best." Spinning back around, Danielle shifted Megan on her hip, gave Colby a bright smile. "Are you ready?"

"Ready for what?" he asked warily.

"We're taking Megan to the zoo."

"The zoo?"

"You know, cute animals, popcorn and peanuts, walking until our feet fall off. Megan's been excited all day." She snapped her fingers as if commanding an obedient pet. "Come on. Time's a-wasting."

He stiffened, trying to salvage whatever tenuous shred of dignity he might still have left. "If you had discussed this with me earlier, you'd have discovered that I'm unavailable this afternoon."

"Of course you're unavailable. You'll be at the zoo."

A titter emanated from the cooler. He silenced it with a look, gritted his teeth. "You misunderstand. I have a lunch meeting with the, er, Family Unity Coalition."

"Ah, that would be us." She smiled brightly. "Personally, I prefer the excitement of spontaneity, but last week when Jo-Jo explained how difficult it was to rearrange your busy schedule, we went ahead and made an appointment."

"You made an appointment?" Colby sputtered, hating the panicked pitch of his normally robust voice. "As a charitable organization?"

"Charity does begin at home," she reminded him, settling Megan into a stroller parked behind his assistant's desk. Straightening, she shouldered the diaper bag, tugged her floppy hat down to her eyebrows and gazed up expectantly. "Shall we go, darling? You're on my time now."

"Oh, for— Stop that. Let...go!" Danielle glared into the bulgy brown eyes, tugged her garment loose, then whirled on Colby, who was squatting in a quiet corner showing Megan how to pet a placid bunny. "Why didn't you tell me that a goat was eating my vest?"

He glanced up, eyes twinkling. "I thought it was doing you a favor."

"Very funny." She straightened the item in question, smoothing the colorful crocheted granny squares with great reverence. "I'll have you know that my favorite sister made this for me with her own arthritic little hands."

"Arthritic, hmm? Well, that explains it." He turned his attention back to Megan, who'd reared away from the bunny and was trying to climb Colby's shoulder. "No, sweetie, it won't hurt you. Look how soft and nice it is." To demonstrate, Colby rubbed a fingertip between the animal's floppy ears. "See? Now you try." The baby jammed both hands against her mouth, let out a frightened wail. Colby sighed, stood, shifted his niece against his shoulder and cast a woeful glance at Danielle. "I told you she was too young for this."

"One is never too young to spend time with the people one loves. Besides, you'd be surprised how much information is being filed away in that curious little mind. For example—" Danielle pointed at the floppy-eared creature bounding across the petting zoo grounds "—that's a bunny rabbit, Megan. Can you say bunny?"

Megan sniffed, peered across the small enclosure. "Yay-agoobeegoo."

"Close enough. Now let's go meet a goat."

"She doesn't want to meet a goat," Colby insisted, seating the squirming child into the stroller where she promptly bit the ear of the stuffed panda Danielle hadn't been able to resist buying her. "She wants lunch."

"Megan has already had lunch."

"I haven't."

"Hmm, I did promise to feed you, didn't I?"

"Yes, you did."

"Well, my dear daddy taught me never to break a promise. This way, troops." Danielle spun, stomped one foot in soldierlike cadence, marched through the petting zoo gate with her tiny entourage hustling on her heels. She headed straight for an umbrella-topped cart beside the polar bear exhibit, dug a few bills from the fanny pack looped around her waist. "Two, please."

The aproned man nodded happily, tonged two giant weenies from a roasting spit.

Colby looked on in horror. "This is a joke, right?"

"Hot dogs are an integral part of the zoo experience." She plopped a frankfurter heaped with relish and onions into his hand, took one for herself, touched it to his in a mock toast. "Enjoy." Taking a massive bite, she ignored the cascade of condiments dripping on her boots. "Mmm-m-m."

Colby stared at her as if she'd entirely lost her mind. "I am not going to eat this."

"No?" Cheeks bulging, Danielle snatched a paper napkin from a display on the hot-dog cart, dabbed at her mouth. "That's okay. I can handle two." She took another bite, savored it, rolled her eyes with pleasure.

Colby watched grimly for a moment, then heaved a resigned sigh, polished off his hot dog in three bites, ordered another and washed it down with a giant cola.

When he'd finished, Danielle handed him a napkin. "Good, huh?"

"Adequate." He tidied himself, tossed the used napkin in a nearby receptacle, brushed his hands together, scanning the bustling pathway like a safari tour guide. "All right, then. I believe the monkeys are this way."

As Danielle wheeled the stroller around, Colby came up beside her, tossed an affectionate arm around her shoulders. She stumbled, looked up in surprise.

"Just portraying the happy family on holiday," he explained. "In case we run into someone we know."

"Oh. Of course." She swallowed hard, tried to ignore the seeping warmth of his fingertips caressing her upper arm. It was all a ruse, she reminded herself. Role-playing. Fakery. Colby Sinclair was a man of many faces, able to easily assimilate into whatever situation was presented to him.

Over the past weeks, she'd learned that about him. And she'd learned more. Despite a stoic demeanor, Colby was not the unfeeling man he pretended to be. Beneath that rigid surface lurked a secret sadness that affected Danielle deeply, because she'd seen another side of Colby Sinclair—the softness he concealed from the rest of the world. He was a man of substance, loyalty and depth, with passionate convictions and a wry sense of the absurd that was particularly evident as he mopped curdled milk off Italian loafers, or chased a bare-bottomed baby while waving a diaper in one hand and a powder can in the other.

Danielle had grown to admire him; even more disturbing, however, was the realization that he was a very special man, a man she could fall in love with.

Naturally she wouldn't allow that to happen. Danielle was much too bohemian to be strapped into the rigors of conventional expectations, and Colby Sinclair was about as conventional as they came. Since a love affair between people so philosophically diverse was an invitation to disaster, she was determined to keep their relationship light, friendly and superficial.

Too bad her heart wasn't listening.

Colby left work early on Friday. He didn't know why exactly. A ton of work begged completion before the next week began, but thoughts of Danielle and Megan pushed business obligations aside. A new Disney film had been released this week. He kept thinking how Megan would enjoy the cheery music and colorful animation. She'd probably never been to a movie theater before. That, too, would be a new and exciting experience, one he was surprisingly eager to share.

So he'd given his startled staff the afternoon off and

headed home, whistling, filled with anticipation, only to find his driveway bristling with activity, his yard littered by strangers. Vehicles were parked everywhere except the front lawn, which was covered by tables ladened with crumpled garments being pawed by a gaggle of chattering individuals, most of whom Colby had never seen in his life.

This was too much.

True, he and Danielle had agreed that she be allowed time to continue her charity work, but he'd never, ever agreed to allow her charity work to invade his home. Furious, he parked at the first available curb space a half block away, strode through his cluttered yard ready for confrontation.

Madeline Rodriguez hurried over, chubby arms ladened with clothing. "Why, Mr. Sinclair, how nice to see you again! Dani said you wouldn't be home for hours. Are you here to help with the drive?"

It was difficult to maintain a scowl in the face of such beaming admiration. Colby managed. "I am here because I live here," he snapped, "although at the moment, it pains me to admit it." Ignoring Madeline's crushed expression, he glowered around the crowd. "Where is my wife?"

"In the sorting room."

"The what?"

"Uh, the garage."

Without so much as a mumbled thanks, Colby strode forward, found Danielle hauling cartons of obviously used clothing out of a rickety white van parked backward in the driveway, rear doors opened to allow easy access. Colby's beloved garage was heaped with similar cartons, along with racks of hanging garments that made the place look like an open-air thrift shop.

Danielle dropped the carton, wiped her forehead, squinted into the yawning belly of the van. "How many more?"

A vaguely familiar bald head emerged. "Six."

The fellow spied Colby, gave a brusque nod that apparently alerted Danielle because she spun around, blinked, pasted on a smile so stiff, it was a wonder her cheeks didn't crack. "You're home early."

"So I've been told."

"Good. We could use the help." To Colby's surprise, she offered no explanation of the chaos. Instead, she spun around, whistled into the van. "Hold up, Jonas. We'll have to sort what we've got before we have room to unload any more."

Jonas nodded, hauled his hefty girth out of the vehicle and ambled over to the back of the garage, where a middle-aged woman and a couple of teenage boys picked through cartons like vultures on carrion.

Danielle moistened her lips, tried to brush past Colby, but he snagged her arm. She angled a wary glance upward. "Would you rather size or sort?" she inquired politely.

"I'd rather know what's going on."

"Ah. Well, it's the end of a monthlong clothing drive, when establishments all over the city put up cute little yellow bins and people drop their usable garments inside. Kind of like Toys for Tots at Christmas, you know?" Danielle tried for a cheery grin, didn't quite pull it off and opted to clear her throat instead. She took a deep breath, gestured toward Jonas's group at the back of the garage. "Anyway, tomorrow morning the food bank's thrift shop opens with all the new stuff we've gathered, so we have to have everything sized and sorted by 8:00 a.m. We're running a bit behind."

"So you decided to invite every down-and-out loser in the city to converge and turn our home into a giant flea market?"

Her gaze hardened. "These are good people, Colby."

"Are they really?" he challenged. "And how can you possibly know that?"

"I just know, that's all. I have instincts about people. It's part of my job."

"Ah, yes, that wonderful intuition about which you're so proud. What, pray tell, did those instincts tell you about dear, misunderstood Sheila, who took advantage of your charitable intent and robbed you blind."

A flicker of real pain flashed through her eyes. It took all of Colby's considerable restraint to keep from gathering her in his arms, offering an apology he didn't owe for observing a truth she couldn't accept.

Danielle tossed her hair, curled a loopy spiral around her finger in an action he now recognized as defensive. "Sheila was an anomaly. My judgment of people is ninety-nine percent sound, and *these* people—" an angry gesture encompassed the entire group of workers "—are my friends."

"They're not *my* friends."

"That's your loss."

The reproach in her voice hurt, although Colby didn't understand why it should. This was his home, after all, his private retreat from the world, a place where intruders were prohibited. He had a right to be angry. "What kind of example does this set for Megan, all these scuzzy strangers scurrying about...?" He frowned, scanned the cluttered chaos. "Where is Megan? My God, you haven't left her alone with these ruffians?"

Danielle regarded him for a moment, with sadness, he thought, or possibly disappointment. She turned away, retrieved a pair of worn denims from the nearest box, held them up for scrutiny. "Megan is inside," she said without looking at him. "Jonas's girls are looking after her."

"Jonas's girls?" Horrified, Colby could only imagine what kind of floozy harem would attach itself to a beer-bellied biker sporting a tattered vest emblazoned by a screen-print eagle riding a motorcycle.

Colby spun so quickly, he nearly tripped over a clothes rack, dashed to the kitchen entrance and found it occupied by three women hunched over ironing boards that were flanked by heaps of crumpled clothing along with neatly pressed garments hanging on more racks.

A thin, older woman greeted him with a snaggle-toothed smile. "That there rack is ready to be loaded," she told him happily. "We'll have us a couple more in half an hour or so."

"Where's my niece?" he blurted.

Startled, she set the iron on end, eyed him suspiciously, then lit up as she figured out who he meant. "Little Meggie? Ah-h-h, she's a sweet one, she is. You must be proud, sir, rightly proud—"

"*Where is she?*"

The woman huffed, frowned, snatched up her iron. "Yonder, playing dolls with the younguns."

Colby swiveled through an obstacle course of ironing boards, emerged into the family room and nearly wept with relief. There was Megan, happily occupied within a circle of four youngsters ranging in age from fourish to about twelve. The oldest glanced up. "Wanna play with us?"

"No. Thank you." Colby took time to fill his lungs, exhale slowly. "You aren't by any chance Jonas's girls?"

The raggedy child, a big-eyed youngster with thin hair and gaunt cheeks, regarded him oddly. "He's our pa. If you want him, he's outside with Ma and the boys."

An image formed of the middle-aged woman and teen-aged boys sorting clothes in the garage. Then a sweet fragrance wafted up. Colby didn't have to look to know that Danielle was standing there. She answered his unspoken question. "These are Jonas's daughters," she said quietly. "His wife and sons are working outside."

Colby felt a slow flush crawl up his throat. "I, ah, that is to say, it's a little difficult to imagine Mr., er, Jonas as a family man."

"Why, because he's bald? Because he's fat? Because his style of dress offends you? Or perhaps because he simply doesn't fit your image of a person worthy of a normal, happy family life?"

Since all her observations were true, Colby said nothing.

Danielle studied him for a moment, then spoke softly. "A couple years ago, Jonas was living the American dream. He had a nice house, five great kids and his wife was expecting their sixth when he was injured in a factory accident. He couldn't work for months, and what little disability he received was barely enough to feed his family. They lost the house, lived out of their car for a while. The baby was nearly born in the back seat."

Colby listened, but found the story implausible. "A responsible man makes provisions for such eventualities, and certainly wouldn't force his family to live in a car."

Danielle shrugged. "Not everyone has a tidy nest egg in the bank, Colby. You'd be surprised how many good, upstanding folks live from paycheck to paycheck, not because they want to but because there's no other way to get by. Jonas was lucky, and he was determined. He's struggling back onto his feet financially, and is working again. Things still aren't easy, but they're getting better, and he's never forgotten the organizations that helped out during those bleak months. He volunteers at the food bank whenever he can, and has been very generous with his time."

Folding his arms, Colby refused to be moved. "That's only proper. The word *bank* implies a loan of goods and services to be repaid with interest."

"More than half of our volunteers have never been clients. They give because they want to, because they understand that the blessings they've received could be taken away in the blink of an eye.''

''Not if they've taken proper precautions, educated themselves, learned to live within their means.''

Danielle opened her mouth as if to argue the point, then simply sighed, took his elbow, guided him away from prying ears around the ironing boards. ''I'm sorry we've created such an inconvenience for you,'' she murmured, ushering him into the gleaming parlor. ''If all goes well, we should have everything sorted and loaded by six, then we'll be out of your hair.''

''Until next year,'' he muttered peevishly.

She stopped abruptly, stared at him. ''There won't be a next year.''

For the first time in days, Colby remembered their contract. This was all fake, he reminded himself. Danielle wasn't really his wife. By next year at this time, the contract would be null and void, their agreed-upon divorce would be finalized and they both will have gone their separate ways. The realization saddened him. He didn't know why.

Pivoting on his heels, he clasped his hands behind his back, gazed out the bay window at the flurry of activity. ''You think I'm being unreasonable.''

It was not a question, although Danielle responded as if it had been. ''I think,'' she said carefully, ''that your view of the world is based on your experience of it. That's neither right or wrong. It simply is.''

''One doesn't have to cut off an arm to understand that the procedure causes pain.''

''No, but the only way you'd understand that is if you'd experienced pain in the first place. There are different hurts in the world, Colby. To understand them all, you'd have to experience them all. Fortunately, few of us are so cursed.''

''Pain is pain,'' he insisted, more because he realized

that when the debate ended, Danielle would leave this sparkling sanctum. And Colby would be alone. "The semantical variations are meaningless."

She cocked her head, little-girlish and sweetly appealing, then spoke like a woman evolved beyond her years. "Have you ever been hungry, Colby? I don't mean ready for your evening meal. I mean days without food, so malnourished that you can't walk six steps without dizziness, so sick that you can't even keep down broth because starved internal organs have begun feeding on themselves."

He flinched, repulsed by the image. "Good God, Danielle, there's no reason to become melodramatic. This is America. People don't starve here."

"Yes, Colby, they do." It was a whisper that struck like a scream. She avoided his gaze, moved toward the door. "Your mail and newspaper are on the table. I'll try to keep the noise down outside so you won't be disturbed. We'll be gone soon."

With that, she closed the door, leaving Colby alone in perfect pristine sterility. He stood where she'd left him, feeling deserted, abandoned, swallowing a sense of panic he hadn't felt since childhood. His mind swam through currents of chaos, a pandemonium of images both real and imagined; images of himself as an emotionally deprived youngster, praying to be loved; images of Danielle as a physically deprived child simply praying to be fed.

That's why she felt such affinity for people of poverty. She'd experienced it, lived it. Colby had known she'd been poor as a child, although he hadn't given much credence to her comments about her parents' financial struggles. After all, she'd pulled herself out of the abyss, become a productive citizen. One couldn't ask more. Nor could one ask less. At least, that had always been Colby's belief. Perhaps he was wrong. He didn't think so…but perhaps.

Frustrated and confused, Colby poured himself a stiff

drink, settled on his supple sofa, scanned his mail, then reached for the newspaper and studied the headlines without interest. The activity outside was merely a dull whisper, not nearly enough to break his concentration, yet he was unreasonably focused on it.

He refolded the paper, went to the window. This time, he actually studied the faces of those working there, and was surprised by what he saw. There was a well-groomed young woman in a business suit, several clean-cut young men who could have been college students, women in slacks and department store sweaters, senior citizens, teenagers, children. All were working together for a common cause.

They were also cluttering up his lawn.

The more help the industrious group was given, the faster they'd be gone, motive enough to rationalize a decision to join them. Which was exactly what Colby did.

Chapter Nine

"Smile!"

Flash, whir.

"Again, sweetums, give me a big, fat giggle…yes!"

Flash, whir.

"Wonderful."

Straightening, Danielle returned the Polaroid camera to the grinning woman beside her. "Thanks, Maddie. I'll pay you for the film," she promised, positioning each foggy photograph across her desk to dry and develop. More precisely, she used the warehouse corner that used to be her desk. City staff had since turned it into a coffee area.

"You'll do no such thing. If you hadn't been so charitable to a certain sticky-fingered adolescent ingrate, you'd still have a camera of your own." Madeline tucked the Polaroid camera into a bulging tote, retrieved one of her famous, homemade rag dolls, which she wiggled in front of Megan's rosy little face. "Look what I found," she cooed in that silly-sweet, high-pitched tone adults are prone to use with babies. "What's that?" Holding the doll's cloth face to her ear, Madeline pretended to listen a moment, then feigned shock. "Oh, my goodness! Dolly wants to play with Megan."

Megan lurched forward in the stroller, extended her fat little arms, grunting madly. When Madeline gave her the doll, she promptly stuffed its yarn-studded head into her mouth, then yanked it out with a grimace, concentrated on trying to scratch its embroidered nose off.

Danielle laughed. "I think she said 'Thank you.' If she didn't, I will. That was very nice of you, Maddie."

"Just a little something I thought she might like." The woman scanned the nearly dry photographs, emitted a soft whistle. "I'll admit she's a photogenic tyke, but why on earth do you need so many copies of the same basic shot?"

Answering with a shrug, Danielle gave the pictures a final admiring glance, then tucked them in an envelope, slipped them into her roomy woven shoulder pouch and changed the subject. "Love what they've done with the place," she murmured, glancing around the disorganized food bank warehouse. "Think how much time they must save by simply piling stuff on the floor instead of labeling and shelving it."

"Things haven't been the same since you left," Madeline agreed. "The new folks mean well, but this is just another assignment to them. They haven't enough time, or enough heart."

"But they're keeping it alive," Danielle murmured. "That's all that counts."

"I suppose." Unconvinced, Madeline tossed a dour glance around, hoisted her tote and followed Danielle, who was wheeling Megan's stroller out the loading dock and down the ramp toward the bustling thrift store on the opposite side of the building. "You know, that man of yours sure did come around yesterday. When he first showed up and saw all of us scurrying across the front yard, I thought he'd bust a blood vessel. Next thing I know, he's folding, sorting and barking orders like a drill sergeant. Could have knocked me over with a feather.''

''Me, too,'' Danielle muttered. ''Although I shouldn't have been totally surprised. I handle the laundry, but Colby commandeered the chore of folding clothes because I couldn't make every T-shirt and pair of shorts look like it had just come out of a package. As for giving orders, let's just say he's had a lot of practice, and he's darned good at it.''

Madeline got an evil gleam in her eye, leaned over to whisper, ''I'll bet that's not all he's good at, hmm?'' She tugged Danielle's sleeve to prevent her from turning away. ''C'mon, girl, share. I want details.''

A slow heat worked its way up Danielle's throat. ''Stop it, Madeline.''

''Stop what? You always confide the good stuff, and frankly, after keeping that hunky husband of yours under wraps for so long, I figure you owe me big-time. Now, fess up. When did you realize that despite a professed distrust of rich, handsome and powerful men, that one of the richest, handsomest and most powerful was actually Mr. Right?''

''Madeline—''

''Inquiring minds and all that rot.''

''Oh, for crying out loud.''

Madeline brightened, snapped her fingers. ''That dreamy first kiss, right? I'll bet your toes curled.''

They'd curled all right. The mere memory made them curl again.

''What about the first—'' Madeline's elbow nudged her playfully ''—horizontal mambo?'' Danielle's annoyed groan only encouraged the woman. "Hot and passionate, hmm? I'd give odds that the sheets melted."

"I'm not going to discuss this with you."

"Oh, oh...I know! Slo-o-ow and sensual." She heaved a yearning sigh, practically swooned against the thrift shop door. "Oooow, I can see it now. Hot, steamy skin, moist lips, erotic desire building from a tiny flame, stoked by passion, spiraling brighter and hotter until melded bodies erupt in volcanoes of hedonistic lust—" The woman stopped abruptly. "Oh my gosh, Dani, what's wrong? You're shaking all over."

"I don't want to talk about this," she said, horrified by a telltale quiver in her voice. "It's not...it's not—" A mortifying flood of tears sprang to her eyes. "Appropriate," she finished lamely.

"Oh, hon, I'm so sorry. You know I was just fooling around. I'd rather yank out my teeth than hurt you." Helpless, clearly bewildered, Madeline held the thrift shop door open, watched her friend wheel the stroller inside, then followed, wringing her hands. "Look, I didn't mean any harm. You know that I'm just a divorced broad getting secondhand jollies from my friends."

"I know." Yanking up the hem of her scratchy tunic sweater, Danielle wiped her wet eyes, tried to control the frightening flood of emotion throbbing its way through her chest. She knew Madeline was confused.

Danielle was confused, too. The women had frequently joked about sex, confided in each other about their dates, disastrous and otherwise. There was no reason for such a volatile reaction to harmless banter. It was completely in character for Madeline to ask intimate prying questions. The fact that she'd based wild speculation on nonexistent activity would normally not have been a problem. Danielle frequently embellished her own responses as much to amuse herself as her nosy but beloved friend. A few fun lies between buddies had never seemed particularly sinful.

This time something was different. This time Danielle could actually envision the moments Madeline had been describing, sweet, succulent, sensual moments that had never occurred—would never occur—and yet Danielle had lived them in her mind, experienced them in her heart with such realism, such clarity that her body had actually responded. The powerful images had shaken her to her soles. And they'd frightened her.

Now she sniffed, gazed across the bustling thrift shop brimming with racks of freshly pressed clothing, and her heart leapt into her throat. There was Colby, tall and strong, his handsome face furrowed with genuine concern as he listened to Frank Lonnigan, who was surrounded by his well-mannered family.

After a moment, Colby nodded, pulled what appeared to be a business card from his pocket. He scribbled something on the back, handed it to the man, who was stoically appreciative. They shook hands, then Colby spoke to Mrs. Lonnigan and each of the Lonnigan children before turning his attention to another family group rummaging through a stack of neatly folded blue jeans.

Danielle watched greedily, absorbing every nuance of Colby's demeanor, from the gentle glow in his eyes to the determined set of his sculpted jaw. Her fingers itched to touch him, to stroke his carved cheekbones, to dally in the curve of that adorable comma-shaped dent in a chin too pronounced to be attractive, but was oddly appealing anyway. Colby Sinclair was a man of extremes, a man of profound contradiction, both gentle and judgmental, compassionate and stern.

Why was it, Danielle wondered, that she hadn't recognized how truly special he was?

The fuzzy-haired woman beside her muttered a soft

curse. "I'm such a fool," Madeline murmured, shaking her head. "How could I not have understood?"

With some effort Danielle tore her gaze from Colby, settled it on her friend. "Understood what?"

"I'm so stupid. I should have known better, but I just had this nagging idea that it was all some kind of elaborate joke."

"A joke?"

"I was wrong, I was so wrong. I see that now."

"Wrong about what?" Danielle released the stroller long enough to toss up her hands. "Honestly, Maddie, I have no idea what you're talking about."

The woman heaved a sigh, gazed up with liquid eyes. "Wrong about you—" she nodded toward Colby "—and about him. The truth is that I never bought into this marriage of yours."

"You…didn't?"

"I figured that for whatever reason, the two of you were trying to pull the mother of all pranks."

Danielle gripped the stroller handle to keep from falling over. "A prank," she murmured with a sick smile. "Whatever gave you that idea?"

"I don't know." She shrugged, her gaze skittered away. "That's not true. I do know. I didn't want to admit that my best friend in the entire world would have kept that kind of secret from me." Madeline licked her lips, looked so forlorn that it was all Danielle could do to keep from hugging her. "I never thought it would happen to you, though. You always seemed so grounded, so completely in control. But it did happen, didn't it, hon?"

"I haven't a clue what you're talking about."

Madeline frowned a moment, then laughed, swatted Danielle's shoulder. "You're teasing me again, bad girl, but you can't fool me twice."

"Oh, for crying out loud, Maddie, stow the gibberish and cut to the chase."

Eyes gentled, Madeline reached out, affectionately stroked a tangled curl above Danielle's brow. "You're crazy in love with him, hon. Any fool could see it. It's written all over your face."

"Dani?" Colby stepped out the sliding glass door onto the patio. "What are you doing out here?"

The answer seemed fairly clear since she was holding a hose, but she responded anyway. "Watering the plants."

"It's dark."

"The plants are too thirsty to care."

Leaves crunched behind her. A branch rustled. When Colby was close enough to radiate body heat, she stepped away, aimed the glistening flow at potted geraniums she'd lovingly arranged at the edge of the manicured lawn.

A strained silence followed. Danielle focused on dancing droplets reflecting amber light from the porch lamps. When she'd first seen this lovely yard, her imagination had soared with ideas. A small reflecting pool at the patio's edge, surrounded by natural stone planters spilling a riot of spring color. Beyond the lawn, a cluster of red maple and sweet-gum trees for privacy. She'd even envisioned a vegetable garden along side the house.

Foolish dreams.

"Things went well today."

She tightened her grip on the hose. "Yes. Thanks for helping out."

"It was interesting. I didn't realize how many people depended on the thrift shop and food bank for basic necessities." Colby was silent for a moment. "Dani?"

"Yes?"

"You're flooding the patio."

"Hmm? Oh." Twisting the nozzle, she cast a weary

glance at the overflowing geranium pots, then picked her way across the puddled concrete to rewind the hose, turn off the spigot.

"You seem distracted."

"Just tired," she lied, wiping her damp soles on the door mat. "It's been a long day."

You're crazy in love with him, hon.

The taunting words replayed in her mind, as they had since the moment Madeline had dared speak them. But it wasn't true, couldn't be true.

It's written all over your face.

No.

Any fool could see it.

No, no, no, no, no.

"Are you sure you're all right, Dani?"

"Hmm?" She glanced over her shoulder, saw Colby flip off the porch light as he followed her inside the house. "I'm fine. Why?"

"You're talking to yourself."

She spun, jammed her hands on her hips. "Is there something in our contract that says I can't?"

"No, of course not," he replied, clearly startled. He started to speak, thought better of it, stuffed his hands in his pockets and rocked back on his heels. "Megan is quite fond of the doll your friend gave her this afternoon."

"Is she?" Danielle mumbled, heading to the kitchen.

Colby eyed her warily. "She insisted that I tuck it under the crib covers so she could sleep with it."

"Madeline will be pleased to hear that." Bustling around the kitchen, Danielle put on the kettle, prepared to make tea. She needed to be busy, needed something to think about, something to look at besides Colby. She could feel his gaze boring into her. He was reading her, she realized, observing every facial tic, every twitchy muscle. If he watched long enough, he'd see the truth. She spun away, retrieved two mugs from the cupboard, dropped a tea bag in each. "I saw you with Frank Lonnigan this afternoon."

"Our Montebello distribution center is hiring. Lonnigan seems a decent fellow. I thought he might find a suitable position there."

"I'm sure he will, particularly after he presents a personally autographed business card from the boss."

"I, ah—" he cleared his throat "—simply jotted a note to the personnel manager asking that Mr. Lonnigan's qualifications be considered, that's all."

"That's quite enough, I'd say." Danielle looked up then. It was a mistake. Colby looked so uncomfortable, so sweetly vulnerable that her heart tightened as if squeezed by an invisible hand. "Don't worry," she whispered. "Your random act of kindness is safe with me. I won't tell a soul."

He grumbled, tugged the short, stretchy sleeves of a golf shirt that fit like a cotton skin. "It was purely a business decision," he muttered. "Obviously I believe the man has enough experience to— Oh, good grief, will you look at that?"

She followed his pained gaze to the counter where Whiskers was investigating the empty mugs. The cat batted one of the tea bag strings with his paw, an activity that apparently set Colby's teeth on edge.

"Make him stop."

"Stop," she said dutifully, then shrugged when the cat continued to play with the strings. "Sorry. Guess you two will have to work this out yourselves."

Scowling, Colby marched over, scooped the animal from the counter, set it firmly on the floor. "Stay there." Whiskers gazed up adoringly, rubbed his head against Colby's shin. "Stop that. Fur sticks to my slacks." Purring happily, Whiskers curled his hairy body around the man's ankle. Colby shook his foot to move the cat aside, then looked to

Danielle for support. "You see? He does it just to annoy me."

"Tea?" she asked, holding up the steaming kettle.

He snorted. "What do you think?"

She filled a mug for herself, took it to the kitchen table. Colby hesitated, then pulled up a chair.

"Are you hungry?" he asked. "I could toast some scones."

"No, thank you. I'm still full from dinner." She dunked the tea bag, forced herself to avoid looking at him. "It was delicious, as usual."

"I'm glad you enjoyed it."

"Always," she murmured, dunking madly. "You like to cook and I like to eat. That's a big score on the roommate compatibility scale."

Colby regarded her thoughtfully. "You consider us to be merely roommates?"

"Seems friendlier than calling you boss."

He flinched as though struck. "I'm not your boss, Dani."

"Employer then, or whatever else you want to call it when one person pays another to do an agreed-upon job."

"Is that how you view our arrangement?"

"That *is* our arrangement." She placed the sloppy tea bag in the bowl of a spoon, sneaked a furtive peek across the table. "Isn't it?"

He shifted, folded his arms. "In the literal sense, I suppose."

"There you have it," she murmured, pushing away the untouched tea when her stomach twisted into a painful knot of disappointment. "It's getting late. I think I'll turn in."

Colby stood. "Good night, then."

She moistened her lips, met his gaze. There was confusion in his eyes, and something else. Something deeper, more poignant, something she dared not consider. "Good night," she whispered.

But she was preparing herself to say goodbye.

The note barely covered a small page of scented stationery, but it took nearly an hour to construct. When it was finished, Danielle read it three times, then folded it into an envelope with two Polaroid photographs of Megan. She sealed it, addressed it, tucked it into her shoulder bag and spent the next hour sitting in her darkened bedroom listening to Colby's restless movement through the house.

First she heard the television, which he'd moved into the family room. After a few moments, the TV fell silent and she heard soft music emanating from the parlor. Rhythmic footsteps revealed that Colby was pacing the room, much as she was pacing her own.

She wondered what he was thinking, what he was feeling. She wondered if he, too, was watching the calendar, watching the court date, the date that would signal the end of their agreement. Barely two weeks away now. There was little doubt that Colby would win custody—Olivia's signed guardianship papers gave him an immense legal edge—and after the judgment had been finalized, he wouldn't need a fraudulent marriage. Wouldn't need Danielle. It would all be over.

The thought hurt. She wondered why, but silent speculation was interrupted as the parlor music died, and she heard Colby enter the hallway. A moment later, the master suite door clicked shut.

She waited a few minutes, then opened her own door a crack, listening, wondering if it was safe to emerge. Her eyes, accustomed to the darkness now, spied a small shadow hunkered in the hallway, at the base of the master suite door. A tiny meow filtered through the darkness, then another, more insistent call.

Colby's door opened long enough for the shadow to slip inside, then closed again.

The shield around Danielle's heart cracked, then shattered, leaving her open, vulnerable, in excruciating pain. Trembling, she clicked her bedroom door shut, stumbled to her bed fighting tears that she couldn't even begin to explain. "Traitor," she whispered into the darkness, not understanding what angered her more—the cat, or the man, or her own renegade heart. All had pretended to be cool, unaffected, dispassionate. All had betrayed her. The cat had gone over to the enemy; the enemy had revealed a human soul; and worst of all, her own heart had forsaken her.

Everything Madeline had said was true. Danielle was deeply, completely, irrevocably, head over heels in love. Playing house wasn't a game anymore. Colby and Megan had become the center of her universe.

It was the worst thing that could have happened.

The following morning, Colby emerged rested, happy, filled with anticipation. It was Sunday, a day of rest and reflection, a day of endless possibilities, each of which was centered around spending the entire day with Danielle and Megan.

Colby couldn't remember when he'd looked forward to anything with such excitement. Unless it was yesterday; or perhaps the day before. In fact, every day was a new adventure now. Through Danielle's eyes and little Megan's, life had blossomed into a series of colorful opportunities, each more surprising than the last. He'd discovered the joy of spontaneity, the thrill of a baby's wet kiss. He'd even decided that cats, animals he'd once considered the most loathsome on earth, had a few redeeming characteristics. They were tidy creatures. They made pleasant foot warmers. They vibrated nicely when stroked.

Yes, life was good. Colby was a happy man.

"Good morning," he boomed, brushing a kiss on Megan's feathery head as he passed the high chair. "Lovely day, isn't it?"

Danielle, who was stirring up a bowl of baby oatmeal, managed a noncommittal grunt without sparing him a glance. Setting the bowl on the counter to cool, she turned away, but not before Colby saw bruiselike crescents beneath her eyes.

"You look awful," he blurted. "Are you ill?"

Without turning, she raked her fingers through her thick hair, stirred a bubbling pot on the stove. "I'm fine."

The assurance was clipped, unconvincing. Still, Colby was reticent to pursue it. She'd been acting strangely. Perhaps a female condition that she was embarrassed to discuss.

He decided to press on with more enjoyable matters. "I was thinking it might be nice to take in a movie this afternoon. There's a Disney film out—"

She spun, stared at him in disbelief. "A cartoon movie?"

"Don't you care for animated features?" Without waiting for her reply, he flicked the suggestion away and went on to another. "All right, then. Perhaps a trip to the beach. I know it's a bit cool for swimming, but Megan might enjoy seeing the water and playing in the sand."

She licked her lips, flounced back to stirring whatever she was stirring on the stove. "It's Sunday."

That was hardly news to Colby. "I'm aware of that."

"Sunday is my day off."

"Your day off?" He'd pulled a chair from the kitchen table, paused in an awkward, half-seated position, then straightened like a starched string. "Well, technically I suppose it is, but during the past weeks, we've spent the weekends together. I naturally assumed—"

"Don't—" she spun to face him, took a forced breath "—assume."

This was more than strange behavior, he decided. Danielle was clearly upset, although he couldn't begin to fathom why. Everything was going so splendidly. "You're right," he said gently. "It was rude to make plans without consulting you. Today we'll do whatever you choose."

She swallowed, spoke between clamped teeth. "I choose to be alone."

"Alone," he repeated, frowning. Surely she didn't mean that literally. It was Colby's challenge to figure out exactly what she *did* mean. He brightened. "Of course. You'd prefer that we spend a quiet day at home."

Heaving a pained sigh, she scoured her forehead with her fingertips, muttered to herself.

Colby was about to suggest renting the video of her choice for their quiet at-home day when a blur at the counter caught his eye.

"I do not want to spend a quiet day at home," she said finally.

"Ah, Dani, you really should—"

"I want to spend a quiet day alone. *Alone.*"

"Yes, of course, but—"

"There's a difference between at home and alone, and if you weren't such an insufferable— Stop that!"

Colby, who'd been persistently pointing toward the counter, instantly balled his fingers, pressed them against his side. "Very well. It's a bit late now, anyway."

Eyes narrowed, she followed his gaze, let out a yelp when she saw Whiskers lapping up Megan's oatmeal. "Oh, for—" She grabbed the cat, stared into his sticky, self-satisfied face. "Bad kitty, bad, bad, *bad* kitty." She put the cat down, gestured helplessly toward the partially eaten oatmeal, and to Colby's horror, looked as if she was about to cry.

Taken aback by the emotional display, Colby awkwardly extended a comforting hand, was rebuffed when she moved out of reach. Bewildered, he took the kitty-licked bowl from the counter, emptied the contents into the sink. "No harm done," he told the sniffing woman. "I'll just make some more."

She nodded, spun on her sneakered heel and strode into the hall. A moment later she reemerged wearing a felt fedora, an oversize sweatshirt decorated with embroidered elves, and that horrid woven tote slung over her shoulder. "I'm going out," she announced.

"Very well."

She stomped to the front door, yanked it open. When Colby issued no protest, she glared over her shoulder. "I could be gone for hours."

He nodded, afraid to say or do anything else.

She hovered there, muttered under her breath then went outside and slammed the door. A moment later, it opened. "Don't you want to know where I'm going?"

"If you care to tell me."

"I don't."

An invisible hand clutched his shoulder in warning. Colby managed what he hoped was an affable smile. "All right, then. Have a nice day."

"I will." She glowered at him a moment longer, then ducked back outside. This time, the door closed more quietly.

Colby held his breath until he heard her car drive away, then leaned against the counter, absently stirring a fresh bowl of baby oatmeal. "Utterly unpredictable," he told the cat, which ceased face-washing to issue an agreeable mew. "You see my problem." With the feline equivalent of a shrug, Whiskers went back to grooming, and Colby returned to listing Danielle McCullough's peculiar personality traits in his mind. Impetuous, emotionally volatile, totally illogical.

Whimsical, playful, adorably frivolous.

Indisputably wonderful.

Without doubt, Danielle was the best thing that had ever happened to Colby. And he knew it.

It was dark when Danielle finally returned. After mailing the letter, she'd driven to a nearby park, sat by the pond watching a young family feed the ducks. All she could think about was how Megan would enjoy feeding ducks, and how Colby would enjoy watching her. Danielle's mind had drifted then, remembering when Colby had put too much liquid soap into Megan's bath, and a mound of bubbles had climbed halfway up the tiled wall. Then she recalled the afternoon they'd discovered that the baby had cut a new tooth, and Colby had baked a fudge sponge cake to celebrate.

So many memories in such a short time. But there wouldn't be many more. Their time together was nearly over. That was sad enough, but the worst part was that the thought of losing Colby and Megan broke Danielle's heart.

It also made her angry. She wasn't angry at Colby, and she certainly wasn't angry at Megan. Danielle was angry at herself, at her own stupidity in having made an emotional investment in a family that never existed. At least, not for her. Someday, another woman would take her place. The family would be real then, the marriage would be real, and not the fraudulent lie Danielle was living.

So she'd spent the day distancing herself, first at the park, then at a mall, then at a restaurant where she'd spent hours dawdling over lunch. She'd hoped to sever her emotional ties with Colby and Megan, or at least to begin the process. In the end, unable to shut off the flood of memories, she'd accomplished nothing more than increasing her grief, her sense of eventual loss. In a few short days, a judge would hear evidence. Somebody would win; somebody would lose.

Danielle had failed, failed to bring peace between Colby and his parents, failed to keep her own heart in check.

Straightening her shoulders, she entered the house, was startled by shouting. She opened the parlor doors, heard Colby's angry voice. He was on the telephone, she realized, and he was clearly furious.

"No...I won't have it! We'll subpoena that Manhattan shyster, put him on the stand and— What do you mean it's too late? Get a continuance." A sharp thud emanated from the study, as if Colby had pounded the desk with his fist. "How the hell am I supposed to answer that? You're the lawyer. Just do it."

The plastic crack of a slammed receiver was followed by the frightened squeak of Colby's swivel chair. A moment later he strode into the parlor looking ashen, sick.

"Colby, my God."

He looked up, his fingers still tangled in his hair, and froze. "You're back."

Since that was obvious, Danielle ignored it. "What is it, Colby, what's happened?"

He stared at her, then went to the bay window and stood there, gazing out. "A document was delivered to the judge this weekend."

"What kind of document?"

"A will."

Danielle digested that slowly. "Olivia's will?"

"It appears to be." He hesitated, cleared his throat. "Apparently my parents located the document through a lawyer in Manhattan."

Realization struck with a sickening thud. "Does it indicate that Olivia wanted her daughter placed with them?" When he nodded, panic surged into her throat, nearly choking her. "Well, it's not the final word. I mean, judges overturn wills all the time, especially when the best interest of the child is at stake. It doesn't mean anything, Colby, not a thing—"

She gasped as Colby spun around, took hold of her shoulders. His eyes were filled with pain, his expression, shattered. "I'm going to lose her," he whispered. "I'm going to lose Megan. I don't think I can live with that."

Chapter Ten

It was Colby's worst nightmare. He was losing everything, the niece he'd grown to love, the woman who had given his life new meaning, even his coveted control. He was trembling, on the brink of emotional meltdown.

And Danielle was watching.

She gazed up, eyes filled with empathy, and pressed her cool and gentle palm to his cheek with a touch so loving, he wanted to weep. "Talk to Eugenia and Kingsley," she whispered. "Find middle ground that can give Megan *all* of her family."

"There is no middle ground with those people."

"'Those people' are your parents. You've already told me that you don't hate them. Deep down, I think you truly care about them, care about what they think of you. Please, don't let this battle tear all of you apart."

Colby shuddered, turned away from her soothing touch even though it took all of his willpower to do so. "I don't expect you to understand."

"Then explain it to me. Make me understand. Every time I bring up your parents you blow me off, change the subject." She snagged his elbow, urged him to face her. "Talk to me."

He didn't want to look at her, didn't want to be sucked into the compassionate abyss of those huge, liquid eyes, warm as golden cognac and just as intoxicating. Danielle didn't know about his family; Colby didn't want her to know. "This isn't your fight."

She stepped back as if staggered by his words. "Yes, it is. You made it my fight. I love—" Her voice broke, her gaze wavered. "I love Megan, I love her dearly. What you and your parents are doing to her is unconscionable."

Colby's head snapped around. "Unconscionable?"

"I know you don't mean to hurt her," Danielle added quickly. "But if this custody fight proceeds to the bitter end, you can't help but hurt her whether you mean to or not."

There was no way to convince her, Colby realized. Until this moment, he'd never even wanted to. Danielle was too trusting, too blinded by light to recognize darkness hidden in the souls of men. And women, he thought bitterly.

But the reproach in her eyes sliced him to the quick. She mattered to him more than he'd realized; what she thought mattered. Which made it even more important that she never, ever know the secret that had destroyed his sister, destroyed him and now threatened Megan in ways that Danielle could never understand.

Because Colby needed to touch her, he stroked her cheek with his fingertip, allowed it to linger longingly at the corner of her mouth. She trembled slightly, a telltale quiver that sliced him to the core. He'd known she cared about him. Danielle cared about everyone. For a fleeting second, he wondered if she cared more deeply than he'd dared hope.

Then her eyelashes fluttered, she averted her gaze. Colby lowered his hand to his side, mustered the cool restraint that had served him throughout his life. "I know you're trying to help, Dani, but you must trust me on this. My parents cannot have custody of Megan."

Danielle moistened her lips, forced herself to look at him. "Apparently Olivia didn't agree, Colby, or she wouldn't have specified the custody arrangement in her will."

"The will is a fake."

That startled her. "What?"

"My parents papered New York City's legal community with announcements of Olivia's death, promising huge rewards for any attorney who could produce a recent copy of her will. Photographs were sent—" a caustic edge sharpened his tone "—along with facsimiles of her signature. They did everything except forge the damned thing themselves."

Clearly shaken by the news, Danielle nonetheless struggled to make sense of it. "Olivia lived in New York for years. Megan was born there. It's reasonable that your sister would have contacted a local attorney to provide for her daughter's future." When Colby set his jaw, stared over her head, she heaved a sad sigh. "All right, can you prove the will isn't genuine?"

"No."

"Then how do you know that it isn't?"

"Because Olivia despised our parents."

"That's very harsh."

He shrugged, said nothing.

Danielle pressed for answers. "Why, Colby, why would your sister feel that way?"

"She had her reasons."

"What reasons?"

Good reasons, Colby thought to himself, reasons he couldn't put into words, couldn't expose to the world. It was a secret Olivia had taken to her grave. Colby respected that, was grateful for it. In a sense, he even loved her for it, assuming that he was even capable of such noble emotion.

As a naive and trusting child, Colby had been capable of love, had in fact been imprisoned by it, dependent to the point of despair. All that had changed with a whisper in the dark.

Colby's world died that day; part of him died with it.

It was his tenth birthday. Cook and Au Pair prepared a small cake—chocolate, which was his favorite. Only Olivia came down to share his party. She didn't really give a hang about her brother's birthday, but she was quite fond of cake. Young Colby held no illusions about his sister's motives. Still, he was grateful for the company. He secretly hoped his mother might come down, too. She didn't.

They ate in silence, then Olivia left. Colby opened his present. It was an encyclopedia set. The card was one of those embossed replies that his mother routinely sent out with social gifts. It simply said, "Best wishes from Mr. and Mrs. Kingsley F. Sinclair." Colby turned it over, looking for a handwritten note. There wasn't one.

Cook gushed about his wonderful present, but Au Pair looked very sad. Colby felt bad for her. Au Pair had always been nice. It upset him when she was sad.

So Colby tucked the card inside the first volume, went upstairs and saw his sister listening at their mother's bedroom door. She pressed her finger to her lips, motioned him over. There was a strange look on her face, so he joined her, heard voices beyond the door.

Their father was inside, Colby realized, and was shocked. As far as he knew, Father had never entered Mother's room, nor had she entered his. But they were both in there now. Together.

The children knew it was wrong to listen, but they did it anyway. What they heard changed their lives forever....

"Colby?"

Images of the past dissolved slowly, painfully. A face blurred before his eyes, a beautiful face, pale with shock, stiff with fear. He blinked to focus as Danielle touched a fingertip below the bridge of his nose.

It came away glistening with moisture.

Danielle stared at her damp fingertip, then up at Colby's shattered expression. He shook his head, bit his lower lip. "What is it, Colby?" she whispered. "Please, tell me."

He closed his eyes, rubbed the lids roughly, then took a shuddering breath and met her frightened gaze. "I can't go back to the person I was before you and Megan came into my life."

Colby's despair shook Danielle to the marrow. She embraced him, hugged him fiercely, desperately wanted to assure him that he wouldn't have to go back, that everything would be all right.

The words stuck in her throat. At that moment, Danielle didn't know if anything would ever be right again. Because she knew what had to be done, and it terrified her.

"One moment, please."

Danielle clutched the telephone as if it were a lifeline in a storm-tossed sea. Her stomach churned. Her lungs burned. Her stiff shoulders ached in protest.

It was Tuesday afternoon, two days since Colby had learned about Olivia's alleged will; two days since Danielle had mailed the letter.

A cautious "hello" was uttered by a voice both cool and wary.

Danielle stiffened, took a rushed breath. "Good afternoon, Mrs. Sinclair."

The voice sharpened. "Who is this?"

"I'm Danielle... Colby's wife. We met briefly at the funeral." The announcement was greeted with icy silence. "I wondered if you and Mr. Sinclair received the photographs of Megan that I sent."

It took a moment, but Eugenia Sinclair finally said, "We received them."

Thank God, Danielle thought, massively relieved. At least she had something to keep the conversation going. "The pictures turned out wonderfully, don't you think? Megan is such a beautiful child. I think she favors you, particularly around the eyes—"

"What do you want?"

Danielle was taken aback for a moment, then moistened her lips and forced a cheerful tone. "I just thought we should get to know each other. We're family now."

"No, we are not."

The brittle statement cracked Danielle's hopes, but didn't crush them. "Actually, we are, although I'm disappointed that doesn't please you. It pleases me."

"It shouldn't. We have nothing in common but a name, and if I could change that, I would."

Danielle flinched, felt the receiver slip through beads of moisture gathering on her palm. She'd expected reticence; she hadn't expected overt hostility. "I care deeply for your son and your grandchild, Mrs. Sinclair. Surely we share that."

The silence was deafening.

Afraid the woman might hang up, Danielle rushed on. "Megan has grown so much since you last saw her. She pulls herself up now, and will actually walk when you hold her hands. Of course, she's not very steady because she gets so excited, her feet go all over the place, but she's a gutsy girl. Why, she might even be walking by her birthday, which, ah..." Danielle paused, wiped her forehead with her free hand. "Which brings me to one of the reasons I called.

Megan will be a year old soon. I thought you and Mr. Sinclair might like to help plan a celebration. Nothing fancy, just an intimate little party with friends and family—''

Eugenia interrupted. "Megan will be with us on her birthday. We shall celebrate as we see fit."

The caustic announcement jarred Danielle, left her temporarily speechless. "That assumption may be a bit premature," she said finally. "The initial hearing isn't until tomorrow, and I understand that a continuance will be requested."

A contemptuous snort filtered over the line. "A stalling tactic. Our attorneys assure us the motion will be soundly rejected. My daughter's child should be with us. The judge understands that."

"With all due respect, Mrs. Sinclair, I think that the judge will listen to all sides before making a decision, assuming the matter even goes that far."

That got Eugenia's attention. "Excuse me?"

"Megan needs you." Startled silence. "She needs her grandparents, and she needs her uncle. Megan needs her entire family, Mrs. Sinclair. There must be a way we can work together to meet those needs."

For a moment, Danielle thought she had gotten through. She could hear the woman breathing, slow, hopefully thoughtful breaths. Danielle held her own, waiting.

"Do you truly believe that?" Eugenia finally asked.

Danielle exhaled all at once. "Yes, yes I do."

"Then you are a fool."

The line went dead. Danielle sat rigid, listening to the dial tone buzz her ear like a trapped insect. After a long moment, she cradled the receiver, replayed the conversation in her mind. She was a fool, of course. Colby had warned her that his mother wouldn't be receptive to compromise.

Of course, Colby wasn't receptive, either, or so he'd have her believe.

But Danielle didn't believe him. She'd seen beyond the mask of indifference, knew the wounded soul within. He was a man, she realized, who craved love so desperately that he'd spent a lifetime avoiding the attachments he feared would lead to inevitable loss.

That stoic facade cracked whenever Colby was with little Megan, when Danielle saw the warmth in his eyes, and the love. She'd learned not to accept Colby's words at face value. She believed only what she saw in his eyes.

If Colby was indeed his mother's son, Danielle knew that she had to dig beneath the surface to truly understand Eugenia Sinclair. After all, the woman didn't know Danielle. Given current circumstance, a certain amount of caution was understandable.

Danielle convinced herself that she simply required a slight change in tactics, a face-to-face meeting with the Sinclairs to discuss the terms of a custody compromise to save their fractured family.

Danielle was certain that Eugenia Sinclair would eventually agree. It never occurred to her that a mother, any mother, would rather destroy her son's life than share it.

When the front door opened, Danielle dropped the chopping knife, grabbed a towel to sop tomato juice from her hands and rounded the counter so quickly that she bruised her hip against the corner. Colby, looking exhausted and gaunt, laid his briefcase on the foyer table. Danielle jerked to a stop, felt as if her feet were rooted in slate. "Well?"

A tired smile couldn't erase the worry in his eyes. "The continuance was granted. We have another month."

"Oh, thank God." She exhaled all at once, slipped comfortably into his arms. All thoughts of future loss, of the end of a marriage that for Danielle had become all too real, dissipated instantly. This moment was real. And she cherished it. "You must be so relieved."

Without confirming that, he brushed a kiss on her brow, nested his cheek in her tangled curls, held her warmly against his chest. She closed her eyes, soothed by the steady rhythm of his heart beating beneath her ear. Her arms encircled him, the dish towel pressed in the hollow of his back. It was so natural to hold him, to have him holding her. So natural, and so very real.

A telltale tension rippled his spine, a caution that despite having received the news they'd been praying for, all may not be as it seemed.

Danielle shifted in his arms, gazed up at his haggard face. "And...?"

They were so closely attuned now that Colby knew what she was asking. "And the case has been referred to social services for investigation."

Her heart sank so fast, her knees nearly buckled. As a trained counselor and social worker, Danielle knew exactly what that meant. Every detail of their lives, public and private, would be subjected to intense scrutiny. Background investigation would be performed; academic records examined; friends and family repeatedly interviewed. Every aspect of their marriage, their personal relationship would be microscopically scrutinized, dissected, laid bare.

Worst of all, their home would be subjected to unannounced inspection, the same home in which Danielle's personal possessions occupied one bedroom and Colby's occupied another.

She staggered half a step back, rested her fingertips against the lapel of his suit coat. "What are we going to do?"

Studying her, Colby brushed the back of his knuckles against her cheek, then stroked his palms along her upper arms. "I can't ask you to continue the charade," he said quietly.

"Charade," Danielle repeated dumbly, as if she'd never heard the word before.

"Our make-believe marriage."

She swallowed, moistened her lips. "Is that what it is to you, Colby. Make-believe?"

He considered that, brows furrowed, eyes puzzled, lips pursed in thoughtful reverence. "No," he replied, and seemed as startled by his answer as was Danielle. He gazed at her for a long moment, then shook his head with more vehemence than necessary. "That isn't the point, Dani. You'll be directly questioned by individuals with authority to inflict legal consequence if you answer falsely."

Danielle's mouth was dry as a desert. *No,* he'd said. He didn't consider their marriage to be make-believe. It was real to him. Real. She closed her eyes, thought she might die of happiness.

"This can't go on," Colby said firmly, bursting her golden bubble.

She blinked, looked up, was frightened by the decision reflected in his wintry eyes. "Are you saying that you're giving up?"

"No, I'm saying that I won't allow you to risk your future for a battle that isn't yours."

"What I'm willing to risk is for me to decide." Brave words, she thought, considering the ominous possibilities. But that didn't matter anymore. Colby cared about her. He cared.

For a long moment, Colby gazed at Danielle as if she were the most precious thing on earth. When he spoke, his voice was soft, loving, strained by emotion. "There's no reason to put yourself in jeopardy, Dani. If it can be proven that the will was forged and my parents knew it, there's little chance they would be given custody."

Danielle considered that. "All right, for the sake of argument let's assume that happens. Let's also assume that the terms of our original agreement somehow come to light—"

"Impossible. Attorney-client privilege—"

She held up a palm, silencing him. "Nonetheless, if I leave now, speculation alone could be enough to cast doubt on your suitability as Megan's guardian. If the judge decides that neither you nor your parents are suitable, she could actually be taken from both of you and made a ward of the court."

"I won't let that happen."

"How would you stop it?"

"I don't know," he said miserably. "Take her away, perhaps."

"Kidnap her?" Danielle shook her head. "You won't do that, Colby, you love Megan too much to subject her to life on the lam. So to speak," she added, when his eyes widened in horror. "Look, I know you'd never deliberately hurt Megan, but spiriting her away, forcing her to live in fear of shadows, good Lord, Colby, that's not even an option."

His unhappy expression quite clearly indicated that he was well aware of that; his eyes, however, revealed a desperate man teetering on the brink of despair.

Cradling his face between her palms, Danielle urged him to look at her. When he did, she whispered gently. "It's time, Colby."

He blinked, bewildered, before his lips hardened with comprehension and he jerked from her grasp.

"For Megan's sake, you and your parents simply have to hash out some kind of agreement."

"No."

"It's the only way."

"I said no." With that, he went into the parlor and closed the door.

"I know how you feel," Jack said. "I've already lined up two handwriting experts, and have a subpoena winging its way to the attorney who produced the document. Depending on the outcome of his deposition, we might even issue a formal complaint with the Bar Association."

"That would take months to play out."

"Yes, but it's an effective negotiating tool." The weary guy yawned loudly enough to send a message.

Colby ignored it. "I'm sorry, Jack, I know it's late but—"

"Nearly midnight."

"Just a few more minutes. I've been thinking about hiring a private investigator." Colby flinched as Jack yawned in his ear again. "What do you think?"

"I think," the man replied in a voice heavy with fatigue, "we should talk about it in the morning."

"But—"

"Good night, Colby."

"Wait a minute, Jack... Jack?" There was a soft click. Cursing, Colby hung up, rubbed his own stinging eyes. His lawyer was right, of course. There was nothing more that could be effectively accomplished tonight.

Giving in to exhaustion, Colby pushed away from his desk, turned off the study lamp and reluctantly headed toward the master bedroom. He paused at the closed door, glanced toward the end of the hallway. No light sprayed from beneath the door of Danielle's room. He was disappointed, but not surprised. If she'd been awake, he'd have been tempted to knock, suggest some tea and conversation. Danielle could always make him feel better, more optimistic. It was a special gift she possessed, one of many he'd come to appreciate over the weeks.

A special gift belonging to a special woman.

Just thinking of her soothed his soul. Warmth settled like a blanket around his shoulders, easing tense muscles, calming strained nerves. He felt a peculiar tug below his cheekbones, realized that he was smiling. Alone. In the dark. Smiling at the mental image of the sensuous woman who shared his life. But not for long.

The smile stiffened and died.

A soft vibration on his shin shifted his attention. He glanced down, heaved a silent sigh, then opened his own bedroom door. Whiskers sauntered inside, disappeared into the darkness, presumably to claim a comfortable nest at the foot of Colby's bed. Colby grumbled about the obstinate animal's sleeping habits, but never seriously considered banishment. The pitiful yowling of a thwarted cat was hardly conducive to a restful night's sleep.

Besides, there was something comforting in sharing one's bed with a warm body, even if the price for that comfort was an occasional fur ball on designer bedclothes.

Closing the door behind him, Colby automatically tugged his necktie loose, dropped his wallet in the polished walnut valet at the corner of his dresser. His knuckle knocked something over, something cool and smooth. He felt around the dark surface, located what felt like a bottle. A heady fragrance wafted up. Cologne? Colby kept no cologne on his dresser, and certainly couldn't recall owning any that smelled so sensually feminine.

If he hadn't been so weary, curiosity would have propelled him to the lamp switch to investigate. As it was, he simply righted the bottle, ambled through the shadows toward his huge walk-in closet. Over the past weeks, objects had frequently moved from one location to another without any apparent means of transport. Colby supposed that was par for the course when sharing one's abode. Considering the benefits, the minor inconvenience seemed reasonable.

Yawning, Colby flipped on the closet light, entered and disrobed routinely, replacing his tie on the carousel of neckwear meticulously arranged by pattern and color, rehanging his jacket in the precise position from which he'd retrieved it earlier in the day, then smoothing his slacks over a padded pants hanger. Everything else was stripped off, tossed in the laundry basket nested beneath a column of built-in drawers. Colby was quite fond of his closet, which was perfectly organized, and so roomy that his entire wardrobe took up only half the available space.

Except that something seemed different now. As he tugged up the pajama bottoms he now wore, the corner of his tired eye caught a flash of clutter, a riot of color. He straightened, slid a cautious glance over his shoulder and nearly fell over.

The vacant side of his closet was now a pandemonium of garments all crushed together like a poorly organized garage sale. Above the squashed hangers, the shelf was piled with various hats, some so ratty, they looked as if they'd been rescued from a trash bin. The floor was a tangle of shoes, a lumpy heap of utter chaos bristling with chunky heels and twisted straps of every conceivable color and style.

Chaos and clutter. In *his* closet.

He spun around, stumbled out into the room, fumbled for the light switch. "My God," he murmured, and could say no more.

Danielle stood beside the bed wearing a spaghetti-strapped, thigh-length, champagne satin gown and a nervous smile. "Hi," she whispered.

"My God," Colby said.

She licked her lips, clasped her hands together. "I was beginning to wonder if you were ever going to come to bed."

"My God."

Shifting, she smoothed the front of her gown, took a shaky breath. "I, uh, moved in." She encompassed the room with an awkward flip of the hand, managed a thin smile. "I guess you can see that."

"My—" Colby shook his head, batted his temple with an open palm. He stared at the dresser, saw the cologne bottle he'd knocked over was one of nearly a dozen bunched on the polished wood surface. "—God."

"I'm sure He heard you the first time." An annoyed quirk tugged her brow, dissipated quickly. She took a nervous breath, glided toward him, smiling gently. Her gaze slipped to his bare chest, glowed in approval. "Nice," she murmured. "Very nice." Danielle moved so close that the exotic scent of her perfume drifted through his senses like an erotic cloud. She brushed his bare chest with her fingertips and she smiled as his nipples jerked in response.

"What are—?" Colby coughed away the humiliating squeak, tried again. "What on earth are you doing here?"

"I live here."

"Yes, yes, of course, but I mean what are you doing—" he sucked a noisy breath, pointed to the floor in front of his trembling feet "—*here.*"

She followed the gesture, repeated it. "Here?"

"Yes, here, in my bedroom."

"In our bedroom."

"*Our* bedroom?"

"Our bedroom. I *am* your wife."

"Well, technically, of course—"

"A wife is allowed to make mad, passionate love to her husband." Colby gulped so hard, he nearly swallowed his Adam's apple. "Which is," Danielle whispered, looping her arms around his neck, "exactly what I'm going to do."

Chapter Eleven

If Danielle hadn't been too paralyzed to draw breath, the room might not have spun so wildly out of control. In her entire life, some twenty-eight years and counting, she'd never done anything as blatantly brazen. Since her feet felt as if they'd been encased in lead slippers, running away was not an option, yet every fiber of her being pleaded for her to do just that.

Colby stared at her as if she'd completely lost her mind.

Maybe she had. "You said it was real to you," she managed to whisper. "You said our marriage was real."

A slight nod, or perhaps his neck simply slackened enough for his head to flop forward.

"It's real to me, too, Colby. I can't even tell you exactly when it happened. All I know is that I looked around one day and realized that everything I'd ever wanted out of my life, everything I'd ever hoped for, I already had. With you," she added, "and with Megan."

His eyes clouded with puzzlement, perhaps something deeper, more ominous. He caressed her upper arms, her shoulders, paused to slip a fingertip beneath the rolled satin strap of her gown. At her shiver of anticipation, he withdrew quickly, pressed his hands to his side. "You don't have to do this, Dani."

"I'm not offering myself as a sacrificial lamb," she replied softly. "I'll admit that the social services investigation directed my focus toward the ethics of attempting to deceive a system I truly believe in. That's when I had to stop and think, and take a hard look at my motives in agreeing to this in the first place."

A glimmer of apprehension. "Have you come to any conclusions?"

"Yes, I have." Danielle moistened her lips, rested her palms against the sparsely furred warmth of his bare chest. "I wouldn't admit it then, not even to myself, but the truth is that I agreed to marry you because I wanted to be your wife, Colby, and I wanted to be a mother to Megan."

Colby's expression crumpled into confusion, conflict. He turned away, raked his hair like a man at war with himself. Finally he held one fist on his hip, pressed the other to the side of his head. But he said absolutely nothing.

Danielle's heart froze in an instant. She stumbled back a step, wanted to flee. Instead, she touched her throat, reassured by her throbbing pulse that she hadn't really died of mortification. "Don't you ever think about me, Colby, about how things between us might be if we followed our hearts?"

A sharp whistle, breath sucked through clamped teeth. He straightened, lowered the hand that had been braced against his temple. After a moment, he spoke, so quietly that she could barely hear. "There are times when I can't think about anything else." He turned slowly, reluctantly. "Sometimes in a business meeting your image flashes into my mind. I picture the giddy grin that warns me you're about to do something outrageous, or I recall a flash of thigh peeking from beneath your robe when you stretch out on the sofa. I imagine how it would be to join you on that sofa, how sweet your hair would smell, how soft your skin would feel.'' He took a ragged breath, lifted her hand to toy with the plain gold band on her finger. ''Then I look up. My staff is staring at me. I realize that it was all a dream. And I'm empty inside.''

''It doesn't have to be a dream.''

He smiled, rather sadly, she thought, and caressed her cheek. ''This has been difficult for you.''

Her ankles trembled. ''You have no idea.''

''I mean putting your social life on hold, depriving yourself of companionship.''

It took a moment for her to follow his meaning. Then embarrassment dissipated in a flash of anger. ''You think I'm standing here spilling my guts because I'm, I'm—'' she sputtered, gestured furiously ''—sexually frustrated? What gall.''

''It's normal,'' Colby said quickly, flinching when she pulled away from his touch. ''I am, too. We're healthy adults, after all. Such feelings are to be expected.''

This was awful, horrible, the worst thing that could have happened. A moment Danielle had dreamed would be the most beautiful of her life had become tawdry, unthinkably common. ''You're right, of course, because you're always right. Either one of us would leap upon anything with the appropriate plumbing, because after all, we're just a couple of perfectly normal, horny-as-hell adults.'' She slapped her forehead dramatically. ''How could I have missed that?''

''Dani—''

''Hey, I really do appreciate you pointing it out, Colby, otherwise I would have gone through with this farce believing we had something special, perhaps even sacred. Thank you so much for sparing me.''

She spun with appropriate indignation, would have flounced out of the room with some small shred of dignity intact, if her feet hadn't been paddling thin air.

When the room steadied, she was firmly ensconced in Colby's embrace. One arm encircled her waist, lifting her off the floor while his free hand tangled in her hair. She sucked in a startled breath, held it as Colby's mouth pressed warmly against hers in a kiss that vibrated all the way to her toes.

He parted her lips with his own, tasted her warmly, then deeply, then with exquisite wonder, ethereal awe. Danielle was swept away by the power of his kiss, shattered by its sweetness, a dizzying euphoria that left her limp and trembling.

''Only you, Danielle,'' he whispered, rubbing his lips along the crease of her swollen mouth. ''No one else. For me, there is only you.''

Danielle could have fainted in sheer bliss. Colby wanted her, only her.

If happiness had been fatal, Danielle would have died on the spot. ''Colby,'' she murmured, tracing the sweet little dent in his chin with her fingertip. He blinked at the caress, seemed slightly taken back by it, but Danielle barely noticed. Overcome with emotion, she flung her arms around his neck and could say no more, because his mouth was on hers again, hot and seeking, fanning flames of fiery passion that exploded into a desperate inferno. She returned his kiss with wild abandon, wanted him so badly, she could have swallowed him whole.

Breathing was a limited option, gasping gulps of air between frantic kisses while fingers dove clumsily, tearing at any scant fabric thwarting their progress. A fastener snapped open. Colby's pajama bottoms slithered to the floor.

Danielle spotted his exposed manhood, made a futile grab as a thin satin strap slid off one shoulder, restricting her reach. When she shrugged the strap off, one breast popped out of the sagging gown.

Colby dove on it with wild wet kisses, only to be thwarted as Danielle did some diving of her own. She took hold of what she sought, pleased by Colby's groan of pleasure. She wanted to caress him, stroke him to ecstasy. But he refused to relinquish the conquered breast, forcing her to twist awkwardly, thrash her way through a tangle of limbs.

The frenetic tussle was awkward enough to be comical, wild enough to be frustrating.

Finally Colby straightened, cupped his palms under her arms and lifted her up. "Enough," he croaked, clearly shaken. "To the bed."

"The bed," she muttered agreeably, although she was kneeling in midair, and continued to clutch the most sensitive part of him between her palms. When she made no effort to stand on her own let alone release that which she'd fought so tenaciously to retrieve, Colby gritted his teeth, struggled onward while Danielle dangled from his grasp like a human safety pin.

He grunted, fell forward, pinning Danielle to the mattress with his weight. They wrestled for position, panting and frantic, ignoring an ominous rumble at the foot of the bed. Triumphant, Colby reclaimed the exposed breast, suckling it as he heaved his legs onto the mattress.

The rumble became a hiss.

Colby lifted his head. "What the—? Arghhhh!" He thrashed madly, kicked at the spitting lump of fur clinging to his ankle.

Danielle scooted onto her knees. "Bad cat!" She made

a grab. The animal hissed, yowled, raked the bellowing man's leg once more for good measure, then leapt from the bed and hunkered under the dressing room vanity, scowling furiously. "Oh my gosh, Colby, are you hurt?"

"Not at all," he snapped, pivoting to sit on the edge of the mattress. "I bleed for pleasure."

"You should know better than to kick a cat."

"How insensitive of me. Next time I'll let him tear off all the flesh he wants."

Danielle scrambled off the bed, hurried to the bathroom to retrieve a damp cloth, paused to shake it at the sulking feline. "You see what you've done?" Since the animal displayed no visible remorse, she returned to the bedroom, knelt to inspect the damage. "That doesn't look too bad," she murmured, dabbing a row of reddened welts. "Just a few little scratches."

"It hurts," Colby complained.

"Poor baby." She angled a teasing glance. "Want me to kiss it and make it better?"

He brightened. "If you wouldn't mind."

"It would be my pleasure," she murmured, lifting his wounded ankle. She brushed her lips seductively along his calf, lingered to nuzzle his knee, boldly slid upward, leaving a trail of moist kisses on his inner thigh. A furtive glance confirmed that his manhood, soundly deflated during the kitty crisis, now vibrated at attention.

Colby swallowed hard, pursed his lips as if struggling to control the rate of air escaping his lungs. When he refilled them, breath whistled through his teeth. Beads of moisture gathered on his upper lip, glimmered above his brow. "I don't believe that the scratches extend quite that far."

She smiled against his thigh, continued a leisurely inspection. "Just being thorough."

"Exquisitely thorough." Colby sucked a startled breath

when her hair caressed his sex, which was pulsing frantically and stiff enough to pound nails.

Danielle stroked her cheek against his thigh, saw him looming in front of her eyes, so vibrant and masculine that the sight took her breath away. She touched him there, tentatively sliding a fingertip along the quivering shaft. Encouraged by his groan of pleasure, she caressed him more boldly, kissed him, tasted him, stroked him with building passion until his desire and hers had exploded into a fiery conflagration.

A soft growl rumbled low in his throat. Colby reached down, drew her into his lap. Cupping her breast with his hand, he stroked her nipple between his thumb and fingers, whispered against her throat. "I see now that I have more than one wildcat to deal with."

A witty response died in her throat, crushed by a gasp of pure ecstasy. Colby's gentle fingers continued to probe, to tease, to elicit the most exciting sensations Danielle had ever experienced in her life. It was as if he'd fastened red-hot wire from her breast to the core of her womanhood, and with every sensual stroke, the wire glowed hotter, sharper, more exquisitely intense.

Tiny sounds engulfed her, musical mews, lyrical ah-h-hs and o-o-ohs, harmonious puffs of moist air from lungs that alternately filled to bursting, then emptied to the state of total collapse. Her body danced with indescribable sensation, every nerve frolicked with life, sang out in sheer joy.

The exquisite torture eased as Colby released her breast, lifted her left hand. He studied her wedding band, a thin circle of glittering gold that meant more to Danielle than she'd ever dared admit. He touched the ring, rotated it around her finger, then bent his head, kissed it with great reverence, as if consecrating both the ring and that which it symbolized.

The gesture touched Danielle to the core. Moisture gathered in her eyes, threatened to spill down her cheeks, revealing the depth of her emotion. She wanted to stop them, but couldn't. The moment was so poignant, so precious that even her heart wept.

Colby straightened, looked so deeply into her eyes that he must have seen the secrets hidden there. He wiped her tears with his thumb, slipped his fingers into the thicket of curls at her temple, and kissed her so sweetly that Danielle feared she might faint. The world spun crazily, wildly, a bewildering blur of color and sound and feelings from a place so deep that she'd never even known it was there.

Softness pressed against her back; it was the downy fluff of his quilted bedspread. The satin chemise slipped away as if by magic. A moment later, her shoulders nested in fleecy flannel sheets. Colby knelt between her thighs, whispering softly. Danielle was vaguely surprised to realize that her legs were draped over his shoulders, but couldn't recall how they'd gotten there, nor did she care, because her pulse was pounding and her heart was racing and his wonderful hands were sliding beneath her bottom.

He raised her hips, opened her secrets. "So beautiful," he murmured, brushing his cheek in the nest of soft curls. "So incredibly perfect."

Colby wanted to say more, he wanted to tell her what he was feeling inside, what she made him feel, but couldn't express what he couldn't understand. The sensation swelling inside his chest was so unique, so profoundly intense that it frightened him. No words could describe the exquisite beauty of this incredible woman, her radiant eyes gleaming like amber jewels, the incandescence of creamy skin glowing like moonlight, an erotic helix of sweet, scented hair spiraling across his pillow. He felt blessed, humbled by a gift too precious to be deserved.

Colby wanted to say all of that, but words were swept away in the flood of emotion, of passion far beyond his experience. And so he showed her what he could not say. He cherished his wife with his eyes, and with his lips, and when she cried out for fulfillment, he slipped over her, into her and cherished her with his love.

The face in the mirror was familiar enough—Colby had stared at it every day of his life—yet something had definitely changed. Perhaps it was a warmth in his eyes that made them seem more blue than gray; perhaps it was a softening around his mouth, a slight thaw in the creases that he'd always thought gave him a harsh appearance. All in all, Colby thought he was looking rather dapper this morning, and not entirely unattractive.

Except for the comma-shaped cleft in his chin that Danielle had once referred to as silly. At the time, he'd been bent out of shape by the comment. He was, after all, quite fond of that feature, and thought it made him look distinguished. Still, if Danielle found it unappealing—

An image appeared in the clouded area of the mirror where he hadn't wiped away the steam from his morning shower. Soft arms slid around him from behind, slender fingers teased the edge of the towel twisted around his waist.

"Good morning," Danielle whispered, punctuating the greeting with a kiss on each shoulder blade. She peered around him, frowned up. "Why are you poking at your chin?"

"Hmm?" Startled, Colby lowered his hand, tried for a nonchalant shrug. "I was, ah, just thinking about something."

"Oooh, sounds like fun. Tell me."

"I was just, well, wondering if I should grow a beard." She stared up, burst into laughter. "That amuses you?"

"Uh-huh." She sniffed, wiped her eyes. "Why on earth

would you want to walk around with a hairy pelt on your face?''

The image wasn't particularly enticing, but he felt required to defend it. ''A neatly trimmed beard is quite professional and dignified.''

''Dignified, huh?''

He saw the goofy grin, the evil gleam in her eye, but before he could stop her, she'd reached into the medicine cabinet to retrieve a can of shaving soap.

She shook the can, advanced on him. ''Let's check that out, shall we?''

''I think not.'' He backed up until his back hit the shower stall.

''You said a beard would make you look distinguished. I have a right, as your wife, to see for myself.'' She squirted a massive pile of foam into her palm. ''Come here, husband.''

''Really, Danielle, this is most—'' A splat of foam hit him square in the mouth. He spit, wiped his lips, heaved a resigned sigh. ''Inappropriate,'' he finished, as Danielle happily sculpted the shaving cream into a lumpy goatee and mustache.

When she'd finished, she hauled him back to the mirror. ''There. Do you look distinguished?''

''I look like a drunken Santa.''

She regarded him for a moment. ''You're right. Sideburns might help.'' Another squirt of foam and two white globs hung precariously in front of his ears. ''Hey, now that's kind of cool.''

Colby flinched at his reflection. ''Good Lord, Elvis lives.''

Chuckling, Danielle grabbed a towel, flopped it against his stomach. ''Still want to grow a beard?''

''Perhaps not.'' He wiped the foam off his face, tossed the towel aside. ''I guess I'm doomed to plastic surgery.''

Her double take would have been comical if Colby hadn't been serious. "For *what?*"

"For this," he mumbled, pointing to his chin.

"Your dent?"

"You see? A dent. You called it a dent."

"It *is* a dent."

"It's a cleft, Danielle, a *cleft*. Kirk Douglas has one, so did Cary Grant. Some women find them very attractive."

"Kirk Douglas has a dimple," Danielle argued. "Cary Grant didn't have a cleft, he had a chasm. You, on the other hand, have this itsy-bitsy comma-shaped notch." Her lips twitched when she added, "also known as a dent."

His gaze narrowed. "Thank you for clearing that up."

"Glad to be of help." Her fingers danced on the towel at his hip, whipped it off and tossed it over her shoulder. "Of course," she purred, circling a fingertip around his navel, "I probably should mention that the mere sight of a dented chin makes me go all limp and buttery inside. It's so-o-o sexy."

"Sexy is good," Colby murmured.

"Oh, yes, sexy is very good." She sashayed a step closer, cupped him between her palms. "I wish I could show you how good, but alas, it's a workday and you're already—" she glanced at his watch on the sink "—three and a half minutes behind schedule."

"So I am." Colby scooped her into his arms. "And do you know what? I don't care." Then he carried her to bed, and proved it.

"Good morning, Jo-Jo. Beautiful day, isn't it?" Colby laid a vibrant crimson rose on his startled assistant's desk, barely noticed her jaw sag in shock. He glanced down the somber, carpeted hall, toward the offices of his management staff. "Is Mira in yet? I wanted to discuss the day-care center with her."

Ms. Reese yanked her gaze from the rose laying prostrate across her account ledger, blinked twice, closed her mouth, cleared her throat. "Uh, Ms. Wilkins? I, ah, believe so—"

"Excellent." Colby spun on his heel, paused to glance over his shoulder. "By the way, you look exceptionally nice today. That color suits you."

The astounded woman regarded herself quickly, as if expecting to discover breakfast smeared on her sleeve. Finding nothing, she looked up again, clearly shocked. "Thank you."

Colby acknowledged her with a nod, would have continued down the hall if Ms. Reese hadn't stopped him.

"Mr. Sinclair?" When he glanced back, she was holding the rose. "Is this for, ah, me?"

"Of course."

She blushed to her gray roots. "It's lovely. Thank you."

"You're welcome," he mumbled, feeling a bit agitated by her grateful smile. It was simply a flower, after all, quite insignificant in comparison to all the years of efficient expertise she'd provided. The fact that she was so touched by the gesture stung, as did the realization that he'd never made a point of expressing his appreciation to her, or anyone else, for that matter.

It was a situation Colby planned to remedy.

He brushed past the startled finance staff, entered Ms. Wilkins's office without knocking. "Good morning, Mira," he said, paying little heed to either her startled expression or the fact that she was on the telephone. "I spoke with the day-care supervisor this morning. She tells me that the center is full, and further staffing is required to accommodate those on the waiting list."

To her credit, Mira Wilkins managed to keep her jaw from sagging. She did, however, look exceedingly perplexed. That wasn't completely unexpected, since Colby habitually summoned his staff into his own office, and rarely visited theirs.

Ms. Wilkins ended her telephone conversation abruptly, then stood, clearly uncomfortable. "Mr. Sinclair, what a pleasant surprise. How may I assist you this morning?"

Motioning for her to be seated, Colby pulled up a guest chair for himself. "The day-care center staffing."

She sat stiffly, clasped her hands on her desk. "I'm preparing a report, sir. The response has been considerably larger than we'd anticipated—"

"I'm not surprised," he interrupted, propping his elbows on the chair arms, and steepling his fingers. "The center is excellent, well-planned, perfectly organized to entertain older children while protecting and nurturing the younger ones. I'd even consider allowing Megan to use it, should the occasion arise."

"You would?" Her jaw was sagging now, but she corrected the revealing response quickly enough to be forgiven. "I mean, of course you would, sir. All of us working on the project understood that you wouldn't accept anything less."

Colby nodded, stood. Mira Wilkins shot to her own feet with appropriate speed. "I see you're on top of things as usual, Mira. I look forward to your report."

With that, he strode to his own office, whistling happily.

"Good morning, precious girl," Danielle cooed, covering the giggling baby's face with happy kisses. She scooped Megan out of the crib, changed her, fed and bathed her, then returned to the nursery, tingling with anticipation for the day ahead.

A week had passed since Danielle and Colby first made love, a week of wonder and so much joy that it should be illegal. Every night had been filled with tenderness, lovemaking that was sometimes wild with passion, sometimes playful and silly, sometimes so emotionally intense that tears sprang to her eyes.

Life was perfect for Danielle, so perfect that the thought that any part of that life could be ripped away was terrifying. The handwriting expert had determined that the signature on the will was indeed Olivia's, but further tests were required to determine if Olivia had actually signed the will itself, or if her signature had been "lifted" from another document. Preliminary indications seemed to support the forgery theory, which left Danielle both massively relieved and supremely sad.

She and Megan and Colby were a family now, in every sense of the word. Losing any part of that family would be like severing a limb, and yet she couldn't keep from thinking about the Sinclairs' grief. Megan was part of their family, too, and they'd already suffered the loss of their daughter. If the custody battle wasn't settled amicably, they'd lose their son, as well. Danielle couldn't let that happen.

At least, not without a fight.

"Let's see, sweetums, what is our very favorite dress in the whole world, hmm?" Danielle dug through the dresser, found a neatly folded cotton pinafore with an adorable bunny appliqué and displayed it to Megan, who was beating a rattle on the carpeted floor. "How about this? You can wear it with your favorite shirt, the pretty white one with the eyelet lace trim."

Actually, Megan considered wearing any clothing at all to be more of an annoying distraction than a fashion statement, but she nonetheless issued a happy squeal that Danielle accepted as agreement. "The pinafore it is," she announced, smoothing the garment on the changing table. "Now, let's find just the perfect hair accessory to go with it."

Megan flopped forward, crawled under her crib.

"All right, then, I'll pick one out." Suddenly apprehensive, Danielle shuffled through the drawers, pulled out a white elastic headband with a perky lace bow. Was it too dressy? Not dressy enough? The decision was more than merely a matter of style. Everything had to be exactly right because today was special.

Today, Danielle would return to the Sinclairs' Brentwood estate, and not simply to lurk in the driveway. Today, Megan would meet her grandparents for the very first time.

Danielle envisioned every moment of the momentous occasion. Emotions would surface in a flurry of hugs and kisses. The Sinclairs would smother their adorable grandbaby with affection and realize, of course, that the best interests of the child would be served by mending family fences. The lawsuit would be dropped. Colby and his parents would be reunited. Everyone would be happy, and peace would reign throughout the Sinclair clan.

Thus fortified, Danielle dressed Megan to spotless perfection, drove to the Sinclairs' sprawling estate and carried her precious sweetums directly to the front door, confident that a harmonious family reconciliation was moments away.

Danielle soon discovered that she couldn't have been more wrong.

Chapter Twelve

"The good news," Jack drawled over the phone, "is that one of the country's most respected handwriting analysts is willing to testify that Olivia's will is a forgery. The bad news is that the Sinclairs have another expert lined up to swear that it's not."

Colby swiveled to face the window, rolled his tense shoulders, felt his world crash down around his ears. "So it's a wash."

"I'm afraid so."

"The judge might believe our expert."

"Uh-huh." Papers rustled in the background. "Or she might believe theirs. Most likely she'll toss them both out and decide the case on other issues." After a pregnant pause, the attorney added, "Without compelling evidence to the contrary, grandparent custody is usually preferred in cases like this, Colby. I wish I could be more optimistic."

"So do I, Jack. So do I."

The conversation ended abruptly. Colby hung up, stared at the seasonal marketing study he'd been reviewing when his attorney called. The solvency of his company depended on that study. At the moment, Colby couldn't have cared less. It didn't matter to him anymore. He was losing Megan. Dear God, he was losing his baby.

Blood pounded past his ears, focused his thoughts inward. *Without compelling evidence to the contrary,* Jack had said. What he'd meant was that the only way Colby could hope to gain custody of Megan was to prove that Eugenia and Kingsley were unfit guardians.

Colby could do that, but not without exposing the family secret, revealing a scandalous past that would bring the entire Sinclair clan to its knees. It meant public ridicule, humiliation, perhaps even financial ruin. Colby would be embarrassed by the exposure; his parents would be utterly destroyed.

Now he grappled with the most difficult decision of his life. Colby alone had the power to stop his parents from gaining custody of his beloved niece. He'd always had the power, yet he'd never considered using it. Revenge had never been his motive; it still wasn't. Desperation was, desperation to save Megan from the same fate that her mother and uncle had endured.

There was only one way to force his parents into dropping the custody suit. It was called blackmail, and he was desperate enough to use it.

The pleasant woman eyed him warily. "Are you expected, sir?"

Colby brushed by the startled servant, strode directly into the massive parlor. He jerked to a stop, balled his hands at his side.

Danielle bolted forward on the faded brocade wing chair, would have stood if Megan hadn't been squirming in her lap. She said nothing. She didn't have to. The guilt in her stunned eyes spoke volumes.

Colby tightened his fists with quiet fury. "I saw your car in the driveway. I'd hoped I was hallucinating."

She bit her lip, shifted the restless child in her arms. "Colby, I—"

He cut her off with a look, turned toward his parents, identically perched on the antique davenport like a pair of preening penguins. His gaze swept the familiar room, taking in the opulence, the formality that he'd so detested as a child.

Nothing had changed really. Wealth was displayed tastefully, an ambience of gentle grace meant to garner both admiration and envy. Entertaining was accomplished by sophisticated formality designed to accentuate host superiority rather than enhance guest comfort.

This occasion appeared no different. Along with a crystal plate of delicate hors d'oeuvres, a gleaming silver tea set was set out upon a burnished rosewood coffee table. It was the same table, Colby realized, on which his cherished crayoned gift had lain before his mother destroyed it.

The memory fueled his fury, stiffened his resolve. "What a charming family scene," he said coldly. "I presume my invitation was lost in the mail."

Eugenia rose like royalty, smoothing her linen skirt with admirable panache. "When confronting such boorish breach of manners, one wonders where one went wrong. Rowena—" When Eugenia snapped her fingers, the woman who'd opened the front door appeared as if by magic. "Fetch another service. Mr. Sinclair prefers lemon and milk with his tea."

Rowena issued a courteous nod. "Yes, ma'am."

"Don't bother. I won't be staying."

The woman slid a bewildered glance toward Eugenia,

then slipped out of the room as unobtrusively as she'd entered.

Eugenia stiffened her shoulders, gave a haughty sniff. "Still the epitome of genteel grace, I see."

Colby ignored the biting comment, focusing instead on his father. He'd aged badly, Colby realized. Eyes that once glittered with power were weary, dull. Defeated. Kingsley's handsome face was haggard, ashen, the robust physical stature young Colby had so admired was now wounded and worn.

A stab of regret startled him. The years had taken a heavy toll on both of his parents. Colby was surprised to realize that he cared.

Movement caught his eye. Danielle stood, balancing the wriggling baby in her arms. "I was going to discuss this with you tonight," she said cautiously. "Perhaps it's just as well that you're here now. We can all talk together."

He skewered her with a frigid gaze. "Nothing I'm about to say concerns you, Danielle. Please take Megan and leave."

She withered before his eyes. "Please, Colby, I understand you might be annoyed—"

"Annoyed?" His laugh was dry, unpleasant. "Betrayal is many things, Danielle, all of which are considerably more strident than mere annoyance."

"I didn't betray you, Colby." The pain in her eyes was like a blade to his heart. "I simply wanted your parents to know what a wonderful father you have been to Megan."

"Ah." He clasped his hands behind his back, rocked on his heels. "And were they suitably impressed?" He knew the answer even before Danielle's gaze skittered away. "I didn't think so. I, on the other hand, have a unique understanding as to exactly what is required to capture my parents' attention. Isn't that true...Mother?" His gaze was as caustic, his enunciation precise.

Eugenia paled instantly. She understood the inference, and was clearly frightened by it.

There was no triumph in Colby's heart, only weariness and regret. "Please leave, Danielle. My parents and I have family business to discuss."

Danielle wavered there a moment before her chin jutted stubbornly. "I'm part of this family, too. So is Megan. We're not leaving."

God, he was tired. "Go home, Dani." She responded by sitting down again. Colby heaved a pained sigh, faced his parents, both of whom were as ashen as the condemned at a gallows party. "If you don't dismiss the custody suit," he said quietly, "I'm prepared to testify as to what Olivia and I overheard on the night of my tenth birthday."

Eugenia swayed, clutched her husband's sleeve. "You wouldn't dare."

"Try me."

Supporting his fragile wife, Kingsley made a vain attempt to square his stooped shoulders. "You heard nothing, Colby, nothing at all." There was fear in the old man's eyes. And exquisite sadness.

From her seat across from the elder Sinclairs, Danielle saw every nuance of their transformation, was awed by it. She felt invisible, as if she and Megan had suddenly metamorphosed into proverbial flies on the wall to observe a human melodrama too theatrical to be real. The lack of emotional warmth between Colby and his parents was shocking, but there was something else going on here, something even more ominous.

Across the room, Colby pursed his lips. His gaze never wavered. "After I opened my birthday present, I went upstairs. Olivia was listening at your door, Eugenia. I joined her. It was a game at first, because we heard Father's voice inside. That was very unusual, of course, since the two of you so rarely spoke. But you spoke that night, and quite loudly if I recall.''

Eugenia's thin body stiffened, quivered like a twig in the breeze. ''Sneaking around like little thieves, poking grubby noses into things that didn't concern you—'' Kingsley grasped her elbow in warning. The woman lifted her chin, composed herself. ''Your father is correct, Colby. Whatever you and your sister heard, or believed that you heard, was clearly misunderstood.''

''Ah, I see. Tell me, how does one misunderstand the phrase, 'the dead whore's bastard?'''

Danielle gasped, pressed her hand to her mouth. No one spared her a glance. Kingsley wavered slightly, tightened his grasp on his wife's arm. Other than a slight thinning of her mouth, Eugenia gave no indication she'd even heard her son's words.

''Yes,'' Colby murmured. ''It does seem rather self-explanatory, doesn't it? That's probably why you didn't feel a need to discuss it when Father opened the door and saw us standing there.''

Kingsley extended a hand. ''Please, son, listen—''

''I'll never forget the shock in your eyes,'' Colby continued, and although he was staring into space, everyone in the room knew he was speaking to his father. ''To your credit, you appeared quite horrified. On the other hand—'' his gaze settled on Eugenia's stiff face ''—I'll never forget your expression, either. When Father opened the door, Olivia practically fell inside. I recall standing there like a statue, too terrified to move. I saw you in the bedroom, wrapped in that silk-and-feather robe that made you look like a movie star, and I remember thinking how beautiful you were.''

Eugenia blinked, maintained composure by clasping her hands together.

''I stood there,'' Colby whispered, ''staring at you, waiting for assurance that it wasn't true. But I saw only contempt in your eyes, and I finally understood why you had never loved me.''

Eugenia appeared jarred by that, but didn't dispute it. ''Wild speculation, incoherent ramblings from the memory of an imaginative child. If you breathe a word of it outside this room, we shall sue for slander.''

''Don't insult my intelligence,'' Colby said tiredly. ''I'm not a foolish ten-year-old anymore. Years ago I researched my past, and located an unaltered copy of my birth certificate. I know who I am. You know who I am. The question now becomes, what is it worth to you to keep the world from knowing?''

Eugenia shook with rage. ''Your father would be ruined. You are despicable.''

Colby shook his head, smiled sadly. ''Don't you think you've protected him long enough, Eugenia?''

For the first time, Kingsley stepped forward, silenced his wife with a gentle nod. He regarded his son quietly. ''You're right, of course. I should have discussed this with you years ago. You may not believe it, but your mother and I were trying to protect you.''

''She is not my mother,'' Colby snapped. ''And you're right, I don't believe you. The only person you wanted to protect was yourself, and your precious reputation. Imagine the headlines—Patriarch Of Rich, Powerful Family Impregnates Impressionable College Student Half His Age.''

''Please, son, you don't understand—''

''I understand that my mother, my *real* mother, died giving me life when her own had barely begun. You seduced her, took advantage of her youth, then buried her memory like so much garbage and thrust me into your wife's home, where she'd be forced to relive your tawdry affair every time she looked into my face. No wonder she despises me.''

With a soft cry, Eugenia collapsed on the davenport, staring straight ahead with wide, dry eyes.

Danielle wanted to reach out and comfort the woman, but was afraid to put Megan down long enough to do so. Besides, she was in her own state of shock, haunted by the image of that shattered little boy who'd learned a bitter truth, and realized that he had no hope of earning a mother's love. Because he had no mother.

Across the burnished rosewood coffee table, Kingsley laid a hand on his wife's shoulder, but continued to stand, staring sadly at his son. "Eugenia is your mother," he said softly. "She adopted you when you were barely an infant, and she raised you like her own."

"Yes, I found the adoption papers." Colby quirked a smile at his father's stunned look. "Money, I've discovered, can uncover even those records sealed by a bribed judge. As for who raised me, there are a series of fine au pairs to whom that dubious distinction should be allotted." His face softened, remembering what he'd learned, how she'd been so distraught by her husband's affair that she'd withdrawn from public view for months. Eventually that disappearance had provided substance to the story, widely circulated, that Eugenia had been bedridden by a difficult pregnancy. "Eugenia, I don't blame you. I've never blamed you. You did the best you could in an impossible situation, but the anger, no matter how righteous, still warped you, twisted your heart. I can't let you have Megan. I won't let you have her. She deserves better."

The woman made no response. She simply perched on the elegant upholstered brocade, rigid and stoic, her thin hands clasped in her lap as if she was conducting a formal tea. Kingsley angled a glance at Danielle, looked away when their eyes met. He said nothing. There was nothing left to say.

For a moment, Colby seemed to have forgotten Danielle

was there, forgotten that anyone was there. He was mesmerized by an antique curio table in the west corner of the parlor. "There was a vase there once," he murmured to no one in particular. "It always had fresh flowers in it."

Something in his voice caught Eugenia, drew her to look at him. "European lead crystal. A stupid servant broke it years ago."

"I broke it," Colby said quietly. "Childish revenge when you destroyed my drawing."

"Your drawing?"

His sad smile pierced Danielle's heart. "I knew how much you loved flowers, how sad you became when they finally wilted and died, so I created a colorful, crayoned bouquet, flowers that would live forever, make you smile forever. But you threw it away." He blinked, stiffened, turned away from the past. "Send my accountant a bill for the vase," he said, then spoke to Danielle without looking at her. "It's time to leave."

She moistened her lips, shifted Megan in her arms, rose shakily from the chair. A moment later, she felt a hand on her arm, realized that Colby had scooped up the baby's diaper bag and was escorting them both out of the room. He opened the massive entry door, stepped politely aside. Danielle tottered out, trembling, sick at heart, utterly devastated.

Clearly, she'd been wrong about the Sinclairs, just as she'd been wrong about Sheila, the teenage runaway who'd burglarized her apartment. This time, her faulty judgment had far-reaching consequences affecting lives other than her own. By ignoring Colby's wishes and forcing a toxic family reunion, she'd caused unbelievable pain, a hurtful confrontation that destroyed any hope that the Sinclairs could become a family again.

Even worse, Colby felt as if she'd betrayed him, taken his family's side against him. In a sense, she had, because she'd acted irresponsibly without understanding the facts. Altruistic motive aside, she had repeatedly misled him, deceived him, betrayed his trust.

And as Danielle had just learned, Colby Sinclair was not a forgiving man.

Colby slept in the guest room that night, and every night for the next week. Danielle's attempts to discuss their meeting with his parents, or anything else for that matter, were met by frigid silence. He'd spent eighteen hours a day at the office, communicating with Danielle only by messages conveyed via his bewildered assistant.

Danielle learned through her that the Sinclairs had dropped the lawsuit, and that a hastily convened custody hearing had resulted in Colby being named sole guardian of his niece.

There would be no celebration that day.

Danielle had put champagne on ice, but it was after eleven before Colby returned home. He went straight into his study and closed the doors.

Danielle didn't intrude. She knew her husband now, knew his moods, his hopes, his secret terrors. She understood that the emotional void he'd created was his way of suppressing the rage of betrayal and childhood abandonment. Her heart went out to the tormented child that he'd once been, and to the wounded man he'd become. She yearned to hold him, heal him, shower him with the love that he'd always deserved.

But Colby had turned away from her now, and Danielle couldn't blame him. She'd violated his trust, sneaking behind his back to reunite him with a cold, contemptuous mother and a spineless father who'd never stood up for his son.

There was nothing she could do to take back the pain

she'd caused him, to bring back those cherished moments that they'd once shared.

So she went to bed, hugged a pillow suffused in his scent and she wept.

"You look terrible."

Colby glowered at his hapless assistant, who adjusted her glasses, shuffled papers on her desk.

"I meant only that you appear quite tired, Mr. Sinclair. You've been working extremely long hours."

"Work does not do itself, Ms. Reese, a concept certain employees have yet to grasp."

She flushed. "Yes, sir."

He swallowed a stab of guilt, retreated back into the comfort of dispassion. "Have the revised marketing studies been completed?"

"I haven't seen them."

"Call Malony," he snapped. "I want them on my desk by noon."

"Yes, sir."

"And get the San Francisco distribution center on the phone. Their inventory discrepancies are intolerable."

"Of course." The woman scribbled madly. "Anything else, Mr. Sinclair?"

"Call my attorney. Schedule a meeting to review the custody papers—"

"Oh, I nearly forgot." Ms. Reese rummaged through a tidy stack of notes, retrieved one. "Your attorney called earlier. He'll be out of town this week, but has couriered documents to your home for review. He also says that he'll be happy to discuss any questions or corrections when he returns."

"Very well. Hold my calls for the next hour." Colby issued a curt nod, strode into his office, closing the door behind him. He sagged against it, rubbing his eyes. Exhaustion wasn't working. He couldn't get Danielle's image out of his mind, couldn't forget the horror on her face when she'd discovered his secret shame.

Colby Sinclair, respected, blue-blooded son of wealth and privilege was in reality a fake and a phony, the illegitimate child of a tawdry affair between a powerful man and a gullible young woman. That revelation had been shocking enough, yet Colby knew that Danielle could have accepted his flawed bloodline. He'd seen her compassion, felt the power of her boundless love. His heritage wouldn't have made her think less of him as a man. She could accept human flaws, embrace them, then erase them with a kindness that flowed from her heart like sweet honey.

Yes, she could accept his bastard identity, but she could never accept a man so ethically blemished that he'd stooped to blackmail, and had threatened to ruin his own parents simply to get his way.

It was more than that, of course; it was a moral dilemma that pitted the rights of his parents against the future of an innocent child.

But the deed was done. The desired result had been achieved. Megan would never know her grandparents. In the eyes of the world, Colby had won. In his heart, he knew that he'd lost everything. He hadn't been able to face Danielle; he hadn't even been able to face himself. The blame was his; the shame was his. For the rest of his life, Colby would bear the burden of guilt for what he'd done. It was a burden he could never ask Danielle to share.

"It's no problem, Madeline. I'll be happy to take over your volunteer shift tomorrow evening." Clamping the portable phone between her chin and shoulder, Danielle finished filling the bottle, a last-ditch effort to sooth Megan, who'd been fussy since breakfast. "Here you go, sweetums."

"Why, thank you, darling," Madeline replied with a chuckle.

"I was talking to Megan," Danielle muttered, relieved when the child snatched the bottle greedily. "She's been cranky all morning."

"Maybe she's coming down with something."

"Maybe."

"But you don't think so."

Danielle sighed, propped a hip against the family room sofa. "She doesn't have any symptom of illness. I think all the tension around here is affecting her."

"Kids are sensitive to problems," Madeline acknowledged. Her voice softened. "Things still aren't going well between you and Colby?"

It took a minute to clear a sudden lump from her throat. "He won't talk to me, Maddie. He won't even look at me."

"Give him time, hon. He'll get over it."

Danielle wished she believed that, but since she couldn't tell her friend without betraying Colby's confidence, all she said was, "You're probably right." A sharp buzz startled her. "Someone's at the door, Maddie. You have fun at the party tomorrow night, okay?"

Danielle clicked off the phone, dropped it on the counter as she hurried to answer the door.

A uniformed courier stood on the porch with two manila envelopes in one hand and a clipboard in the other. "Delivery for Colby Sinclair and—" he glanced at the second envelope "—Mr. and Mrs. C. E. Sinclair."

That startled her. There had been many such deliveries over the past weeks, all from Colby's lawyer and all concerning the custody matter. None had ever been addressed to them both. "I'll sign."

The courier thrust out the clipboard, waited while Danielle scrawled her name, then left without ceremony.

Danielle laid Colby's envelope on the kitchen table, eyed

hers with trepidation. There was no reason that documents relating to the custody agreement should be forwarded to both of them. The court had appointed Colby as Megan's sole guardian.

Presuming there had been a simple mistake in labeling the envelopes, she considered leaving both unopened on Colby's desk. A niggling dread crept along her nape. *Mr. and Mrs. C. E. Sinclair.* So ominously legal.

Of course, attorneys were notorious for proper decorum, except that Jack had always forwarded documents addressed simply to Colby Sinclair, as was the first envelope. The second was different. Formal. Frightening.

Her fingers trembled at the flap, withdrew the contents sheathed in blue binding. She read Jack's scrawled note and the first line of the first page before her vision blurred with tears. The documents had nothing to do with Megan's custody. They were divorce papers.

Colby returned home late that night, nearly tripped over a suitcase and packed duffel set out by the front door. He frowned, laid his briefcase on the foyer table. "Danielle?"

A sound from the hallway captured his attention. Danielle emerged with a molded plastic pet carrier. Two sad yellow eyes peered out from behind the carrier's wire gate. "There's a plate in the microwave if you're hungry," she said without looking at him. "The laundry is done, and I washed the linens, too." She set the carrier down long enough to hoist the duffel strap over her shoulder. "There's a list of child care providers on the refrigerator. All of them come highly recommended. I've made arrangements for Megan to stay at your office day-care center until you find someone else."

"Find someone else?" Colby grasped her arm as she reached for the small suitcase. "Wait a minute. What's going on here?"

She seemed startled. "I'm leaving."

The question raced to the tip of his tongue before he swallowed it. There was no reason to ask why she was leaving. Clearly she couldn't bear to remain in the same home with a man who'd use such cruel coercion against his own parents.

Colby released her, clasped his hands behind his back. "I see."

Something in her gaze melted, but she looked away before he could interpret what he saw there. "I'll be staying with Madeline. There's no room for my furniture there, so I hope you won't mind if I leave it here. Just for a while," she added quickly. "Until I can make other arrangements."

"Of course."

She hesitated, cast an unhappy glance toward the kitchen. "Well, then…" A flash of white as her teeth scraped her lower lip. "I guess that's everything."

It took every ounce of willpower for Colby to keep from grabbing her, screaming that she couldn't go, couldn't leave him, not now, not ever. "Do you require assistance?" he inquired politely.

"No, thanks. The rest of my stuff is already in the car." She turned away, slipped a furtive thumb across her cheek. Then she took a shuddering breath, hoisted the suitcase in one hand and the kitty carrier in the other.

Suppressing an urge to block the front door with his body, Colby chivalrously stepped forward to open it for her.

Danielle paused on the porch, glanced over her shoulder. "The papers are on the kitchen table. I think you'll find them in order. Goodbye, Colby."

Before he could react, she'd disappeared into the darkness. A car door slammed, an engine revved. A burst of light bathed the yard as the vehicle backed from the driveway.

Colby stood there until the final glow of red taillights

dissolved into night. "Goodbye, Dani," he whispered after she'd gone. His heart felt as if it would explode with grief.

He closed the door, swallowed a nauseous surge. Dear God, how could he live without her? He would, of course, for Megan's sake. But at that moment, Colby felt as if his life was over.

Shoulders slumped, Colby shuffled to the family room, which was barren and hostile without the clutter of knick-knacks and sprawling plants. He moved through the room, gliding his palm across the worn sofa. Danielle's sofa. At least he had something left of her.

He turned away, scoured his burning eyes with the back of his hand, gazed toward the breakfast nook, where the hanging lamp illuminated an unopened manila envelope along with a neat stack of legal documents in the center of the kitchen table. Danielle had commented about papers when she'd left. Colby hadn't understood her meaning then, but when he perused the documents in question, he understood all too well.

The cover note was scrawled by a familiar hand. "As requested," Jack had written. "Please review and return executed copies to my office for recordation."

He laid the note down, flipped through the first document and found what he'd expected: Danielle's signature, properly notarized, with today's date.

Colby wasn't surprised that Danielle was divorcing him. She had, after all, fulfilled her part of their agreement, and was clearly anxious to get on with her life. Colby couldn't blame her for that. Deep down, he'd always expected to lose her someday; but he'd never anticipated the pain.

Chapter Thirteen

"You have to eat." Madeline sighed, shoved the plate under Danielle's nose. "Just a few bites, hon. It will make you feel better."

Danielle dutifully lifted a fork, poked at her radicchio salad, then laid the utensil aside. "Maybe later, Maddie. I'm just not hungry."

The grumbling woman snatched up the plate, covered it with plastic wrap. "You haven't been hungry for three days," she complained, placing the wrapped salad in the fridge.

"Quit nagging me." Pivoting from the table, Danielle stood, raked her hair, wandered toward the cramped living room of her friend's small apartment. Whiskers, snoozing beneath the coffee table, deigned open one eye as she approached. More out of habit than interest, Danielle flipped through the newspaper, scanned the want ads. "That retail outlet across from the mall is looking for sales clerks."

Madeline entered the room, wiping her hands on a towel. "Sounds perfect for someone with a master's degree in psychology. Far be it for me to suggest something as radical as, say—" she snapped her fingers "—family counseling! Is that a bizarre concept or what?"

Danielle tossed the folded paper onto the table, where it scooted across an untidy scramble of magazines and slid to the floor. The startled cat shot out, gave Danielle a disgruntled glance, then stalked out of the room.

Weary to the bone, Danielle sank onto the sofa, leaned forward to prop her elbows on her thighs. "I am not going back into social work."

"So you've said." Madeline sat beside her, tossed a chummy arm around her shoulders. "My question is, why not?"

"I'm through messing with people's lives," she said simply.

More precisely, Danielle was through messing *up* people's lives. Having always viewed the world through a rosy lens of optimism, she'd believed that any problem could be solved with a hot meal and an empathetic ear. She'd been naive. Worse, she'd been selfish. Because she had personally wanted the Sinclairs to be a warm, loving family, she'd ignored reality, betrayed Colby's trust, hurt him deeply and lost him forever.

Still Danielle could accept her own fate. If heartbreak was her destiny, she'd created it herself by pushing her own agenda onto a family wreaked with chaos and despair. What Danielle could never accept, however, was the pain she'd inflicted, not only on the elder Sinclairs but on Colby and Megan. Because of her idiotic interference, all hope of reunification had been destroyed. Megan would be raised in an environment of family secrets, and anger so deep, so destructive, that it was bound to affect the child's sense of security, if not her entire future.

The sofa cushion dipped as Madeline settled beside her. She lifted Danielle's hand, regarded it as if some secret was revealed in the web of fine lines around each knuckle. "You know, hon, it's none of my business but—"

"You're right." Danielle withdrew her hand, folded her arms. "It isn't your business."

The woman sighed. "You and Colby have only been married a few weeks. Regardless of the problems you two are having, you haven't really given yourselves a chance to work them out."

"Please, Maddie, you just don't understand."

"I want to, Dani. Explain it to me."

All Danielle could do was shake her head. Explain what? she thought to herself. That her husband had never loved her? That their marriage was a sham, a fake, a cruel hoax specifically designed for deception? In that context, it had been a roaring success. Even her own heart had been fooled.

"Listen, Dani, after two divorces I'm certainly no expert on the subject of marriage, but—" She was interrupted by the peal of the doorbell. "Damn." Annoyed, Madeline rose, glanced at the clock. "Jimmy must have forgotten his wallet and keys again," she muttered, referring to her teenage son who'd flown out the door an hour earlier on his way to a hot date. She yanked the door open. "I'm going to get you a belt chain for your birthday— Oh, hi."

"Is, ah, Danielle available?"

At the sound of his voice, Danielle's heart dropped to her knees, which wobbled dangerously as she struggled to her feet.

Madeline cast a smug glance over her shoulder, stepped away from the open door. "Sure, come on in."

Colby entered hesitantly, carrying Megan in his arms. He paused just inside the door, swayed slightly when he saw Danielle. His eyes softened and glowed. "Hello, Dani."

Since her voice had failed, she mouthed "Hello."

Megan spotted Danielle, issued a joyous shriek and flung her arms out, grunting madly. Danielle's feet wouldn't move, so she waited while Colby crossed the room to deposit the giggling child in her open arms.

Danielle hugged her fiercely, fighting tears. "Oh, sweetums," she whispered against the baby's warm little cheek. "I've missed you so much."

"Ungee be-ba!" she announced, pinched a handful of facial flesh with each baby claw, then plopped a wet kiss on Danielle's mouth. "Mamamamama!"

Mama? Had Megan actually called her Mama? Danielle's knees nearly buckled at the thought. It took a moment to reel in her spinning heart, remind herself that childish gibberish was little more than a peculiar assortment of vowels punctuated with a few of the more interesting consonants. The only words Megan spoke with any recognizable regularity were *uncle, juice, bye-bye* and *cat*. She also grunted "Uh-uh" rather well, although Danielle was hesitant to elevate negative slang to word status.

As Danielle ducked her head to covertly wipe an escaped tear, she saw Madeline slip quietly into the kitchen. They were alone now, the three of them. Four, actually, since Whiskers had reappeared and was affectionately rubbing against Colby's calf.

"Hey, boy," Colby murmured, bending to stroke the purring cat. "Have you been getting enough tuna?"

Whiskers issued a soft trill, butted his head on Colby's ankle, contorted his furry neck to allow a satisfying throat scratch. Colby complied with a gentle smile, then straightened awkwardly, glancing around the cluttered quarters. "It didn't take long for you to make yourself at home."

"The place looked like this when I got here," Danielle said. "Maddie isn't any better at housekeeping than I am."

Colby nodded, rolled his lips together, clamped them with his teeth.

A strained silence followed. Danielle hugged Megan, shifted her in her arms. "So," she murmured finally, "what brings you here?"

"Hmm? Oh." Colby dug into the inside pocket of his sport coat. "You left some things at the house." He withdrew a rumpled plastic wad, laid it on the skewered magazine pile.

"My shower cap?"

"I thought you might need it," he replied defensively. Digging back into his pocket, he placed a wrinkled piece of scratch paper beside the crumpled cap. "There's a phone number on it," he explained. "I thought it might be important."

She spared it a glance, bit back a smile. "It's for the dry cleaner. I wanted to make sure your things were ready."

"Oh. Well, I have these, too." Three hair clips joined the pile. "I, ah, found them in a bathroom drawer."

Danielle had to turn her head to keep from laughing out loud. "One can never have too many hair clips."

"That's what I thought," Colby replied in all seriousness. "I presumed you'd be upset to discover they were missing."

She could have gone the rest of her life without noticing, but would have sawed off an arm before letting him know that. "Thank you for returning them."

"You're welcome." He folded his arms, watched Megan twist a lock of Danielle's hair around her chubby little hand. His eyes glowed softly, sadly, reminding Danielle more acutely than words just how very much she had lost. He blinked, turned away, shoved both hands in his slacks' pockets, immediately withdrew one hand and mumbled, "I almost forgot."

Bending, he dangled a furry fake mouse in front of

Whiskers. The cat sniffed the toy, then snatched it in his mouth and scurried off, presumably to deposit the creature in one of his new hidey-holes.

Colby straightened, angled a sheepish glance. "I found it under the kitchen table. Since it was his favorite toy, I figured he'd been kind of, well, upset about losing it."

Far be it from Danielle to point out that the furry item in question was merely one of a half-dozen identical fake mice that the animal had squirreled away. "I'm sure Whiskers appreciates your thoughtfulness."

"He seemed pleased," Colby acknowledged, then shoved his hands back into his pockets. "So you're doing well?"

She cleared her throat, fought a quiver in her voice. "Sure, fine. And you?"

"Yes, thank you."

"Good, that's good."

"It's good that you're doing well, too."

"I'm doing great," she lied. "Things couldn't be better."

"For me, either," he said quickly. "Couldn't be better."

"That's good."

"Yes, good."

The lame reply dissipated like so much steam while they both glanced around the room as if searching for something, anything, that required discussion. Finding none, they shifted from foot to foot in awkward silence until Megan, apparently bored with Danielle's hair, rubbed her eyes, bucked restlessly.

"She's tired," Colby said, seeming disappointed.

Danielle didn't want to let her go. "Maybe she'd like a cookie."

"It's past her bedtime. She'll be cranky in day care tomorrow."

Since Danielle couldn't argue that without seeming selfish, she reluctantly relented, handed the fussy baby back to her uncle. "Is that working out for you? Day care, I mean."

"It's all right." Colby shifted as Megan laid her head on his shoulder. A moment after popping her thumb in her mouth, her eyelids began to droop. "Megan enjoys the other children, but after a couple of hours, I understand she gets restless and seems distressed."

A telltale glance indicated that he considered Danielle responsible for that, although she couldn't understand why he would. He was the one who wanted to end the marriage.

Of course, Danielle's stupidity had given him little choice.

"Megan's a bright little girl," she murmured, avoiding his reproachful gaze. "She'll adjust."

"I've found a provider willing to care for Megan at home three days a week," Colby replied. "She comes highly recommended."

"That's good," Danielle mumbled without conviction. "I'm sure that's best for Megan."

Colby made no reply to that. Instead, he glanced around the room once more as if assuring himself there was nothing more to say. "We should be going." He hesitated a moment, then turned toward the door.

Danielle met him there, opened it for him. "Thank you for returning my, ah, our things."

He regarded her for a long moment, then focused his gaze out into the darkness. "You're welcome," he murmured, and then he was gone.

The moment the door closed, a tear glided down her cheek. She wiped it away as Madeline entered the room.

"Well," the woman said gruffly, "that was the most pathetic thing I've ever seen in my life."

"You wouldn't have seen anything if you hadn't been spying."

"My entire apartment would fit in the walk-in closet of

your house," Madeline observed caustically. "The only way I could avoid that pitiful spectacle you two put on was crawl into the oven. Which, by the way, doesn't sound like such a bad idea at the moment."

"You're beginning to aggravate me." Danielle swung away from the door, flopped into a battered easy chair and hoped her dour expression would send a message to her friend.

Apparently it didn't. "How in the devil could you let him leave?" Madeline demanded. "Are you completely out of your mind?"

Danielle gritted her teeth, busied herself flipping through a dog-eared magazine. "He had to put Megan to bed."

"Yeah, right." Madeline snatched the magazine out of her hands. "That man loves you, Dani, and you just let him walk out of your life."

Frustrated, infuriated by her own broken heart, Danielle shot to her feet, let anger cover the pain. "Stay out of this, Madeline. The only reason Colby came by was to return my things. Period, end of discussion."

She would have pushed past her friend except that the woman planted her palms on Danielle's shoulder, pushed her back into the chair, then shook a finger in her face like a scolding parent. "If you honestly believe that man drove halfway across town just to hand over a disposable shower cap, a wad of trash, three hair clips and a stuffed mouse, then, honey, you're even more hopeless than I thought." With an impatient snort, Madeline tossed up her hands and stalked out of the room.

Danielle sagged back in the chair, closed her weary eyes. She was hopeless, all right. Hopelessly in love. But she was through mooning like an angst-ridden adolescent, through thrusting her misery on her best friend, and through blaming the world for her own stupidity. The only way she'd ever get over Colby was to throw herself back into life, ignore the ache of her own selfish heart and devote herself to the needs of others.

Tomorrow she'd return to the food bank, volunteer every shift until her body couldn't stay upright and her mind was blank with fatigue. Then maybe she could sleep without dreaming, without remembering that she'd held love in the palm of her hand, then allowed it to slip through her fingers.

Colby parked at the edge of the lot, well beyond the open chain-link gate leading into the food bank. Slumped down in the car seat, he felt like a covert operative in a bad spy movie.

If someone had asked why he was here, he couldn't have come up with a reasonable response. During a routine commute home from the office, he'd been fretting about his last fumbled meeting with Danielle, how foolish he must have seemed tracking her down to return a pocketful of useless trash.

The next thing he knew, he'd found himself turning right instead of left. Now he stupidly scooped out the food bank loading dock, watching pallets of baked goods being unloaded from a bread truck.

Colby scanned the workers in disappointment. He hadn't really expected to find Danielle driving a forklift. Still, he'd hoped for a glimpse of her. Instead, he was studying a truck driver who tucked a clipboard under his arm, waved to the volunteers and sauntered back toward the cab of his truck.

From the corner of his eye, Colby noticed rustling in the shrubbery separating the parking lot from an adjacent alley. A moment later, a gaunt form leapt out, dashed through the open gate and accosted the driver. She pulled at his arms, appeared to be pleading with him. The driver shook his head, pushed the young woman away.

Colby straightened, leaned forward against the steering wheel for a better look at the scrawny girl who continued to tug at the driver until he'd climbed into the cab and closed the door in her face.

A man on the loading dock shouted down at the girl, who responded by sprinting like a frightened rabbit back into the bushes.

As the truck rumbled past his car, Colby leaned back, stunned and deflated. Stringy blond hair, sallow cheeks, sunken eyes. There was no doubt in his mind.

He exited the vehicle, moved toward the rustling shrubbery. A flash of white darted from the bush. He snagged her arm, held the struggling girl firmly. "It's all right, Sheila. I'm not going to hurt you." Her eyes widened in terror, cracked lips open in a silent scream that tore at his conscience. "We met once, at Danielle's apartment. Do you remember me?"

A cloud of confusion dulled the fear. She licked her lips, squinted at him. "You're the neighbor guy."

"Yes. What are you doing here, Sheila?"

Her gaze darted toward the loading dock, where a burly volunteer was watching the scene with obvious suspicion. "Looking for Dani. They said she won't be back until morning."

"Don't you think you've done enough to Dani?"

The girl's gaze jarred back to Colby, then jittered away. "It wasn't my fault. He made me do it."

"'He' who?"

"My, umm—" She bit her lip, stared at her feet, rotated her bony shoulders in a listless shrug. "You know."

"Your pimp?"

She flinched, nodded.

"So when you told Dani that you weren't prostituting yourself, that was a lie?" When she didn't respond, Colby lifted the arm he held, shoved up the sleeve of her dirty white sweatshirt, glimpsed what he'd expected before she yanked away. "That looks like a bad habit."

"Ain't no such thing as a good one." Sheila sniffed, wiped her nose with her sleeve. "I'm going clean, though, honest I am. Dani said she'd help."

Colby regarded her. "That's not quite true, either, Sheila. Danielle had no idea you were on drugs."

The girl didn't dispute that. "Dani wouldn't care. She's helped lots of girls like me."

"How many of them stole from her?"

A shimmer of tears brightened her blue eyes. "He made me," she whispered miserably. "I couldn't stop him."

The fact that Colby believed her was mute testament to how much he had changed over the past few months. It hadn't been that long ago that he would have brushed past this pathetic creature without a backward glance. In his arrogance and his ignorance he'd have presumed her to be responsible for her own predicament, and wouldn't have felt the slightest twinge of guilt in allowing her to figure her own way out of it.

Odd, he thought, how different things appeared to him now. Initially he'd viewed Danielle's charitable heart as an example of good intentions weakened by poor judgment and a woeful lack of guile. That image had been challenged over the past months.

Through Danielle, Colby had met good, hardworking people who'd been knocked down by life, yet continued their struggle with dignity and grace. He'd seen the hope-lessness of abject poverty, and children whose ability to learn had been irreparably damaged by malnutrition. He'd seen women cowed by violence, and despondent men dis-illusioned by an inability to cope with a technologically advanced world that had passed them by. He'd seen chil-dren cast into the streets to survive as thieves and prosti-tutes.

One of those misguided youngsters stood in front of him now—trembling, filthy, half-starved and desperate. Danielle wouldn't have been able to turn her back on this pitiful young girl. Colby couldn't, either. "Come with me."

She reared back fearfully. "Why?"

He gentled his grasp. "First, we're going to get you something to eat," he said quietly. "Then you're going to decide what you want to do with the rest of your life."

She wiped a string of hair from her face, regarded him skeptically.

Colby laid his hand on her shoulder. "I can promise that for tonight at least, you won't be cold, and you won't be hungry. What happens tomorrow is up to you."

A light of hope flickered in her eyes, not brightly, but it was enough to warm Colby's heart. After a moment's hesitation, the girl turned, trailed him to his car.

Shadows from the setting sun followed them out of the parking lot, a dusky darkness enveloping the dilapidated warehouse that held hope for so many.

A silhouette stepped out of those shadows, hovered just beyond the reach of the loading dock floodlights and watched Colby Sinclair's vehicle disappear into the night.

Later that evening Colby flexed his fingers over the telephone, paused, then turned away. He wanted to talk to Danielle, tell her that Megan had cut a new tooth. They'd celebrated the last one with ice cream and party hats. Colby missed that. He missed the fun and the laughter, especially the laughter, the melodic sound of Danielle's infectious chuckle when she watched a silly television commercial, or was tickled by Megan's baby antics.

Yes, Colby missed that laughter. He missed the sound of her voice, the clutter of magazines strewn across the tables, the clipped-up newspapers piled on the floor. Hell, he even missed the stupid cat.

Even the lovely house that had once vibrated with warmth was now a cold, foreboding place. After Megan was asleep, the silence was stifling, and Colby no longer found joy in the solitude he'd once cherished. Everything was different without Danielle. Colby was different, too.

For the first time in his life Colby Sinclair was in love, deeply, irrevocably in love. But there would be no happy ending, for his was a tragic, unrequited love. Colby had never expected Danielle to return his feelings, never believed that a woman of such vibrant warmth could ever love a man so flawed that even his own parents had rejected him.

He rubbed his eyes, wandered into his study. There was always work. He could bury himself in facts, figures, marketing projections. Work had always been his salvation. Always.

Until now.

Disgusted, he flipped the computer off, swiveled his chair around. The study was incredibly neat, well organized. He hated it.

He dropped a couple of books on the floor. That was better. A few bound marketing studies joined the pile. Colby liked the effect, and was about to empty his briefcase contents onto the heap when the doorbell rang.

Assuming that the delivery service was working late that night, he strode to the foyer, muttering to himself. He wasn't in the mood to handle anything urgent, which was why he'd disconnected the telephone and flipped off his beeper. At the moment, he couldn't think of anything earthshattering enough to merit his attention.

But there was one thing. As soon as he opened the front door, he saw what it was.

Chapter Fourteen

For a moment, Colby thought he was hallucinating.

The hallucination spoke. "Hello, son." Kingsley Sinclair stood stiff and rigid, grasping his dour wife's arm as if expecting her to sprint away. "May we come in?"

"Ah…" Colby swallowed shock, rearranged his features into a mask of dispassion and stepped aside. "Yes, of course."

With a polite nod, Kingsley attempted to move forward, and would have, had his wife not remained firmly planted on the porch.

"It does not appear that we are welcome." Eugenia's thin lips curled in upon themselves as if she were sucking a sour grape. "Take me home at once."

A pucker of annoyance fluttered between the older man's brows, settled into a furious frown. "We have already discussed this matter," he told her quietly. "Our son has invited us into his home, and we shall accept. You may choose between entering graciously under your own power or being carried over my shoulder like a petulant child."

Colby nearly fell over. In eighteen-plus years of living beneath his parents' roof, not once had Colby seen his father display visible anger toward his wife, or conduct himself in a manner beyond utter acquiescence to her wishes.

Eugenia vibrated as if struck. "How dare you speak to me with such disrespect? I am your wife."

"Yes, you are my wife." Kingsley's eyes softened, saddened. "And as such, I expect you to behave with appropriate decorum." He took one step back, gestured toward the open door. "After you, my dear."

Beneath her frigid gaze was a flicker of something strange, a nervous fear completely out of character for a woman so self-assured that Colby had thought her invincible to mortal pain. Before he could analyze that, Eugenia pivoted with a haughty huff, hiked her pointed chin and stepped through the doorway.

Kingsley followed, hovered uncomfortably in the foyer as Colby closed the entry door, offered to take their coats.

"We won't be staying," Eugenia said, reinforcing that statement by clutching both a small designer handbag and a thin flat package to her fragile bosom. The package was tastefully wrapped in white satin, accented by a beige lace bow.

Kingsley heaved a sigh, slipped off his tailored overcoat, handed it to Colby with a polite nod. He leaned forward, whispered in his wife's ear. After a strained pause, Eugenia shifted the package long enough to shrug out of her mink dinner jacket, stood rigid as a naked statue while her son hung both garments in the hall closet.

Colby returned and showed his parents into the parlor. "May I get you something? A cup of tea, some sherry, perhaps?"

"Sherry would be pleasant, thank you." Eugenia glanced

around without further comment, perched uncomfortably on the leather sofa and laid the package on her lap. Kingsley sat beside her, stiff as a corpse and just as pale.

Colby poured the sherry, placed a crystal wine goblet in front of each of his parents, then took one for himself and settled into the leather lounge chair with what he hoped was a pleasant expression. Inside, the frightened boy of his childhood fought to emerge and run screaming from the room. Colby kept that terrified child in check, held his ground, maintained his composure. Composure was everything to a Sinclair—the appearance of control, of confidence, of superiority. It was the only thing his parents respected.

And deep down, Colby wanted their respect. He'd always wanted it.

Kingsley sipped his sherry, murmured, "Excellent."

Colby nodded an acknowledgment, watched Eugenia dutifully raise the crystal rim to her lips.

She tasted, set the goblet down without comment, cast another dispassionate glance around the gleaming room. "Where is Danielle?" she asked reproachfully. "A good hostess must personally attend to the comfort of her guests."

Colby twirled the sparkling crystal stem between his palms. "Danielle is visiting a friend." Eugenia quirked a penciled brow, but said nothing. She did, however, appear disappointed, which surprised Colby and honed an edge on his suspicion. "I'm certain that if she'd been aware of your impending visit, she would have made every effort to greet you."

"Of course," Kingsley said, setting his sherry glass on the coffee table. "We'd hoped to thank her personally. Perhaps another time."

"Thank her?" Colby leaned forward, felt the muscles of his cheeks stiffen like leather. "Excuse my confusion, but it was my understanding that you were less than pleased with my wife, or more precisely, with what you considered to be her interference in family matters.''

Eugenia's chin wrinkled. She downed her sherry in one swallow, stared straight ahead as Colby retrieved the bottle to refill her glass.

Kingsley waved off a refill, unbuttoned his suit coat. His eyes were stoic, determined, filled with a strength of purpose Colby had never seen in his father. ''You're right, of course. We were less than gracious to your lovely wife, and we regret that. In retrospect, we understand that she went to great lengths to include us in Megan's life, although at the time we believed that the letters and photographs were intended to manipulate a more favorable legal position.''

Colby held up a palm, turned it to rub his forehead. ''Exactly what letters and photographs are we talking about here?''

The question startled Kingsley, but he merely glanced at his wife, who hesitated only a moment before retrieving a monogrammed wallet from her handbag. Eugenia opened the wallet to display a carefully laminated photograph.

Colby sucked in a breath, held out his hand. ''May I?''

He waited while Eugenia removed the picture, gazed at it with blatant affection, then laid it in her son's outstretched hand. Colby studied it carefully, noting that the picture was clearly a Polaroid that had been trimmed to wallet size. Megan, grinning happily, was decked out in her best red gingham dress, the one she'd worn at the food bank's thrift sale. Colby recalled Madeline carrying a Polaroid camera that day. Danielle must have borrowed it to take this photograph.

He returned the picture to Eugenia, who carefully tucked it back into her wallet.

''There were two others,'' Kingsley continued cautiously. "I have one in my billfold. The other is framed on the parlor mantel."

Colby nodded, leaned back, steepled his fingers.

"I didn't realize you were unaware," Kingsley added, apparently misinterpreting his son's confusion for annoyance. "I assure you, no deception was intended." He glanced away from Colby's skeptical gaze. "At least, not on our part."

"My wife was…is quite distressed by the lack of Sinclair family unity," Colby said quietly. "I can assure you that her intentions were honorable."

"We realized that when we received her last letter."

Colby hesitated, not certain he wanted an answer to the question he was about to ask. "Which letter might that be?"

"The one we received after the custody decision," Kingsley replied. "Danielle apologized for any pain she had caused, and made it quite clear that you had no responsibility for, nor any knowledge of, her actions. She indicated great sorrow that the family had been unable to come to agreement for Megan's sake, and urged us to continue to search for any common ground that would allow our family to heal past wounds."

Colby couldn't have been more shocked if a giraffe had walked through the parlor door and kicked him square in the chest. "Danielle wrote that?"

"She's a fine woman," Kingsley replied. "You must be very proud of her."

Closing his eyes, Colby covered his face with his hands, felt his coveted control slipping away. "If anyone is owed an apology in this ludicrous mess, it's Danielle. She's been treated abysmally by all of us."

Kingsley regarded him thoughtfully. "You're right, of course. Certainly your mother and I were less than gracious, and your anger with her was quite obvious during the, ah, unpleasant altercation at our home. It was at that point we realized that you had not sent your wife to plead on your own behalf, and that Danielle was completely unaware of our family's—'' he paused to moisten his lips, straighten his spine ''—historical difficulties.''

Colby stared at his father in disbelief. ''Historical difficulties? Is that what you call it?''

Kingsley's flinch was subtle, covered well. To his credit, his gaze never wavered. ''Would you prefer the term 'moral bankruptcy,' or 'pathological dysfunction'? Semantics no longer matter, Colby. What's done is done. We were poor parents, too engrossed in public appearance and private sorrows to notice what was happening to our children. For that, we are deeply sorry. Speaking for myself, I confess to having been a failure as a father, and as a husband, and yes, even as a man. I betrayed your mother, and I betrayed my children. I've spent the past thirty-five years trying to earn my wife's forgiveness, but I never tried to earn yours, Colby. That's a mistake I plan to rectify, if you'll allow it.''

The pronouncement was so stunning that Colby couldn't even grasp its significance. He stood, raked his hair. Bitterness surged into his throat, a cold, cynical lump threatening to choke off his airway. All his life he'd wanted this, dreamed of the day when his father would come to him, reclaim him as his son.

Now that it had happened, Colby didn't know how to respond. His heart was numb, his mind fuzzy with confusion. He slumped forward, shook his head.

Kingsley extended a hand, then let it drop to his own knee. ''Do you hate me so much, son?''

''No.'' Colby drew a shuddering breath, steadied himself against the leather lounge chair. ''I never hated you.''

''But you don't want me to be a part of your life, either.''

''That's not entirely correct.'' Colby stood, rubbed his

hands together, walked toward the bar simply to give himself a moment. He lifted a bottle of aged Scotch, idly scanned the label. "Tell him, Eugenia. Tell my father why I can never be part of his life."

There was a soft hiss from behind him, the sudden intake of air through clamped teeth. Colby returned the Scotch bottle to the bar, turned to face his parents. Kingsley appeared merely perplexed, but Eugenia's expression was cool, almost scornful.

"It's all right," Colby told her gently. "Talk to your husband, tell him how it felt being forced to relive his betrayal every time you looked into my face. You have a right to those feelings, Eugenia. No one can blame you for despising a child of disgrace."

The woman lifted her chin, gave him the same haughty stare that had shriveled him as a child. This time, something was different. There was a peculiar repentance in her gaze along with a flicker of insecurity that Colby had been too hurt to notice earlier.

As she clasped her hands in her lap, Colby noticed that they were trembling. "It was your father I despised, Colby, never you."

Kingsley paled at the harsh words, but said nothing. He covered both of his wife's knotted hands with one of his own, and waited quietly for her to continue.

After a moment she did, in a halting voice that touched Colby to the core. "When your father told me that another woman carried his child, I thought I would die of the shame. I didn't, of course. Your birth mother did. I told myself that her death had been God's plan to punish the guilty and heal my heartache by blessing me with the son that I never thought I'd have." She moistened her lips, gazed into space. "After Olivia's birth, I was barren, you see."

Kingsley squeezed his wife's hand, met Colby's gaze

with pleading eyes. "When your mother discovered that she could no longer bear children, she was devastated. I feared for her health, and for her sanity. I was not as patient as I could have been. I didn't understand her pain." He lowered his gaze. "I sought comfort elsewhere."

"Enough." Eugenia squared her shoulders, finally made eye contact with her stunned son. "I pushed your father away, Colby. I pushed him out of my bed, and had I not been so terrified of being socially ostracized, I would have pushed him out of my life. Then you came along, and I believed that your birth was an omen, a gift to appease my suffering." She jerked her head, lifted her chin. "But I wasn't through suffering, and I wasn't through punishing your father for his adulterous affair. I never realized that I was also punishing you."

Even from across the room, Colby could see tears sparkling in his mother's eyes. Her pain sliced him to the quick, but he couldn't move, couldn't even speak to offer comfort.

Eugenia took the handkerchief her husband offered, dabbed at her face. "In my parents' home affection was assumed, not displayed. I never realized how that had affected my own ability to parent until a few weeks ago, when I saw the agony in your eyes and realized how deeply you'd been wounded."

She blew her nose, sniffed, shook her head when her husband whispered in her ear. Kingsley lifted the wrapped package from her lap, urged her to take it. She did.

"You are my son, Colby. You have always been my son, and I have always loved you." Eugenia fingered the beige lace bow with peculiar reverence, then held the gift out to him. "I've always cherished this. I hope you will, too."

Colby hesitated, then crossed the room on wobbly legs, angling a curious glance at his father before accepting the gift.

Kingsley nodded. "Take it, son."

With a nervous shrug, Colby slipped off the lace ribbon, removed the satin wrapping, then sucked in a sharp breath and dropped into the leather lounge. There it was, professionally framed and matted, protected beneath a shield of gleaming glass, a riot of crayoned color, immortal blooms created from a child's unconditional love.

"My drawing," Colby whispered. "You kept it."

"I adored it," she said simply. "It was a gift from my son."

With those simple words, the healing process had begun.

"Are you sure, Jonas?"

"Yep."

"But you said yourself that it was dark out. It might have been someone else, someone who resembles Colby from a distance."

"It was him." Jonas shrugged, spat on the concrete loading dock. "And that Sheila girl."

Danielle was stunned. After burglarizing her apartment, Sheila had disappeared completely. No one had seen her for weeks. Even if the girl had returned to the food bank, Danielle couldn't understand why Colby had been here. She hadn't had any contact with him since he'd stopped by Madeline's apartment nearly a week ago.

Not that Danielle hadn't wanted to see Colby. She'd picked up the telephone a dozen times, only to hang up when she realized that there was nothing she could say to him, nothing that would recapture the life she'd destroyed with her own stupidity and ego.

In retrospect, she realized that she'd been filled with the same pompous arrogance that she'd once attributed to Colby. She'd considered him a person of privilege, unable to understand the problems of common folks. Instead, it had been Danielle herself who'd been privileged, raised with love and acceptance while Colby had struggled against incredible odds.

The lesson was a bitter one, and she'd learned it far too late.

"Too late," she murmured aloud, having forgotten that she wasn't alone.

"Maybe not," Jonas replied, startling her.

Danielle followed the scruffy dockworker's gaze, and her heart leapt into her throat.

Jonas shifted, heaved his belly. "Got work," he mumbled, then sauntered into the adjacent warehouse just as Colby wheeled the stroller onto the dock.

"Aren't there any ramps around here?" he complained. "I had to carry this thing up two flights of stairs." He rolled the stroller to a protected space in the warehouse's coffee area, set the parking brake and angled a nervous glance in Danielle's direction.

In the padded stroller seat, Megan squealed happily, pounded a cookie into dust. As soon as the numbness dissipated from Danielle's legs, she hurried over, gave her precious sweetums a fervent hug. She murmured loving words, wiped crumbs from the baby's face, then occupied her with a stuffed toy.

Danielle stood shakily, wiped her damp palms on her slacks. "I heard that you were here last night. Jonas saw you," she added when his eyes widened in surprise. "He saw Sheila, too."

Colby's gaze skittered away. "I found her lurking in the bushes out by the parking lot. She said that she was waiting for you."

"Is she all right?"

"She will be, I think."

"What happened?"

Colby shrugged, seemed uncomfortable. "She was

half-starved, looking for help. I fed her, then took her to a place where she'd be safe and get the help she needed.''

''Where did you take her? All the public shelters have been full for weeks.''

Squatting down, Colby grabbed a towel from the stroller bar, made a production of wiping Megan's sticky hands.

Danielle had lived with him long enough to recognize one of his favorite avoidance tactics. ''What is it that you don't want to tell me, Colby?''

He heaved a sigh, stood, replaced the towel. ''I took her to Heaven House.''

''No, you couldn't have.'' Danielle shook her head so hard that a clip vibrated out of her hair and bounced onto the concrete floor. ''Heaven House is a private institution, and they only take drug rehab cases.'' One look into Colby's sad eyes revealed a truth Danielle didn't want to accept. ''Oh, God.'' She stumbled back a step, folded her arms. ''Why didn't she tell me?''

''She was ashamed, Dani. She didn't want you to know.''

''But last night—?''

''Last night she was desperate. She would have told you if you'd been here.''

''Even if I had been here, there's no way I could have gotten her into Heaven House. That place costs a fortune, and they want every dime up front at the door.'' Danielle watched Colby busy himself by refolding the baby's wiping towel over the stroller handle. ''You paid out of your own pocket, didn't you?'' The embarrassed flush crawling up his throat was all the answer she needed. ''That was a wonderful thing you did, Colby. You've given Sheila the greatest gift of all, hope for a better life.''

''Speaking of which...'' He stroked the neatly creased terry-cloth, spoke without looking up. ''After I returned home last night, my parents showed up.''

Danielle went rigid, touched her throat as images of screamed accusations flew through her mind. "And…?"

"And we talked." He licked his lips, puckered his brows adorably. "The scars run deep, but for the first time, I believe there is hope that we can come together as a family, and give Megan a brighter future."

"Oh, Colby." Her breath gushed out all at once, and she struggled against an almost overwhelming urge to throw herself into his arms. "I'm so glad for you."

"You did it, you know."

"Me?" She shook her head. "I'm the one who nearly destroyed everything."

A gentle smile touched his lips. "No, you're the one who forced us to look beyond ourselves and our own petty hurts. I should have been grateful. Instead, I turned my back on you just as I'd turned my back on the sister that I'd never allowed myself to know." His eyes glazed reflectively, fixed somewhere in the past. "I lost Olivia long before her death because I was afraid to reach out, afraid of being rejected. I lost you the same way."

"Lost me?" Extending her hand, she flexed her fingers and withdrew nervously. "I don't understand. You're the one who wanted a divorce."

He shook his head, issued a throaty chuckle that irked her to the core. "I never wanted a divorce."

"But the papers—"

"The divorce documents spit out of the computer automatically with the final custody papers, just as Jack had programmed them to do when our original marriage agreement was executed. His assistant simply forwarded them on."

She squinted in disbelief. "You didn't want the divorce?"

"No."

"Then why did you let me leave?"

"*Let* you leave? I thought you *wanted* to leave."

"Why would I want to leave?"

"Because staying meant living with me." He blinked, stiffened, folded his arms. "I realize that I am not an easy man to, ah, appreciate. I would, however, ask that you reconsider that decision. Megan needs you."

"Megan needs me."

"Yes, clearly." He wiped his brow, fidgeted uncomfortably. "The child has been distraught, feeling abandoned and is at considerable risk of being emotionally scarred by the loss of the woman she loves as a mother."

"I see."

"There are other considerations, as well," he muttered, yanking out a handkerchief to mop down his sweaty face. "Is it hot in here?"

"Barely sixty-five degrees," Danielle replied. "You were discussing other considerations?"

"Ah, yes, there are, er, financial incentives, of course."

"Of course."

"I will make arrangements to transfer joint title of the house, and you will become prime beneficiary on my life insurance policies. They are substantial, actually."

"Are you saying that you'll be worth more to me dead than alive?" she inquired politely.

His eyes widened. "One hopes not."

"Good. With all this talk of financial security, I was wondering where emotions might fit in."

"Megan's emotional security is of paramount concern."

"Megan again." Danielle turned away, heaved an exaggerated sigh. "I'm sorry, Colby, I want more."

"More?"

She tossed a glance over her shoulder. "Much more."

"Well—" he tugged his crisp white collar "—we'll establish a personal stock portfolio in your name."

"Not interested."

"Something safer, perhaps government bonds—"

"No."

"Short-term certificates of deposit are highly liquid—"

"Dammit, Colby, I don't want your money!" She spun to face him, poked a finger in the center of his chest. "All I want is your heart, and if I can't have that, I don't want anything at all."

His eyes softened with reverence. "You already have that, Dani."

"Then tell me."

"I just did."

"No, I mean *tell* me." Sighing, she dropped her hands to her side, spoke with deadpan futility. "You don't have any problem articulating what you believe Megan wants and feels. Why can't you just tell me in your own words what you want and feel?"

He considered that, clasped his hands behind his back. "Very well. I, too, am distraught by your absence."

"Go on."

"I'm, er, lonely and I feel abandoned."

She nodded. "And...?"

"And I, too, am at risk of being emotionally scarred—" his voice rasped, broke "—by the loss of the woman I love as a wife."

"You love me?" It was a whisper.

"With all my heart." His eyes reddened, shone with moisture. "Will you marry me, Danielle? I mean, really marry me. Be my real wife, through sickness and health, forever and always."

Emotion clogged her throat, rendered her mute. She stepped into the circle of his arms, accepted with the sweetness of her kiss. After all the years and all the tears, Colby Sinclair had finally opened the door to his heart. Danielle entered joyfully.

Epilogue

"Breathe, son, breathe." The paper bag expanded and collapsed with every frantic puff. "That's it," Kingsley murmured, patting his son's tuxedo-clad back. "Slower, slower, deep breaths, that's good."

The dizziness eased. Colby lowered the bag, took an experimental gulp of fresh air. This time, the room graciously refrained from spinning. He steadied himself on a dressing chair, puffed his cheeks as his father pried the crumpled bag out of his hands.

Chuckling softly, the older man fussed with the white rosebud pinned to his son's lapel. "The same thing happened to me on my wedding day. Your uncle George, God rest his soul, was my best man. He went through the entire ceremony with that bag tucked under his tuxedo vest, just in case."

Colby licked his lips, blinked his stinging eyes. "You didn't forget the rings."

"Right here in my pocket."

"They're new rings," Colby murmured for no particular reason. "Dani wanted to keep the other ones, but they were just plain, gold-plated bands. She deserves solid gold and diamonds, lots of diamonds. Would you please turn down the heat? It's stifling in here." Fanning his face with his hand, Colby made a dive for a small disk mounted on the wall, lowered the thermostat from sixty-eight degrees to somewhere around fifty. He spun, sagged against the wall, felt the sweat ooze across his brow. "The cummerbund is too tight. It's squeezing my lungs."

Kingsley smiled, held out the paper bag.

Colby panted into it until the chamber door opened. Organ music from the chapel vibrated through his skull like a rhythmic air gun. A firm hand grasped his shoulder, another urged the bag from his face. "They're ready for us, son."

Colby nodded, vaguely noticed his father tucking the bag under his own tuxedo vest. He managed two steps toward the open chamber door, then froze. "Are you sure she's here?"

"She's here," Kingsley assured him. "Mother has been with her all morning."

"What if she's changed her mind?"

"She hasn't changed her mind."

"But what if she has?" Colby spun, clutched his father's satin lapels, shook the poor man until his jowls jiggled. "What if she's decided that she can't live with a man who sets a watch timer to brush his teeth, and, and—" He abruptly released his father, skewered him with a squinty stare. "This amuses you?"

Kingsley wiped his eyes, shook his head. "I was just remembering that I refused to leave the groom's chamber until three witnesses filed in and swore to me that your mother was physically on the premises, dressed in her wedding gown and fully prepared to spend the rest of her life with a man who couldn't knot a necktie without watching himself in the mirror."

Colby stiffened. "That's ludicrous."

"Yes," he murmured, still chuckling as he took a firm grasp of his son's elbow and propelled him toward the door. "I suppose it is."

Before Colby could issue further protest, he was ushered past the booming organ toward an altar surrounded by cascades of white roses tied with intricate satin bows. A buzz of conversation instantly dropped to a hushed murmur. Colby tottered in place, angled a frantic glance at the reverend, who simply smiled with maddening serenity, clearly unconcerned that the groom was in danger of pitching nose-first into a wicker vase.

The organ music changed tempo, alerting the crowd that the ceremony had begun. Colby wobbled, felt his father's hand on his arm.

"Pretend it's a board meeting," Kingsley whispered. "And you are preparing to conduct the most important presentation of your life."

Colby squeezed his eyes shut, clasped his hands behind his back, and imagined an auditorium of potential investors. His heart slowed, his breathing deepened, his pulse throbbed with rhythmic power. When he opened his eyes, one of Danielle's brothers, all of whom were serving as ushers, escorted Eugenia and her lace-bedecked granddaughter down the aisle.

Megan wriggled in Eugenia's arms, waved happily at Colby and her beloved grandpa. "Ungee, gampee!" She shrieked, eliciting muffled laughter from the guests.

Eugenia's smile brightened. She graciously seated herself in the front pew with Megan on her lap, and winked at her son. Colby grinned stupidly, wishing he could step away from his appointed spot long enough to give his mother a hug. Much had changed over the past few months.

Not only had Colby reestablished a relationship with his own family, he and Megan had also become a cherished part of Danielle's family.

The mother of the bride, now being escorted to her place on the arm of one of her usher sons, beamed at Colby with genuine affection. The affection was mutual. Colby had instantly adored Danielle's jovial, high-spirited mother, who possessed the same bizarre humor and sparkling laugh as her daughter.

Suddenly a nervous hush rippled the chapel. Colby went rigid, realized the organ had fallen silent. Beside him, Kingsley whispered, "Here we go, son."

The procession began with Danielle's curly-haired sisters gliding down the aisle in a cloud of mauve satin. Then Madeline Rodriguez appeared looking radiant but pale as she clutched her bouquet like a lifeline.

As each attendant reached the altar, Megan clapped and squealed happily, even reached out to snag a fistful of Madeline's dress, forcing the anxious maid of honor to stop long enough to receive a baby kiss before taking her place beside the two bridesmaids.

The organist hit a chord so resonant that the entire floor vibrated to life, and the thrilling strains of "Here Comes The Bride" shook Colby to the soles of his feet. He shifted awkwardly, forced his jittery hands away from the sadistic bow tie that threatened to strangle him on the spot and riveted his gaze on the open door at the rear of the chapel. The doorway was empty.

Behind him, the organist continued to play as if Colby's world hadn't just crashed down on his shoulders.

The doorway was empty.

"She's not there," Colby croaked.

Kingsley leaned over to whisper, "She will be."

And suddenly she was, floating on a luminous cloud of wispy white tulle and pearlescent lace, the most beautiful woman on the face of the earth. Colby's lungs emptied all at once. Danielle hadn't run away. She was gliding toward him on her father's arm with a cascade of white roses flowing from her hands and a radiant smile glowing from beneath the gossamer veil.

Colby couldn't move, couldn't breathe, couldn't take his eyes off the woman he loved more than life itself.

It seemed an eternity before Danielle was standing beside him, and he was enveloped by her sweet fragrance. He took her hand, caressed its softness, its warmth.

It was real. Danielle was real. This wasn't a dream anymore. Everything Colby had yearned for was actually within his grasp. A real marriage; a true family; an enduring love. Forever had just begun.

* * * * *

Silhouette Special Edition delivers Diana Whitney's next STORK EXPRESS book, BABY IN HIS CRADLE, in May 1998.

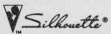

BEVERLY BARTON

Continues the twelve-book series— 36 Hours—in April 1998 with Book Ten

NINE MONTHS

Paige Summers couldn't have been more shocked when she learned that the man with whom she had spent one passionate, stormy night was none other than her arrogant new boss! And just because he was the father of her unborn baby didn't give him the right to claim her as his wife. Especially when he wasn't offering the one thing she wanted: his heart.

For Jared and Paige and *all* the residents of Grand Springs, Colorado, the storm-induced blackout was just the beginning of 36 Hours that changed *everything!* You won't want to miss a single book.

Available at your favorite retail outlet.

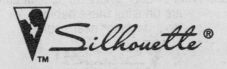

Silhouette ®

Silhouette®

SPECIAL EDITION™

COMING NEXT MONTH

#1171 UNEXPECTED MOMMY—Sherryl Woods
That Special Woman!
And Baby Makes Three: The Next Generation
Single father Chance Adams was hell-bent on claiming his share of the family ranch. Even if it meant trying to seduce his uncle's lovely stepdaughter. But when Chance fell in love with the spirited beauty for real, could he convince Jenny to be his wife—and his son's new mommy?

#1172 A FATHER'S VOW—Myrna Temte
Montana Mavericks: Return to Whitehorn
Traditional Native American Sam Brightwater was perfectly content with his life. Until vivacious schoolteacher Julia Stedman stormed into Whitehorn and wrapped herself around his hardened heart. With fatherhood beckoning, Sam vowed to swallow his pride and fight for his woman and child....

#1173 STALLION TAMER—Lindsay McKenna
Cowboys of the Southwest
Vulnerable Jessica Donovan sought solace on the home front, but what she found was a soul mate in lone horse wrangler Dan Black. She identified with the war veteran's pain, as well as with the secret yearning in his eyes. Would the healing force of their love grant them a beautiful life together?

#1174 PRACTICALLY MARRIED—Christine Rimmer
Conveniently Yours
Rancher Zach Bravo vowed to never get burned by a woman again. But he knew that soft-spoken single mom Tess DeMarley would be the perfect wife. And he was positively *livid* at the notion that Tess's heart belonged to someone else. Could he turn this practical union into a true love match?

#1175 THE PATERNITY QUESTION—Andrea Edwards
Double Wedding
Sophisticated city-dweller Neal Sheridan was elated when he secretly swapped places with his country-based twin. Until he accidentally agreed to father gorgeous Lisa Hughes's child! He had no intention of fulfilling that promise, but could he really resist Lisa's baby-making seduction?

#1176 BABY IN HIS CRADLE—Diana Whitney
Stork Express
On the run from her manipulative ex, very pregnant Ellie Malone wound up on the doorstep of Samuel Evans's mountain retreat. When the brooding recluse delivered her baby and tenderly nursed her back to health, her heart filled with hope. Would love bring joy and laughter back into their lives?

Silhouette Books

is proud to announce the arrival of

A MOTHER'S GIFT

This May, for three women, the perfect Mother's Day gift is mother*hood!* With the help of a lonely child in need of a home and the love of a very special man, these three heroines are about to receive this most precious gift as they surrender their single lives for a future as a family.

Waiting for Mom
by Kathleen Eagle
Nobody's Child
by Emilie Richards
Mother's Day Baby
by Joan Elliott Pickart

Three brand-new, heartwarming stories by three of your favorite authors in one collection—it's the best Mother's Day gift the rest of us could hope for.

Available May 1998 at your favorite retail outlet.